FREED

AMANDA CARLSON

FREED

A PHOEBE MEADOWS NOVEL: BOOK TWO

Copyright © 2016 Amanda Carlson

ISBN-13: 978-1-537661-83-4
ISBN-10: 1-537661-83-3

This book is a work of fiction. The characters, events, and places portrayed in this book are products of the author's imagination and are either fictitious or are used fictitiously. Any similarity to real persons, living or dead, is purely coincidental and not intended by the author.

For Jane. You amaze me.

1

"Don't worry about it, Phoebe. It'll come." Ingrid's voice was confident as she handed me a new weapon. "Here, try this. It's the mighty pickax."

I took the ax begrudgingly. It felt like a child's toy after hefting a fifty-pound spiked cudgel all day. It was lightweight and nondescript, and the blade wasn't even sharp. "There is nothing mighty about this weapon," I told her. "I'm pretty sure you just dug this out of a storage closet."

I didn't blame Ingrid in the least for trying. As it stood, we were running out of options. I'd been training at the Valkyrie stronghold for over a month, and the weapon that was supposed to "choose me" had yet to reveal itself. I'd tried swords of every flavor and size, bows, maces, machetes, and battle-axes, just to name a few.

Nothing felt right.

"I'm not going to say I did or I didn't," Ingrid answered wryly with a wink. She'd been my champion since the very day I'd arrived. She rose at dawn without fail and tirelessly worked on bettering my skills, teaching me how to fight and defend myself and, overall, being a great aunt and friend. "One never knows with these things. We have to try them all, from storage or not, until The One finally makes its way into your meaty fist."

"What if my perfect weapon is not actually *in* the Valkyrie compound?" I twirled the pickax around my head, getting a feel for the weapon like I'd been taught. It was unbalanced, much heavier on top, which made my movements clunky. I had to be careful it didn't catch on my sleeve, or it might come down on my head.

I wore the standard Valkyrie fighting regalia. The same clothes Ingrid had shown up in on that fateful day in my apartment. Today I had on a black overtunic, called a kirtle, which fell to my upper thighs, and soft pair of dark gray leather pants. I wore a sword belt called a balteus secured at my waist, which currently held Gram and the ice pick I'd taken off the dark elf I'd killed. Over everything, sat a protective metal breastplate that had been crafted to my exact measurements. It was held in place by thick leather straps that crisscrossed my back. Some Valkyries preferred a longer kirtle and no pants so that nothing impeded their movements, but I liked the pants. These were pretty kickass. I'd never been tempted to wear leather before, but these were by far the softest pants I'd ever owned.

To finish the ensemble off were a pair of beautifully detailed arm bracers. They were my favorite. They felt strong and sturdy, making me feel every inch the shieldmaiden.

The only thing I'd insisted on doing my own way was the footwear.

Valkyries wore simple leather shoes, but I needed more. Growing up in Midgard, I was used to wearing shoes that had some girth to them. My request had been granted within days, but no Valkyrie knew any shoe brands, so I'd drawn a detailed map of the shoe department at Macy's where I'd worked, and the next day I'd found a beautiful pair of high black boots waiting for me outside my door.

Well, *door* was a guideline. It was more of an *opening*.

The entire stronghold was carved out of the side of a sandstone mesa, just like the Pueblo Indians had done with their cliff dwellings. The only differences were the modern conveniences, such as beds, furniture, you name it. The Valkyries had everything, including electricity that ran on energy harnessed by the sun, which was why the Valkyries had chosen New Mexico in the first place. Sunny days were the norm around here. The technology was much more advanced than solar, but they assured me that humans would catch up someday.

Because of the arrangement we'd made to let the guys in, Fen and Tyr were not allowed in the main compound. So the three of us, and Sam, had separate quarters the equivalent of a few blocks away. Our accommodations were a little less high-tech, but they worked fine. I'd been happy here thus far.

I continued to whirl the pickax above my head and down around my legs in figure eights, making sure to keep its balance in check.

"Don't worry, Phoebe. Your weapon is around here someplace," Ingrid said. "They have a funny knack of showing up right when we need them most. My guess is you're still a little too green. You haven't learned to harness your energy yet, so it's waiting to reveal itself like a present on Christmas morning at exactly the right time."

"I hope so." I took a few practice swings, air whizzing by the blade as the pickax came down swiftly. I'd grown immeasurably stronger during my stay. Ingrid had insisted I feed from Yggdrasil, the tree of life, every other day, and because of that, I'd gained a lot of muscle weight. All-day training had taken that muscle and shaped it. I'd never been this toned and fit in my entire life. People who'd gone to high school with me would freak if they saw me. Phoebe Meadows from marching band and the swim team had come a long way. My balance had also improved, and I'd learned to fight with my hands, which was extra exciting.

The only thing I was waiting to learn was how to harness my inner energy. Ingrid had insisted I wait until she was sure I was ready, as it was "a tricky thing to master." So far it hadn't happened, and I wasn't in a position to dictate anything, even though I was eager to learn.

I swung the pickax again, pinwheeling it this time with one arm as I made my way over to the bales of hay set up in a small practice yard made just for us. Each bale was a different shape and size.

With thoughts of rescuing my mother, who was currently trapped in Svartalfheim, the land of the dark elves, I swung the ax down with everything I had, embedding it solidly in the middle of the painted red X.

The bale exploded handily, hay flying everywhere, each side toppling to the ground, rocking precariously a few times before they both lay still.

"That was great!" Ingrid clapped, coming toward me, her voice sounding genuinely appreciative. She looked fierce as always. Her blonde hair was military short, but she was undeniably beautiful. Her hazel eyes sparked with humor. "That was much better than what you did all day with the cudgel. How does it feel in your hands? I mean, with a blow like that, it has promise." With the cudgel, I'd managed only to spray hay everywhere, beating the bales to death like a frustrated child punching a feather pillow.

4

I shrugged as I brought the pickax up to inspect it, turning it over in my hand. "Honestly, it's nothing special." I gave her a look. "I have a hard time believing this is what would choose me." Not only was the blade incredibly dull, but calling it a blade was iffy at best. It was more like a helpful tool you'd use to get up the icy parts of Mount Everest than an intimidating appendage a Valkyrie referred to as her *war weapon*. The handle was chipped and worn, and literally no one would take this weapon seriously. Zero people would run from me if I waved this at them.

"No, you're right, this likely isn't it. But we gotta go with the weapons we have," Ingrid said. "Give it another try. Maybe it'll sing this time."

There was no way this was going to do any singing. I eyed it. "Ingrid, this is a glorified garden tool. It's something folks back home in Wisconsin use to chip ice off their driveway. My dad kept one in our garage. The only time I ever saw him use it was to go after a pile of dirt that had become like concrete from too much rain." I flipped the thing to my left hand, taking a few swings in the air. One of the things Ingrid had been insistent on teaching me was to use both hands. I was pretty proud of my newfound agility. As my brilliant aunt told me time and time again, you never knew when "some asshole" would incapacitate your fighting arm. Not that I would've classified me as a klutz before, but smooth hadn't been in my repertoire either. "Ingrid, if this is truly my weapon, I'm going to be the biggest dork in Valkyrie history."

Ingrid chuckled. "No worries, Phoebe. Our weapons come in all shapes and sizes. You haven't met Helga yet. Her weapon is a hammer. And we're not talking Thor's hammer. We're talking hardware-store hammer. But"—Ingrid shook her head appreciatively—"that girl can make that puppy sing. I've seen her take out more eyes than you can count. She uses the claw like it's an extension of her hand. Brutal." Ingrid swiped her hand like a cat, curling her fingers.

"Shieldmaiden!" Fen called from his usual spectating place on a sandstone ledge in the shade a few yards away. He looked as relaxed and handsome as ever, his blond hair tumbling over his shoulders as he sat up. "Tyr's back from the river." A second later the sound of the stronghold barrier being opened whistled through the air and vibrated the ground. My brother had gone to retrieve his weapon cache from the water. They'd arrived an hour ago by boat. Fen grinned. "Maybe you'll find something of use in there. Don't fret, your weapon will surface." Fen often sparred with me, teaching me what he knew, as did my half brother Tyr, the god of war. I was incredibly lucky to have such a strong team of supporters.

"I'm not fretting." I was definitely fretting. "But you have to admit, this"—I shook the pickax—"is not warrior material. I look like I'm going on an expedition that involves ropes and shoes with spikes."

Fen walked toward me, swinging his huge broadsword. "I'll spar with you, Valkyrie. If you can block my blade with that"—he nodded at the tool—"then it's warrior material."

"Okay," I agreed as I watched him. He moved with an unbelievable fluidity that was all demigod. "What's the deal with Tyr's weapons cache, anyway?" I asked, squaring up. "Why did it take so long to arrive?" Tyr had been arguing with various people from Asgard the entire time we'd been here. The stronghold contained a small, portable mirror-type thing that was connected to other realms. I didn't remotely understand it, nor had anyone taken the time to explain it, so it remained a mystery.

"He had to heavily negotiate for his arsenal to be returned,"

Fen replied, warming up his arm by twirling the broadsword, making his huge biceps jump. "He is the god of war, after all, and he left many weapons behind when he left the realm. Because he hadn't been back to Asgard in too many years to count, they'd been given over to the new war commander. He's had to make a deal to get them released, as they are his by right, but even so, they've only agreed to let some go."

My best friend, Sam, had gone with him, and I heard her animated chatter before I saw them. She was excited about something. As they rounded a corner, Fen, Ingrid, and I walked to meet them.

Tyr cradled a giant chest in his broad arms, which was no small feat, since he had only one hand. Other than Fen, my half brother was one of the biggest men I'd ever seen. His good looks were slightly marred by a long scar that stretched from one eyelid, across his nose, ending at the opposite jawline. But his wavy auburn hair and clear green eyes managed to give him a youthful appearance despite the damage, which was no small feat. I'd been shocked to learn that Fen had given him that scar, and taken his hand, when Tyr had tricked him into being bound, which resulted in Fen's banishment. But the guys were clearly over it. As only men can seem to achieve.

If I'd been given a scar like that, the grudge would've gone on for an eternity, possibly even post-eternity.

Sam's blonde curls bounced into view right behind Tyr. I laughed out loud when I saw her. "Sam, you're covered in weapons."

"I know!" she chirped. "Isn't it cool?" A large bow was draped over one shoulder, what looked to be a huge katana stuck out from behind her back, around her hip hung a large broadsword, and in her arms were several knives along with what looked to be a machete.

"It looks like you finally found a way to channel your inner Xena, Warrior Princess." I grinned. Sam sparred with me occasionally and was always eager to learn from anyone willing to show her a thing or two about combat. The Valkyries had noticed her enthusiasm and had taken her under their wing after she'd worked her charm on them.

Honestly, it was impossible not to adore her.

She was naturally funny, witty, and super smart. It sealed the deal when they found out she had Asgardian blood flowing through her veins.

We'd found this tidbit out almost by accident. Fen had been in his wolf form when we were fighting the Serpent of Midgard and scented her, picking up on her unusual heritage. It's likely from her father's side, since she's never met him. Now she's determined to make a trip to Asgard and find him, and I'd promised to help her.

"I'm way cooler than Xena," she said. "She *wishes* she had my swagger."

"I'm sure she does—"

Tyr set the chest down with a loud clang, and I was immediately drawn to it.

I walked toward it, totally focused, before I even knew I was moving.

"What's up, Phoebe?" Ingrid's voice held curiosity.

I glanced at her, dazed. "My weapon is in there." I pointed dumbly at the large chest.

There was no mistaking it. An unbelievable pull yanked at my insides to get to that chest. My hands began to shake like crazy.

"Well, let's open it up and take a look-see, shall we?" Ingrid turned to Tyr and ordered, "Pry that puppy open so we can get this show on the road."

2

Tyr did the honors, bending over and hefting up the lid. The chest was made of dark wood embellished with ornate carvings of warriors, each clad in armor and brandishing a variety of weapons. It was a large chest, almost the size of a small coffin. It had to be that big to hold all the weapons.

We gathered in a semicircle, gazing down at it.

Once Tyr had lifted the lid, we all exhaled. It'd felt ceremonious.

Try grinned as he glanced inside. "The new commander did well by me. Most of what I requested resides inside."

"Come on, Phoebe," Sam urged excitedly, rubbing her hands together. "Don't leave us hanging. Which one of these beauties is yours?"

I dropped to my knees, tossing the decidedly *unmighty* pickax to the side.

Good riddance, lowly weapon. I hope we never meet again.

My hands trembled. "I'm not sure which one it is," I told the curious onlookers. "Something in here just feels...powerful...and my body craves it." I brushed my hand across the weapon on top. It felt cold. "It's not this one." I lifted out a big scythe. "Not this one either." I started a pile to my right, dumping a large cleaver on top of a sickle.

I knew my chosen one would feel hot or tingle or *something*.

Fen crouched next to me. "I think it's no surprise that you would find your weapon in this chest." His presence comforted me, as always.

I smiled at him. "Why's that?" I asked as I discarded some sort of swinging cudgel with a big loopy chain. It made lots of clanging noise as I added it to the growing pile.

"Because," Ingrid answered first, "Tyr is your brother and these are his weapons. As the god of war, he would have some doozies in his arsenal, and sometimes gene pool trumps everything."

"I wasn't sure your weapon would be here," Tyr agreed, his voice deep and steady, "but I figured it couldn't hurt to try. Plus, we're going to need these weapons once the mission starts." He referred to our upcoming trip to Svartalfheim to find my mother, where she had been trapped for years. "When I was young, I found my weapons among this arsenal as well." He nodded down at the chest. My brother could call up at least five weapons at any time. They flew right into his outstretched hand. Coolest thing *ever*.

As I neared the bottom, my breath caught.

"What?" Sam cried. "Which one is it? Is it that funny-looking sword or the awesome spear? I can't stand the suspense! Hurry up!"

"Neither," I answered, pushing aside the bigger weapons, making my way to the bottom where a tattered leather scabbard lay. It was about three feet long and well worn.

I lifted the thing out, my fingers hot, the weapon feeling electric under my grip.

The straps snagged on another weapon, and I had to patiently free them, my intake of breath increasing as the anticipation rose. The scabbard looked as though it was meant to be strapped on my back. Two beautifully carved handles made of dark onyx stuck out of each end. My hands tingled as they cupped the broken-in leather, almost like when I touched Yggdrasil to feed, but different.

I brought it out as ceremoniously as I could. The weapon demanded reverence, and I was ready to give it.

"That old thing?" Sam asked, skepticism in her voice. "Really?"

Once it was out, Tyr exhaled sharply, and Fen made a noise that sounded like a cough.

I tried to read their faces. Ingrid's appeared semishocked. "What?" I asked. "You guys are freaking me out!" I held the weapon in my open palms, like an offering, not knowing what else to do with it. "What is this thing? It's vibrating my entire body. My heart is literally beating in tandem to the currents of electricity pulsing through me. It's the strangest feeling."

Fen answered first. "If I'm correct, that is Gundren, sister to Gungnir, both crafted for Odin and extremely powerful."

Tyr nodded gravely. "Both weapons were made for our father many years ago," he told me, clearing his throat. "Gungnir never leaves Odin's side. The spear has true aim and always kills. Odin's runes are carved into the side of his spear"—he nodded at the scabbard—"just as you see there on the handles of those swords. The runes make the weapons even more powerful."

"Why would Odin's sword be here?" I asked Tyr, confused. "Shouldn't it be with him?"

"Swords," Tyr corrected. "There are two nestled together, one at each end. The blades are slightly curved and extremely deadly. You are to wear the scabbard on your back and reach around"—he mimicked one hand over one shoulder and one arm around his lower back—"releasing both to fight at once." Then his facial expression changed to something I couldn't read. "I do not know why it is here. I didn't request this weapon to be added to the arsenal, nor would it have been granted to me if I had. In fact, if the commonwealth of Asgard knew Gundren was out of the realm, where someone could steal it, there would be riots. Those blades will cut through any hide, the blow lethal to any creature, wherever it lands, in all Nine Worlds. This is Odin's personal weapon."

"Okay." I had no idea what else to say. It was a lot to take in.

Ingrid leaned over, peering into the chest. "It was at the bottom, covered by the others." She grinned, crossing her brawny arms in front of her, her breastplate shining. "Odin is sneaky, I'll give him that." She met my gaze. "There's no doubt he stuck Gundren in there himself. He wants you to survive at all costs, Phoebe, and that's a very good thing. You'll need those swords, especially when we descend into Svartalfheim. They will deflect dark elf magic." Her eyes gleamed. "Those little suckers have it coming. Can't wait to see their faces."

"The boatman who delivered these weapons," Tyr said as I stood, the scabbard still outstretched in my hands, "also told me to expect something to arrive in the next few days, but he would not elaborate. He is one of Odin's closest advisers."

"How...how do I put this on?" I tried to control my shaking, but it was difficult. Little eddies of energy swirled inside me, mixed with excitement, making me feel like a kid who'd just opened the best gift ever. Ingrid had been right.

Fen grinned. "Hand me the weapon and turn around." I complied, although it was tough to actually let the swords go. My body bucked at the separation, and a prick of physical pain winced through me. Once I had my back to him, Fen leaned over my shoulder and planted a chaste kiss on my cheek. Thoughts about what we did last night crept into my mind. I blushed. The man was passion personified. Having him this near gave me goose bumps on top of my already-hyped adrenaline.

"Good grief, you two," Sam joked. "Is there ever a time when you're not swooning over each other? I'd gag if it wasn't so damn cute."

I chuckled as Fen untangled the straps. "Hold out your left arm."

I did, and he slipped one strap over my shoulder. Electricity rushed through me. I closed my eyes to drink it in.

"Now turn around, and I'll slide it over your other shoulder."

Once it was on, I straightened.

"How does it feel?" he asked.

I didn't have words for how my body felt.

Invincible, electric, powerful, strong.

Gundren had its own current, and once again, it flowed in harmony with the blood pumping through my veins.

"It should feel like a million bucks," Ingrid cracked. "Like the weapon is a part of you, an extension of your limbs. Just go with it, don't force anything." She placed her hands out in front of her. "Drink in the moment."

I nodded as I moved toward a hay bale. I was too overcome to speak.

Needing to feel the dark onyx in my hands, I stopped, and without knowing exactly what I was going to do, I reached around with both hands, one over my shoulder and one around my right side, and clasped the sword hilts simultaneously, drawing them out quickly.

As they left the scabbard, they made a zinging noise.

There was no sweeter sound.

The hilts melded into my hands, like oil coating a pan. The weapon felt like an extension of my body.

As I lashed them both into the bale of hay, one from each side, making a solid X, I noticed how thin the blades were, slightly curved and wicked sharp.

The bale broke neatly into four triangles and fell to the ground. Not one errant piece of straw flew anywhere. The effort it took to make mincemeat out of the bale was equivalent to sliding a warm knife through a stick of butter.

I stood there, stunned. Holy crap!

"Well," Ingrid chuckled, coming up behind me, "that's one way to do it. That pile of hay never saw it coming." She kicked one of the triangles, and it tumbled over.

"That was incredible, Phoebe!" Sam exclaimed. "You were so fast. I didn't even register it until I saw the bale break apart like it was your *bitch*. You know, I'm beginning to rethink those swords. Maybe you did get the best of the bunch."

I snorted, bringing the blades in front of me to inspect them. *Best* was an understatement.

The two swords were identical in every way. The steel was two inches across at the widest. The metal was extremely thin, not more than a few millimeters thick. The blades had matching elegant curves midway up, and they glinted sharply in the sun.

I knew if I ran a hand over either of the edges, it would cut to the bone. They were deadly weapons. The polar opposite of the ninny pickax.

A noise interrupted my reverie, and I turned to look. I

was surprised to see a crowd of Valkyries had amassed. It was the first time they'd come into our tiny training area. I'd been introduced to most of them, but none had chosen to interact with me yet.

Ragnhild, the battle captain, stood slightly in front of the group, her arms crossed. Her jet-black hair was shaved on the sides, plaited on top in intricate braids woven together, ending in a fall of dark waves which flowed freely down her back. She stood taller than all other Valkyries, and that was saying something, since the average height of a shieldmaiden was almost six feet. She nodded once and stated boldly, "You will join us in the Park tomorrow at dawn."

The Park was the area where the Valkyries trained.

She didn't wait for a reply. Instead, she walked away, the other shieldmaidens trailing behind her, some giving me tentative smiles, others cold glares. Once they were gone, I said, "Well, that was unexpected."

Ingrid clasped me on the back. "Way to go, Phoebe!" she said. "Rae is a hard nut to crack. Do you know her name actually translates to *adviser in battle*? I mean, with a name like that, there's no denying your fate. And her weapon is a lethal katana. It's a good thing she didn't want to become a gardener. Lucky for us, too, since she's the fiercest commander we've had since Brynhildr, but that's a story for another day. Come on, let's see what else you can do with those things." She led me toward the edge of our training area.

I brought the blades in front of me, and my brother whistled low, causing me to glance his way.

"Those weapons even make me envious," he said, his mouth going up slightly on one side. "Only Gungnir comes close to those in beauty and grace."

I had a thought. "Do you think Odin will want them back

when we're done with the mission?" My heart pinged. I didn't want to relinquish them. Ever.

"No," Tyr stated evenly. His voice held certainty, and I let myself breathe. "Those swords have clearly changed their allegiance. Once given as a gift, if they find the host agreeable, a magical weapon stays true. If some other picked those up"—he gestured to my blades—"and Gundren did not agree, they would not work to the same capacity. You are safe."

I sighed, relief filling me. "Great."

Fen stood behind us. "Your father chose well," he said, a hint of sarcasm in his voice. Fen wasn't a fan of my father, which was understandable since Odin had been the one to toss him into Muspelheim, a place Fen had been jailed for more years than I could fully comprehend. It didn't help that Fen had been slated to kill Odin during Ragnarok, the fated battle between the gods. I'd never met my birth father, so I had no idea what he was like. I imagined him to be fierce and intimidating, with a big beard and a stern demeanor. I had no idea why I thought he had a beard. No one had said anything, but that's just what popped into my head. Meeting him was going to be beyond weird. Fen cracked, "It seems Odin wants you to live after all."

"Yes, that appears to be true," I replied. The two of us had had many debates about what Odin's true intentions were in all this. We'd thought, on different occasions, that Odin was both actively trying to aid me and not interested in helping at all. Our late-night pillow talk revolved around whether Odin sought to protect himself in the eyes of the Norns or really wanted me to survive. After all, he was *the* god of gods. It made sense that he could step in if he wanted to. But he hadn't. "Like we've said all along, if Odin wanted to, he could go free my mom, or swoop down and bring me up to Asgard until all this blows over with the Norns. But that doesn't mean I'm not grateful for Gundren, because I am. It was nice that he sent it." It made me feel like he cared.

Tyr shook his head. "He can't do either."

"Why not?" I raised my eyebrows. "He's Odin. He's the leader of gods. Why can't he help us?" I'd tried to ask Tyr about this before, but every time I'd broached the subject, he was suddenly busy with another task.

He exhaled, taking his time to answer. I could tell he was reluctant to speak about it, like if he did, he would betray some sacred trust. Tyr had his own way of talking, and much of it was in the form of long sighs. "He must save his interfering until the last possible second. Right now, he's trying to garner formal support for your cause from other gods and goddesses. As I've told you, he cannot kill the Norns outright. It is forbidden. Because he'd kept you a secret for twenty-four years, he has to justify his reasons for doing so. It's a tall order. There will be challenges, and he must contend with them. If he fails to garner any support for you and your mother, everything crumbles."

"What do you mean by *crumbles*, exactly? That sounds kind of hopeless."

Tyr scrubbed his hand over his face, looking tired. "Some gods or goddesses are challenging his authority. It's common practice after finding out a god has lied or killed someone he or she shouldn't have. Keeping a secret like this is considered a big infraction. Many will be angry, and many fear the Norns. If he cannot find the support, you will be exiled, or worse."

Well, that was dire news. "So, he's going to court to defend me?"

"Something like that." Tyr nodded. "The Council is similar to a Midgard court, but it has its own rules, and all the gods and goddess in attendance decide judgment. The room is grand and round, and the speaker must stand in the middle and address the attendees, who sit higher up. If he can succeed in exonerating himself for keeping such a secret, he can gain allies, which is what he will need to save you from the Norns and their wrath. It is no easy task. So thus, he cannot leave the realm."

I positioned my legs apart and raised my swords. "So if he's not successful, I will be banished or worse?" I eyed a pile of stacked tree trunks in front of us. They sat on top of a wooden beam that spanned two sawhorses. I was ready for the next task, especially after this conversation.

"Don't worry about it, Phoebe," Ingrid interjected, angling her head toward the logs to give me permission to have at them. "If anyone can convince a crowd, it's Odin. Your dad had good reason to scuttle you and your mother away, and once the story comes out, they will see his side of things. I'm sure of it. Let's shelve this discussion for later. The day is waning, and you need to keep training. If Rae wants you in the Park tomorrow at dawn, you can't go in green. They will be expecting a Valkyrie to join them, not a greenhorn."

I nodded. "Thanks for letting me know, Tyr. It helps to have all the information." I rallied my concentration back to the task and took a deep breath. I positioned myself in front of the pile and swung my swords down, my right hand a little ahead of my left.

When Gundren collided with the wood, as with the hay, there was little resistance. The blades sliced right through. The kickback from my hands was almost nonexistent.

One second later I realized I was going too fast, the momentum too strong. I couldn't pull back in time. My blades not only cut through the logs, but kept going through the wooden platform, and the entire pile crashed to the ground, sawhorses and all.

I jumped out of the way, yanking my swords up, and missed stabbing them into the ground by an inch. I stumbled backward, trying to regain my footing, panting heavily with the effort it had taken.

I glanced around, wild-eyed.

"That was impressive, bordering on manic." Sam giggled. "I guess we could say the new swords are a success. It took you zero effort to heft through those logs, and they were huge. I'm pretty sure you could sever a torso, and it would be like a cartoon where, after a few moments, the body parts go in two different directions." She used her hands to demonstrate, still laughing. "That would be cool, but so, so gruesome."

"Yes, that would be grisly," I agreed, hoping I never had to witness it.

Ingrid pointed. "Those swords are a couple of zingers. But I can see we're going to have to work on your long game. You can't go in swinging like crazy and end up slicing and dicing the entire place. It will take some practice and control."

I blushed, drawing the blades back to examine them again. They were obviously old, but there wasn't a scratch anywhere to be seen on the steel. The blades were shiny and new, like they'd been forged yesterday. "Yeah," I said. "I think that's a good idea. I don't want to hurt anyone. They're just so light. They don't feel like much in my hands." I took a few practice swings in front of me.

Fen cleared his throat. I suddenly noticed everyone had taken a big step backward. "Easy there, shieldmaiden." He chuckled. "Let's get you working on some stop-and-start drills." He gestured at another hay bale, this one dressed in battle gear, including a breastplate.

I followed him over, trying not to feel silly for not being able to control myself, as Tyr announced, "I'm going to take the rest of these weapons back to the living area and take inventory."

"I'll go with you!" Sam said eagerly. "Staying here with Han Solo is too risky. I might look like Swiss cheese when she's finished with those things."

"Ha-ha," I said. "But Han didn't use a light saber, Luke did. I thought you were smart." I arced both blades above my head in a sweet crisscross maneuver. Or what I *thought* was a sweet maneuver. I might very well have looked ridiculous.

Except no one was laughing.

"You're right," Sam called as she followed Tyr out. "But Han was the closest thing to *hot as shit* I could think of. And you're definitely that, even if you could use a little help from Yoda to find your Valkyrie force." She waved. "See you later. Hit me up when you get back."

"Will do," I answered.

"Okay, time to get down to business," Ingrid said. "We only have a few scant hours until dawn. You can't go into the Park looking like you have no idea what you're doing. Fenrir, do you have your sword on you?" He drew it out of his waistband. "Good. Go stand over there, and let's rock this out." She gestured to the other side of the area. "Phoebe, get your head out of the clouds and put those things down. Follow the wolf. He's going to put you through your paces."

I blushed, dropping the swords from above my head. "Whatever you say, boss."

3

I face-planted in the dirt. For the seventh time.

It was 5:07 a.m.

The sun was barely over the horizon, not even close to breaking through to the valley floor where we were currently situated, and it was already sauna hot.

Rae paced by me, her face devoid of any expression. "Get up," she ordered. "Go again."

Trying to salvage any dignity that was still creeping around inside my bruised and battered body, I scampered up, brushing myself off, trying to be inconspicuous. Fighting with dirt in my eye wasn't an option, so it had to be done.

The two wooden swords I'd been sparring with had each been tossed in different directions and, with my head down, I went to retrieve them.

To my utter humiliation, my shiny new weapons had been sidelined until I could "control myself" better. It had been mortifying to sheathe them and put them away.

Since then, I'd tried to keep a low profile.

If I hadn't face-planted so many times, I might've

succeeded. As it stood, every Valkyrie in attendance had noticed my non-heroic antics as I plowed face first into the red dirt again and again.

Shieldmaidens didn't fall down.

I was a joke.

Anya, my sparring partner, glared at me, her arms crossed tightly against her unmarred breastplate, waiting impatiently for me to get organized. After she'd knocked me down the first few times, she'd appeared triumphant.

Now she just looked bored.

I was wasting her time—time she could've been using to better her own skills. She was a tall beauty, with long blonde hair plaited closely to the sides of her head, the rest hanging freely down her back. She also had a pair of dazzling blue eyes, which were laser-focused on me, more than a little perturbed.

"Let's go," Anya sniffed, her voice carrying what I'd come to refer to as an Asgardian accent. To my ears it sounded like a mix between an Irish brogue and a hint of Australian. Ingrid had told me Old English—meaning *very* Old English—was a direct derivative of the Asgardian language. But it didn't sound like today's British accents. "Go get your *swords*," she ordered. "I don't have all day."

She did have all day, as there was nothing else on the docket except training, which Valkyries took seriously. It was their religion, but that was beside the point. I picked up the wooden stand-ins, wishing for a blissful moment that it was a pickax, which would be better than a pair of toy swords, and paced back to where she stood, trying to summon some much-needed dignity. Anya was positioned in the middle of a small circle rimmed with green paint. I raised my faux weapons, arms braced, as Rae had instructed. Anya's weapon was a double-sided battle ax. The curved blades were almost as intimidating as she was.

Almost.

There were jeers from the sidelines. I tried to ignore them. The Park held only so many sparring areas, so Valkyries rotated in and out. As we readied to spar, I forced my mind to stay on task. No shieldmaiden had come out and directly opposed me being here, but there had been a pall of uncertainty from most in attendance.

I wasn't part of the pack, and at the rate I was going, I might never be.

As the heckling continued, Fen growled from just outside the boundary of the Park. He wasn't allowed inside, but he'd come as close as he could to support me. The sound was so low, I wasn't sure anyone else had heard it.

The jeers stopped instantly.

I hid a grin. Anya hadn't let on she'd heard Fen, but her slight eye movement gave her away. The Valkyries weren't afraid of Fen, per se. They were proud warriors and strong, capable fighters. It was more that they knew he could create mass destruction very quickly, and he was inside their lair. A predator in their safe space. It made them wary.

It was one thing to go into battle ready to fight. It was yet another to have Loki's son turn into a massive wolf and tear apart the stronghold while they slept.

In the month we'd been here, Ingrid never let on there was a problem, but I'd heard her in animated discussions with other Valkyries when she hadn't realized I was near. She always fervently defended him, saying she'd vouch for all of us any day of the week, but that didn't make them any less uneasy. The only reason he had even been allow inside was that he'd saved my life.

Three times.

Valkyries lived by a code of honor. They paid their debts. It was their way.

But without Ingrid defending us, we would've been ejected on the second day. It helped that my aunt was one of the oldest Valkyries and one of the strongest. When she sparred, it was always against Rae. They were evenly matched, and the bouts were fierce. The other shieldmaidens might disagree with Ingrid's choice to harbor me and my friends, but they weren't going to push her.

Hands reached around my waist, startling me, clasping my arms and shifting them upward. "You have to place them here"—Rae lifted one of my hands up and pushed the other arm down—"and here. If you do not, you leave yourself open. Your breastplate will only aid you so much. If the dark elves attack with magic, which is likely, you must protect your most vital areas. Your swords will deflect their magic. It's a perk most of us don't have." Her voice was firm, but not unkind. I had no idea if she just tolerated me or was trying to be nice in her own way, since her nice was about as warm as a punch to the gut. "Learn to use the assets you have." She stepped back.

Anya gave me a look that simultaneously said *you're such a child* and *your ass is grass.* Or, in this case, *your face is awaiting red dirt.*

"Begin," Rae's voice commanded. Normally, the entire Park was busy with activity, Valkyries sparring with one another. But not now.

All eyes were on me, waiting to see if I would go down again.

I wasn't planning on providing their entertainment for the eighth time, so when Anya moved to strike, I decided to duck and spin. I kept my wooden swords strategically positioned out in front to keep her battle ax from slicing me in two.

Surprisingly, the moved confused Anya for a sweet—

although too brief—moment. I received a grunt of approval from Rae.

Now we were getting somewhere.

Anticipating her next move by taking small cues from her feet and eyes, I feigned to the right. Anya snorted her frustration as I ducked her blow again. "Why are you running like a coward?" she raged, stalking forward. "You must fight me!"

"Nobody said I *had* to engage in combat," I countered, dropping my swords to my sides. "This doesn't end until one of us face-plants, and I have news for you, it's not going to be me this time."

"You don't run away in battle," she scoffed. "When the dark elves swarm, you fight. You're a Valkyrie." Her eyes narrowed. "But then again, maybe you're not." She smiled and swung the handle of her weapon down, whizzing through the air a hairsbreadth from my cheek.

I leaped to the side at the last moment, swinging my right arm around as hard as I could, my silly wooden sword slamming into her back. It barely jolted her, but I would take it.

First contact!

How's that for *not* being a Valkyrie, you blonde, smug-faced bully?

I danced away before she could retaliate, panting hard with the supreme effort it had taken me to finesse the maneuver. I'd forced my body to move faster than I had before, and now I was a sweaty mess, perspiration streaming down both sides of my face. The New Mexico heat, paired with my new nifty leather pants, wasn't making things any easier. Sweat pooled in places I hadn't known existed. I was going to have to air these puppies out when we were finished. But it didn't matter.

I'd dodged the shieldmaiden!

If a look could've dropped me in my tracks, Anya's contained enough explosive fury to blow me sky high.

"You must fight! Not run around in circles—"

"No, she doesn't," Rae stated calmly, preempting her diatribe as she moved inside the circle, hands on her hips. "The object for her is to stay alive. That's the first thing a young Valkyrie learns, or have you forgotten that, Anya?"

Anya's face turned purple. She wasn't embarrassed about being reprimanded, she was stone-cold furious. "Yes, that's something a child learns," Anya spat, lifting her battle ax and pointing it directly at me. "She is no child."

"She had no prior training when she was struck," Rae argued. "Which is why she must work harder than any of us. We had the luxury of learning passed down by our mothers, who were shieldmaidens before us. It's a privilege to be blessed by Odin's light. One that you do *not* disdain." Rae's voice took on a hard edge. "Odin not only struck Phoebe, but she is his *daughter*. She was sent to live in the human realm to survive. You do him, and us, a disservice by not teaching her what your mother passed down to you."

I glanced around. Rae's little talk had morphed into a full-on speech for all the Valkyries in attendance.

As she continued, Rae scanned the faces of her shieldmaidens. "It is our duty to help Phoebe grow into the warrior she is meant to be. If not for Odin, then do it for Leela." Murmurs erupted at the mention of my mother's name. "How quickly we forget our devotion to our missing sister. We love Leela. We fight for Leela. This is Leela's child." She glanced at me, her voice tough as nails. "Anya, you're dismissed." She didn't even pretend to look to see if Anya followed her command. "Billie, are you up for the task?"

A Valkyrie with curly brown hair, a warm smile, and shining gray eyes came forward. She'd always been cordial when we passed each other, though we'd never spoken more than a few words.

"I am," she stated, her voice clear. Her weapon was a spiked club. She twirled it absentmindedly as she entered the circle. Her breastplate was dented in a few places and was worn to a dull sheen. Her vanity meter was in the low single digits, which I appreciated.

Anya left without so much as a backward glance.

Good riddance! Go find someone else to antagonize.

Billie turned to face me, squaring up to spar. I brought my arms around in what I thought was the right pose. She shook her head good-naturedly. "No, you need to have them here." She reached out to lift one of my arms up slightly. "The reason is you must protect your heart. It's the first place any worthy adversary will strike, including myself. My club, if I aim it accurately, can puncture armor. One spike to a vital organ, and you can die. Older Valkyries can regenerate a serious injury, because with each year of immortality we grow stronger, but young Valkyries must be close to Yggdrasil for healing. We are immortal, but not immune to death. There is a difference between the two."

"Thank you, I appreciate that." Ingrid had told me the same—that we wouldn't die of old age, but we could be killed in a number of ways. "Honestly, I thought I had it, but holding my hands out this far is a little awkward."

"It is," she agreed. "But you get used to it." Her voice had a sweet, slow cadence. She raised her spiked club, and I eyed the sharp points. They were at least four inches long and covered the entire end of the orb. I knew Billie wouldn't intentionally hurt me, but if I wasn't careful, I could find myself in some moderate-to-severe pain.

Rae said, "Begin." To the other Valkyries who were looking on with some interest to see what Billie would achieve in besting me, she ordered, "Back to work! Let's go. Daylight is waning." They dispersed immediately, but I knew they'd have one eye on me no matter what.

In besting Anya, I had managed to raise my game, and I planned to keep it that way.

*

I fell into bed groaning. "I hurt all over." Fen stood over me, grinning, his arms braced over his head, his chest bare. "You can laugh all you want, but you know what I need? *Solay.*" His expression turned to musing. "Yes, you heard that right. I'd pay some serious cash to plunge into those stinky, healing waters right about now." I groaned as I rubbed a tender spot on my thigh. The sacred waters in Muspelheim had healed me, not once, but twice when I'd first met Fen. The smell was atrocious—rotten, foul garbage mixed with incredibly stinky eggs, and all I could think about was cannonballing into the pool right now.

Fen chuckled as he perched on the edge of the bed, taking one of my legs into his lap. "You worked harder than I've ever seen you. You should be proud of yourself, Valkyrie." He rubbed my calf muscle deliciously, earning a solid groan and a good ten-second murmur of ecstasy.

"Yeah," I said, weaseling my other leg onto his lap. The man was huge, so he had plenty of room. I wiggled my body closer and sighed. "But I still feel like a child. Maybe Anya was right. All Valkyries have a gigantic advantage. They started training much earlier than I did, like day one of their lives. I'm beginning to think I'll never catch up." His warm palm slid up my leg, and I gasped as his energy raced into my soreness, my body gobbling it up.

He was a demigod whose body held energy.

Valkyries fed on energy.

How lucky was I?

I couldn't even think about it without curling my aching toes. Yes, it was that good.

We were bunked down for the night in our small sleeping space, a room carved out of the sandstone mesa. It held a mattress, a small dresser, and nothing else. It was cozy and perfect. We had one fairly large window, cut right into the rock, no glass. Moonlight filtered through the opening. It was a beautiful, starry night and had the bonus of a small breeze.

"I have no doubt you will catch up," Fen stated confidently as his hand edged higher. "You will make up for the time lost with skill."

"How can you be so sure?" I rearranged my legs, lifting the neglected one as an offering. His thigh muscles were as big as tree trunks, and just as firm. They flexed under me as he grabbed on and began to massage.

Holy...yes. I closed my eyes. Heaven wouldn't be any sweeter.

"Because you are a child of both a Valkyrie and a god. A very powerful god."

"There must be other Valkyries with gods for fathers," I said. "I can't be the only one. You said Asgard is full of gods." He moved down to my feet, and I real-live whimpered.

"I've been listening and watching," he told me. "The only other with a god for a father is Ragnhild. He was not a powerful god, from what I've gathered, but a god nonetheless. That is why she is the leader. A god and a Valkyrie make a powerful match. It is undeniable. You will overcome your late training and rise in the ranks, there is no doubt."

It was hard to internalize what Fen was saying when I was trying not to lose consciousness from the foot rub, which was lulling me into a sleep state faster than any medication. I yawned, my eyes firmly shut. "Why aren't there more god-Valkyrie matchups?" My speech was slurred, verging on wistful-drunk.

Fen chuckled. "Because gods prefer to couple with gods. Sleep now, shieldmaiden." He gently removed my legs from his lap and tugged the sheet over my shoulders.

"Remind me," I mumbled as I turned on my side, Fen crawling in behind me, settling his brawny arms around my waist. "I have to call my parents tomorrow. It's time for my weekly check-in."

Frank and Janette Meadows, my adopted parents, who lived in rural Wisconsin, had alerted the police when I disappeared from New York. When we'd found out there had been a missing-persons report filed, I'd gotten a hold of them. I'd been forced to make up a fantastical story about jetting off at the last minute on an unexpected trip with my best friend, Sam. They'd bought it, because, honestly, nothing else made any sense, and they had been beyond relieved, and weepy, that I was okay, not to mention still alive and breathing.

Now I called them regularly with updates on my travels, or they would worry. They were wonderful parents who loved me, and it wasn't fair to disappoint them or make them overly anxious. We'd all agreed it was better for them to think I was fine, than to believe I was in danger.

"I will." Fen kissed my shoulder as I snuggled my back into his warm chest, feeling content, if still achy. "Rest now, Valkyrie. Tomorrow is a new day."

4

"We're having *so* much fun! It's been the trip of a lifetime, really," I said in a mock gushy tone. "Sam is beside herself with the food. South America has such a diverse palate with so much to choose from." Sam socked me in the arm, shaking her head like I was nuts. "It's been amazing." I shrugged at her, inventing stuff as I went.

She made a face, and I mouthed, *Not helpful.* Lying was hard.

"That's so wonderful, Phoebe. Dad and I are so happy for you," my mom said on the other end, genuine love and affection in her voice. I had the cell phone on speaker so Sam could hear the conversation. "It's amazing you found a friend in New York who has so many wonderful connections. Is the area you're staying in safe? We worry about you traveling around in all these exotic places."

"Yes, Mom. It's perfectly safe. In fact, it's completely secure. There's no way to get in without passing through a large gate." I glanced out over the horizon. It stretched out in front of us as far as the eye could see. Not a soul for miles. Sam and I sat on a mesa next to a massive cell tower that had been rigged for this very purpose.

It was the first true thing I'd told my mom since I got on the phone. The stronghold was more than secure—it was completely cloaked. Finding it meant you were a very powerful immortal.

"When do you think you'll be back in the States, sweet pea?" my dad asked, his voice a mixture of serious and good-natured. He ran a hardware store in our small town and specialized in easy rapport with his customers.

"Um…" I hesitated. I couldn't go home. Not for a while, anyway. "I'm not sure. Sam is thinking her parents will be in"—I glanced at her for help, my face imploring, and she mouthed, *Hawaii*—"Hawaii next. So I can't really pass that up. This entire trip has been a dream come true."

Sam gave me a thumbs-up.

"Grandpa Richard's birthday is in two weeks. Can you give him a call? Everyone is missing you here like crazy," my mom said. "It's been so long since we've seen your beautiful face. Maybe we can make a trip out to New York next month for a quick visit?" Her voice was hopeful.

"*Er*," I started, "I'm not sure I'll be back in a month, but once I'm there, yes! Of course. I miss you guys like crazy, too. I can't wait to see you." I gave Sam a nod, and she got up and walked over to the tower, tugging on the side marked with red tape.

The line started to break apart instantly.

My mom said something, but I heard only, "…visit…holidays…hardware store."

"Mom, the line is failing!" I called. "The connections here are so unreliable. I'm so sorry, but I have to run. I'll call you next week! I promise."

"Okay, sweetie," she yelled through the buzzing. "We love you!"

"Bye, sweet pea. Be safe," my father added.

"Goodbye," I said. "I love you both!" I ended the call, meeting Sam's gaze. "I'm a horrible person. They deserve better." I stood, dusting off my pants. I shoved the phone in my back pocket as we headed toward the edge where a steep path would wind us down to the valley below. "If I didn't already think there's a chance I'm going to hell, I'd say I just earned a one-way ticket for being such a skunky liar. My parents are so sweet, and I'm awful. I feel like a dirty cheat."

"Relax, you're not going to hell. You're just doing what you gotta do," Sam assured me. "You can't leave here, and you can't have them worried. It's not like you can say, 'Hey, Mom and Dad, I was struck by lightning and now I'm a Valkyrie! Oh, and Odin's my real dad, and the Norns are out to get me, but have no fear because my boyfriend is a wolf!' Seriously, you're doing them a solid by not saying a single, solitary word."

"That's easy for you to say," I snorted. "You just had to tell your mom you were shacking up with some dude in New Mexico, and all was forgiven."

"My mom doesn't know the definition of 'helicopter parent.' I was on my own at fifteen. But the last time we chatted, I happened to sneak in a question about my real dad." Her voice was jubilant, as it was every time she discussed Asgard.

"And?" I asked as we began to shimmy down the side of the mesa. "Don't leave me in suspense here."

"She was coy at first, but then she totally admitted he was a one-night stand, which didn't surprise me in the least. My mom was never good at hiding her hookups." Sam maneuvered over some rocks in front of me. "I guess he did come around a few times after I was born, but then she said he disappeared and she never heard from him again."

"That sounds very mysterious indeed," I said, sidestepping a small gap. "Did you ask his name?"

"Duh, of course." Sam jumped down onto a short ledge. "But it was really weird. My mom kind of paused for a few seconds before she answered. Then had to come clean with the fact she couldn't remember! She thinks it started with an H, but that's all she had."

"Wow," I said, shimmying over a big boulder. The view was majestic as we made our way down. The horizon was dotted with mesas and buttes, and the valley beneath us shone brightly in the early morning light. The sky was crisp and clear, only a few billowy clouds lazing across the blue expanse. "I wonder if he wiped her memory?"

"That's what I was thinking!" Sam said excitedly as she scooted down onto another ledge. "Like an Asgardian mind-meld. But it could also be that my mom is just too ditzy to remember. I'm kind of bummed out, since a first letter doesn't really help me at all."

"It's better than nothing," I pointed out as we stepped onto a gravel path around a big stone wall. "It narrows the playing field."

"The guys," Sam said, meaning Tyr and Fen, "don't think my father is a god, so that leaves the entire populous of Asgard with a *possible* first name that begins with H. How many people live on Asgard anyway?"

I shrugged. "Honestly, I have no idea. I've never asked. I assume it's metropolitan, but I could be wrong." When I thought of Asgard, I always envisioned a bustling New York City, but instead of dirt and grime, it was ethereal, clean, and shiny, with castles as tall as skyscrapers made of stone, with turrets and waterfalls around every corner, and windy paths of marble.

"I hope we get to find out someday," she mused. "That would be *so* freaking cool."

"I'm sure we will," I answered, not sure in the least. I had no idea if we would be welcome there or not.

We rounded a corner, reaching the halfway point. Fen was perched on a small ledge waiting for us. The tiny space made him look huge. He was dressed in a pair of jeans and a white T-shirt, his sword attached to a belt around his waist. His casual attire belied his focus. He was tense, like a predator stalking prey.

We were technically still inside the Valkyrie stronghold high on this mesa, but he didn't trust it. The first few times I'd made a call, he accompanied me to the top, until he decided something could attack us from the bottom and trap us up there. Then Sam started coming with me and he stayed midway between.

So far my phone calls had happened without incident.

Fen slid his arm around my waist as I approached and gave me a quick kiss. He smelled delicious. "We must get back," he murmured. "Training has already started again."

After I asked this morning, Rae granted me permission to make this call during our first break, but I didn't relish getting special privileges. Billie had sparred with me, but I knew I wasn't going to be so lucky this afternoon. Valkyries changed their partners often to keep fighting styles fresh. I'd spotted Anya whispering with a group of her cohorts. She wasn't going to let today go without comment. I had a feeling it was going to be another grueling session.

"I know," I said, following Sam as we all made our way down. "But maybe I'll be able to use Gundren today."

*

"Midday break!" Rae announced after several long hours of hard combat training. "For evening sparring, I want Phoebe, Ingrid, Elise, Mari, Billie, Anya, and Nadia back. All others are excused for the day."

There was instant chatter from the crowd.

Being excused from training didn't happen very often, if ever. Valkyries rarely got a break if they were on the grounds. The only time they weren't training was when they traveled back to Asgard and other places to visit family. That was considered their downtime. None of them ever seemed bothered by the rigorous schedule. They loved fighting. It was in their blood.

I tossed my wooden swords down and nodded to Billie, who'd ended up being my midday partner, and went to find Ingrid. She was chatting with another Valkyrie outside the Park, so I waited.

Once she was finished, she turned and gave me a warm smile. "Well done, Phoebe. Your skills are coming along nicely. I saw you throw in some fakes that had Billie going right when she should've been dodging left." She clasped my shoulder, like she usually did, draping her arm comfortably around me as we made our way toward Yggdrasil.

It was lunchtime. The shieldmaidens alternated days to feed, or it would've been too hard for everyone to touch the tree at once.

"Yeah." I blew out a tired breath. "But it's still a huge bummer I'm not allowed to use my swords yet."

"That's all about to change," Ingrid said confidently as we turned down a small path.

"How do you know?"

"Rae has ordered the battle team back for training. After today, you will be working with this group exclusively." We rounded a corner. Yggdrasil came into view. It was tucked inside a small valley close to where we trained. Its rich dark drown bark, ribbed with deep, furrowed veins, flowed up through the ground, melding seamlessly into the mesa, giving it an otherworldly effect. It radiated strength and energy. My body responded to it immediately. My fingers curled, and my blood pulsed faster, anticipating what was to come.

Feeding from the tree was a unique experience, one I didn't have a name for. It was euphoric. A high that rivaled any and made me feel invincible in the best way possible. "Only the battle team gets to train?" I asked.

"For a time. These are our best warriors," Ingrid answered as she pressed her back against with the bark, her arms splayed. I joined her. "The team we're bringing to Svartalfheim. We usually take eight on a mission. It's hard to be stealthy with a large group, and eight has worked for us in the past."

"Are they required to go?" I exhaled as raw energy flowed into me, pooling in my extremities first, then filtering through the rest of my body. Ingrid had taught me the optimal way to drink it all in, and relaxation was key. I closed my eyes.

"No, of course not," Ingrid said, her voice steady and calm. "But Valkyries don't say no to a mission, especially when it involves Leela. Your mother is beloved around here. We're taking the best of the best." Ingrid's voice was wistful.

"Twenty-four years is a long time to be gone," I murmured. I didn't want to think about my mother being tortured by the dark elves in Svartalfheim. It was bad enough knowing she'd been gone so long.

"It is. I miss her like crazy," Ingrid said. "I'm just glad she wasn't sent to Helheim. Then we might not ever have gotten her back."

. "Why?" I didn't pretend to know anything about the realms.

"Hel is a dark place inhabited by dark, evil creatures. But I've never been there personally. You can ask Fenrir about it. It's not my place to gossip."

"Gossip?" That was an interesting word choice. I'd reached my energy limit, my body swirling with light. Lighting up like a glow stick was something I'd gotten mostly used to. It was still spectacularly weird to think I fed on electricity and felt full after feeding. Consuming the energy was actually more satisfying than having a meal—it was like eating a five-course dinner, starting with crab cakes drizzled in béarnaise, moving on to lobster bisque, then to a perfect Caesar salad with just enough anchovy paste to make the taste buds tingle, followed by a rich, buttery truffle oil drizzled over sautéed mushrooms, and ending with a porterhouse steak as big as my face. That's how satisfied I was. I gave a sigh as I stepped away from the tree. "Has Fen been to Helheim?"

"Let's just say he has family there," Ingrid said, rubbing her belly. "We can leave it at that."

Family? Before I had a chance to ask what she was talking about, a loud noise reverberated through the valley, shaking the ground like a mini-quake.

A loud bellow followed.

It was the alarm. Something was outside the gates.

Ingrid had her spear in hand before I could blink. We began to run.

"What's going on?" I asked, sprinting after her, wishing I had Gundren on me, cursing for the seventieth time today that I had been forced to use crappy wooden substitutes.

"I'm not sure," she called over her shoulder, "but whatever it is, it's not supposed to be here."

We rushed toward the main entrance, which was located between two buttes. The span of the opening wasn't more than fifty feet across.

Other Valkyries had beaten us there, their weapons drawn. There were shouts and general pandemonium as they tried to determine what the threat was. Ingrid and I couldn't make out what was there, because we were too far back and too many bodies stood in our way.

Then I heard, "What's a troll doing here?"

"That's one mad-looking creature. Look at its horn."

"I say we kill it."

"Yeah, but what the hell is it doing here?"

I began to push my way toward the gate. It might have been a stupid move, since I was likely the only one present without a weapon, but I had an inkling who it was.

Once in front, I let out a gasp of happiness and ran forward, my face breaking into a wide grin. "Junnal!"

5

A hand landed on my shoulder before I reached the invisible barrier, effectively stopping me in my tracks.

"You know this creature?" Rae asked skeptically. "He is a rare breed, a cross between a giant and a troll. They are immune to most magics and are extremely hard to kill."

"Yes, I know him. He saved my life," I answered simply.

Rae glanced at Junnal, who was less than ten feet away, and then back. "Who did he defeat in your favor?" she challenged.

"Verdandi," I answered without pause, "and the ettin Bragnon. I thought Junnal was dead, but I'm happy he's not!" I was so, so relieved. "Odin sent him to the Norns' lair to protect me. He helped me escape."

Rae's eyebrows shot up as she let go of my shoulder, directing her gaze back at Junnal, who had stopped pounding on the barrier and stood watching us. He could clearly see in, so he was definitely immune to the Valkyries' glamour, or whatever they used to ward the entry.

"Drop the gate!" Rae shouted. There were loud grumbles and protests. "Do it. This hybrid was sent by Odin."

Ingrid reached my side. "Tyr said something was coming. I'm thinking this must be it."

The barrier wavered a few times before it completely disappeared, and I ran, not realizing I was moving, and jumped straight into Junnal's arms.

The troll-giant was huge, bigger than I remembered, at least eight or nine feet tall, but his skin was softer than it looked. He was all gray, like a walking boulder. A tusk protruded out of his forehead and he wore some kind of loincloth.

He hugged me back with one hand, careful not to crush me. He held a fierce-looking club in the other. I gazed up at him, smiling. "I thought Bragnon poisoned you! And if that hadn't worked, I was positive Verdandi would've finished you off. I'm so sorry I couldn't stay and help you. I never got a chance to thank you for telling me how to get out, so thank you! I'm alive because of you." There was no doubt in my mind that this giant had saved my life.

He nodded, seeming to smile, but it was hard to tell because his features were so huge. "Safe," he boomed in a low, rumbling voice before he let go of me.

I turned, intending to lead him inside and stopped short.

A line of Valkyries stood in front of us, most of them with stunned looks on their faces. Some had their weapons up, others looked unsure, glancing at Rae to get her read of the situation.

Rae stood stoically, her arms crossed. She was going to leave this up to me.

"Um," I addressed the crowd. "This is Junnal. He saved my life. I believe Odin sent him here to help us get my mother back."

That was it in a nutshell. The best I had. If they retaliated, things were going to get ugly fast.

Ingrid followed me, announcing in a jubilant tone, "Welcome to the stronghold, Junnal. Any friend of Phoebe's and Odin's"—she stressed the word *Odin's*—"is a friend of ours. Please enter. We are grateful for any assistance in finding Leela. I'm certain you will be an asset to our mission."

I took a few tentative steps forward, Junnal following, his footsteps shaking the ground as he lumbered along. Begrudgingly, the Valkyries parted so we could enter. With relief, I spotted Fen and my brother waiting for us behind the group.

The guys looked relaxed, but both had weapons by their sides. Tyr, it seemed, had shoved Sam behind him at some point, and she poked her head out from behind his broad back, smiling, appraising the troll. "Dang, you're a big boy," she said as she maneuvered around the god.

"Nothing to see here," Ingrid announced to the Valkyries who lingered, gawking at the giant. "Time to get back to work."

"The battle team will meet back in the Park in ten," Rae said, her voice carrying. "You heard Ingrid. Disperse."

A few offhanded comments about pet trolls followed in their wake, but it wasn't awful, and I was way too happy my giant friend was alive and well to be bothered.

Rae addressed me, her tone firm. "This is on you, Phoebe. If your troll causes any problems, it's your mess to clean up."

I nodded. "I understand. Thanks for letting him enter."

"See you in the Park in ten."

After she took off, I turned to the guys. "This is Junnal," I said. "He saved me from Verdandi by telling me how to get out of her lair with Gram." I patted my midsection where the trusty dagger was stashed. "Not to mention, he yanked

Bragnon off me and selflessly put himself between me and Verdandi."

Fen glanced up at the troll appraisingly. "My thanks to you, giant. My mother is the giantess Angrboda, Queen of Jotunheim. Is that where you hail from?"

Junnal nodded, his big head bobbing.

Tyr came forward, his face set. "You are a crossbreed." He stated it as fact, not a question. "Both Jotun and troll. That is a rare mix, indeed. Were you born with both resiliencies?"

Junnal nodded again.

"My father makes it his business to be in partnership with powerful beings. Odin is masterful about such things." Tyr finished, "We are grateful for your aid."

Sam craned her neck. "You're tall," she said, stating the obvious, "and big. You're kind of like the best bodyguard ever invented." She gave him a sunny smile. "I'll tell you what, I'm going to let you hang out with me while Phoebe trains. They don't let the boys near the Park." She jabbed a thumb in the guys' direction. "But they can't stop you from doing much of anything, which is super sweet. Honestly, they'd need a bulldozer to remove you. As a bonus, I bet they won't insult Phoebe nearly as much with you around." She stepped boldly in front of him. "Come on." She grabbed on to his meaty fist. "Let's go get front-row seats before they fill up. Only a few Valkyries are training tonight, so there will be more curious onlookers than usual." She shook her head, her curls bouncing. "I can't wait to see their faces when you show up. It's going to be epic."

And just like that, she led him away.

The giant glanced behind him once, and I nodded. Not that I had to give him permission, but he was clearly looking for some sort of sign. I couldn't help but laugh out loud.

Leave it to Sam to have no qualms about befriending a big, scary troll.

The first time I laid eyes on Junnal, I was not nearly as calm and collected. I may have even wet myself a little. It had been a very stressful day.

Tyr scrubbed his hand over his face. "That girl is going to get herself into massive trouble. She's too trusting, especially for a human. She has no idea of the dangers at hand."

"That's what you're for," I told him, patting his shoulder. "But she's also pretty feisty, so I'd lay money down that she could hold her own in a fair fight if pushed hard enough."

We began to walk toward the Park, and Fen settled his arm around my waist. "I'm happy the Jotun is here," he whispered in my ear, "because looking after you is a full-time job. I can use the help."

I elbowed him in the ribs and kept going.

*

The sun had set hours ago, and we were still training. Rae had been ruthless, making us run, battle, and condition nonstop. This was the real deal.

"Phoebe," Rae ordered after a stint of calisthenics that would've made a human collapse in their own vomit, "go get your weapon."

I stopped short of my last lunge. "Really?" I replied, thinking I might not have heard her correctly. I tried to suppress any happiness that threatened to leak out. I didn't want to embarrass myself by raising my arms in the air and doing a hip roll right there.

She answered by placing her hands on her hips. "Yes, really."

I tossed my wooden imitations away with glee and rushed

to where Sam was keeping a solid vigil with Junnal. Sitting on the ground, the giant was still taller than Sam, who was perched on a raised bench.

Sam handed me Gundren, smiling. "Here you go!" she sang with glee. "Go kick some ass."

I slung the scabbard on my back, energy racing into me as I strapped it on. My body had ached for this moment. I petted the leather straps as I walked forward.

Rae halted me before I reached the inner circle. "But you're not sparring...yet. Those weapons could seriously injure a Valkyrie or destroy her weapon. I want you to practice against that." She gestured casually over her left shoulder to the far corner of the Park.

My eyes followed, my eyebrows shooting past my hairline. I darted a confused look back at her. "You want me to use my weapons against...an animal?" My stomach lurched, finding a new home below my kneecaps. I was about to tell her that there was no way I could kill a sheep tied to a tree in cold blood. I wasn't even hunting it for food. It wasn't going to happen.

"Valkyrie, this is all about control, not killing. Only when you can *control* your weapons will you be allowed to spar with another. I want you to shear that sheep, don't harm it. If you cause its death, you've failed the task."

I blinked. "Um. Okay?" It came out as a question.

Snickers erupted from the Valkyries who weren't training. Large lights that had been positioned around the Park, along with the bright moonlight filtering down from the fully dark sky, made it easy to track what everyone was doing.

As I walked toward the sheep, I heard, "I bet she skins that thing alive in under two seconds."

"That poor thing doesn't stand a chance."

"It's too bad I'm a vegetarian."

45

I was about to voice my displeasure, when a low, garbled yowl shook the air, followed by a huge thump. I turned to see Junnal standing, club in hand, towering over the other Valkyries, something akin to a scowl on his face.

Everyone shut up.

The shieldmaidens could've taken Junnal down, eventually. But it would've taken a lot of them to wrestle him to the ground. Plus, they would've earned the ire of Rae and Ingrid. It was easier to shut the hell up.

But it was the boost I needed.

I paced over to the sheep.

It bleated at me, sniffing the air warily.

"I'm not going to hurt you, big guy," I told it in what I hoped were soothing, sheep-appropriate tones. Was it a guy? No horns. Okay, maybe it was female. "I'm just going to…um…give you a haircut?" Again, it came out as a question, because I had no idea how I was going to go about achieving that task. I unsheathed my swords. They exited the scabbard with that same satisfying zing. I was pretty sure I'd never get sick of hearing that sound. I brought them around and positioned them in front of my body.

I thought I would be shaky, because I was nervous I was going to kill this innocent creature, but my hands were rock steady. Not one muscle moved, everything locked up tight.

"When I give you the order, I want you to slash down quickly and sheer the sheep," Rae commanded from ten feet away.

"Okay." This was, bar none, the craziest thing I'd ever been asked to do. Cut sheep wool with magical swords given to me by a god, their blades sharp enough to kill any living creature on all seven realms. I almost laughed out loud. Topping this was going to take some skill.

"Go!" Rae ordered.

I lashed my hand down, and almost immediately, Rae shouted, "Stop!"

My arm was moving quickly, but I managed to jerk it up at the last minute, effectively stopping my motion a mere inch from the terrified sheep.

It had been choppy, but a stop nonetheless.

The sheep gave me a defiant *baa* as I stepped back.

"That was a test, and you barely passed," Rae all but sighed. "This is what I was referring to. You must be able to halt, change your position, or redirect yourself at a moment's notice. No exceptions. Things around you will always be in motion. It's an art form, Phoebe, something we Valkyries learn at an early age. You must master it. Without it, you will be a danger to our group and yourself."

"So, you don't want me to shear the sheep?" I asked dumbly.

I was a teensy bit confused about the plan.

"Yes," she replied, somewhat impatiently. I didn't blame her. "I want you to cut the sheep's wool, but you will do it with constant distractions and redirection. Do you understand? You must master your control above all else."

"Yes, of course," I replied. This was something Fen was working with me on as well. "I understand." Fen referred to my lack of finesse as *my sluggish human carryover*, which was an artful way of saying I sucked and hit like a girl. He kept at me to become more *Zenlike* and less like a *human zombie* while I was fighting.

Although, he didn't call it *Zen*. He called it *centered*.

And he didn't call it *human zombie*, he called it *phlegmatic*.

Same, same.

"Find the center, Phoebe," he'd tell me again and again.

I'd thought I was getting better at it, but apparently not.

I glanced at the sheep. It snorted and dug a hoof in, kicking dirt and flaring its nostrils.

I hadn't sliced it in half, so that was something. I wanted to point that awesome fact out, but kept quiet. It likely wouldn't garner the same reception that was currently playing out in my head.

"Anya!" Rae called. "Come here." Then she turned to me. "Anya will give you directions, and your job is to follow her every command. Got it?"

"Yes," I answered.

Inside, I screamed, *Why her?*

No one would get more joy from my missteps than she would.

Anya sauntered over like she'd been given a serious gift, twirling her battle ax like it weighed nothing, her face dialed to *I'm soooo bored.*

Rae addressed Anya, her face set. "Phoebe is to work on control. You will be her guide. Are we clear?"

"Yes," Anya replied. After a moment, she added, "I won't disappoint you." She accented the *I* ever so slightly.

Rae glanced at me, saying nothing before she turned and left.

"You heard the commander," Anya intoned, like I was daft and already unwilling to work hard. "Get your swords up. We've got a *lot* of work to do." She mumbled low enough for just me to hear, "Likely an insurmountable amount."

I gritted my teeth, refusing to be baited. I had no idea how long Rae was going to make us work together tonight, but I'd be damned if I let this Valkyrie get the best of me. I positioned myself, waiting not-so-patiently for her command.

"You can't do anything with that form. Hold your arms out farther," Anya sniffed. "And can you please not kill the sheep? I don't want to have to clean blood out of my clothes tonight."

"Sure thing," I replied in a monotone, holding my swords higher, not moving a muscle.

What Anya didn't know was I was determined to master this quickly.

I wasn't going to be her tool for long.

6

"She's insufferable!" I pounded my fists into my pillow. Fen climbed into bed next to me. We'd just gotten Junnal situated nearby. Turns out the big guy preferred to sleep under the stars. His first choice had been to take up residence right outside our door, but after some persistent persuasion on our part, we convinced him that wouldn't be necessary, and he finally acquiesced.

We'd found him a nice spot to bed down near the entrance to our small valley. It was the only way in or out, so he was satisfied.

"Anya is toying with you because she can," Fen told me, pulling me close. I collapsed against his shoulder, sighing. The energy felt wonderful. It was late and I was drained from a full day and night of training. But at least I was less sore.

Anya had run me ragged, shouting inane orders left and right. I'd come close to killing the poor sheep more times than I cared to admit.

When Rae had finally called time, I'd given the ovine the worst haircut of its life. Tufts of wool stuck out here and there. Large patches of pink skin lay exposed. It looked like it had gotten into an accident with a deranged chain saw.

But it was alive.

That was the most important thing.

"I know she's just toying with me because she can. I just don't know what I'm supposed to do about it." I shifted onto my back, enjoying the currents of electricity from his body as they licked against my side.

"She knows you will not do anything to her in retaliation, so it emboldens her."

Emboldens? Sometimes Fen sounded like he was straight out of 1923. I found it endearing. "Why would I retaliate?" I craned my head up to look at him. "She's a big bully who's stronger and faster than me. Fighting her wouldn't get me very far, except face first in the dirt. And that's exactly what she wants. Me to look weak in front of everyone."

Fen shook his head. "I don't believe she'd win handily. Leaving the situation alone is a human trait. In Asgard, if someone challenges us, however subtle, we take it head on, settle the matter, and move on."

"Then how do you recommend I go about it?"

"Fight and defeat her, and she won't bother you again. In fact, she will respect you for it."

"You make it sound easy, and I should point out, that's not only an Asgardian trait. Humans do that, too. But usually only if we are ensured a win. If not, we hide in the locker we were stuffed in until the coast is clear." I sighed. "Anya is like the beautiful jock picking on the new girl."

He chuckled. "I have no idea what that means, but fighting to secure your place is what you have to do. We have a hierarchy in Asgard. Physically strongest on top, the weakest at the bottom. Not many are as bold as Anya in their challenges. Not all share her ways, but many do. She is seeking Rae's favor as well as to move up the ranks on the battle team, and she believes picking on the powerless will get her there."

I hated that I was the weakest gazelle in the herd. Defeated, I rolled toward the wall. "I don't think I'm going to catch up." It felt like an insurmountable climb. Every single Valkyrie had the advantage of time and training over me.

"You won't be at the bottom for long," he assured me as he ran his hand along my arm. I sighed for the fifteenth time. "You are improving tenfold daily."

"How do you know? You're not allowed near the Park," I grumbled. Rae had declared the guys were getting too close, so they'd moved back. They were more of a distraction than a threat. I'd seen many Valkyries preening, especially when Tyr was around.

"Look up next time." I heard the grin in his voice.

I turned my head, appraising him. His eyes were soft. He looked so much different than when we'd first met. He was more relaxed now, and it was a welcome sight. "Are you telling me you're scaling the mesa to watch me?" The Park was in a fairly hard-to-access location, encircled by steep rock walls on all sides.

"Of course," he growled. "I keep you in my sights at all times."

"That seems a bit excessive," I told him, even though I was grateful. After what we'd been through, having him close made me feel secure.

He grinned. "It would be like you to tumble into a wormhole. I have to make sure that doesn't happen."

I chuckled. "Yes, that would suck." I ran a hand through my hair. I was exhausted. "Now, back to Anya. So how do you recommend I best her? She's far stronger than I am and quicker on her feet."

He looked thoughtful for a moment. "You wield the most-powerful weapons in the stronghold," he answered smugly. "It wouldn't be that hard."

"Hard to do what?" I arched my neck to gape at him as I gasped. "Are you saying I should *kill* her?"

"Of course not, Valkyrie," Fen replied patiently. "But you should come this close." He spread his fingers less than an inch apart, grinning like a fool. "So everyone knows you *could* if you wanted to."

I let out a poof of air, the sound close to a deflated raspberry. "That might take more skill than I have at the moment. I'd be lucky to get her to face-plant. I'm not getting by her battle ax so easily. She holds that thing close to the vest."

"I believe in you, Valkyrie," he said, stroking my side, his hair tickling my shoulder in the most distracting way. "Stand your ground, and you will prevail." *Prevail*. So. Adorable. "If you do, the abuse will end. Mark my words."

"That's easy for you to say." I yawned. "You can just turn into a wolf and be done with it. You're asking me to defeat a six-foot amazon who's stronger than me by a mile and who likes to dice people up with her trusty ax."

His warm breath hit my neck, and my toes curled. "That may be true," he murmured, "but I'm pretty sure there's a wolf inside you, too. Here, let me help you find it."

I turned, falling into his arms, his lips meeting mine, both of us hungry.

At least one thing would go right today.

*

"Get back up, you imbecile!" Anya shrieked, her voice hoarse from all the spewing she'd managed to accomplish before noon. "If you continue to move that slowly, you'll kill yourself as well as all of us. Valkyries protect each other at all cost. You must react quicker!"

My face was in the dirt.

Again.

Anya had issued an impossible order to turn one hundred and eighty degrees when I was mid-sheep-shear, my swords near several vital organs. So, in order to not kill the innocent animal, this one different from last night, I chose to land on my face.

I spit out red dust and rose.

It'd taken me a long time to simmer, but now that I was here, my anger was at a boiling point.

All morning, while enduring her abuse, my mind had rehashed what Fen and I had talked about last night. I was going to have to push back at some point, but the old Phoebe—the *human* Phoebe—worried about all the things that could go wrong. Challenging Anya could backfire in so many ways. I could end up really hurt and not able to help find my mother. Or Rae could toss me out of the stronghold. Or a million other things, most of which ended in my horrible death, chopped into little pieces by razor-sharp twin blades.

As Anya yelled another insult, I decided it was time to cool off before I did something I'd regret. I had to find the right moment to strike, and I didn't want it to be a gut reaction. I turned my back on the angry shieldmaiden and sheathed my swords.

Junnal and Sam would be the perfect distraction to take my mind off my crappy morning. The Jotun had chosen not to sit down this morning. Instead, the massive troll stood sentinel at the edge of the Park gates, which were a pair of old wooden posts strung together with small pickets that were purely ornamental. I knew his presence made all the other Valkyries uneasy, but none had been brave enough to challenge him to leave.

If I could morph into Junnal for a few minutes, I'd be all set. I'd punch Anya right into the sandstone rock and go about my business.

As I left the Park, I couldn't bring myself to search for Fen or my brother to see if they were watching. The events of the day had been too humiliating. Knowing they'd been witnessing me getting my ass handed to me again and again was almost too much.

I brushed the dirt off me while I walked.

"Don't turn your back on me!" Anya raged. "We're not done until I say so." I didn't even pretend to look at her. "Did you hear me? We are not *finished* here!"

"I'm taking five," I tossed carelessly over my shoulder.

I was almost to the gate.

"You are not taking five," Anya sneered. "Rae tells us when it's break time, and you don't get special treatment just because you're Odin's bastard *spawn*."

I watched Sam's face go from pity to anger, her fists clenching as Junnal raised his club.

We'd all had enough.

But my friends couldn't fight my battles for me. It was time to finish this, even if I wasn't the victor. I turned slowly. "What did you call me?" My voice wasn't above a whisper.

Anya spat on the ground. "Spawn. You're the bastard child of Odin, and you will bring ruin to us all." Her words meant she was a believer in what the Asgardian seer had foretold. That a child born around the same time as I was would be a threat to the well-being of Asgard.

"Say that again. I dare you." My voice was so low it even surprised me. I began to pace toward Anya, unsheathing my weapons, taking no joy in the telltale zing or the currents of energy that raced into my palms as I grasped them both.

Anya's face was hard, but her eyes betrayed her once again. She was unsure, and that bolstered my resolve.

As I advanced, she brought her battle ax up, swinging it in a circle above her head. Then, as she found her confidence, her face broke into a broad grin, her uncertainty morphing into cockiness. "Bastard *spawn*."

I leaped in the air, meeting her head on.

She blocked one of my swords with her steel blade as we clashed, but my left hand whizzed around, biting into her breastplate, searing through it like it was made of liquid.

When she realized what I'd done, she came at me again, cold fury lining her expression.

I was ready. "Give me your best, Anya," I told her. "You're making it too easy."

She screamed as she swung her ax, spinning her body at the last minute, trying to confuse me. But she'd been using the same tired moves since I'd been here, and I anticipated which way she was going. I ducked, one knee hitting the dirt as I whipped my swords around one after the other, grazing them along her shin guards, careful not to put too much weight into it. I wanted to show her I was a boss, not hack off her leg. But using my control let her know I *could* if I wanted to.

Rae had insisted we wear full fighting gear during our battle practices, which included metal leg guards and extended wrist guards. Some Valkyries even opted to wear chain mail, but Anya hadn't worn it today, and neither had I.

Her protection split in half, the bottoms of the guards tumbling to the ground with pinging noises.

Satisfaction ran through me like a rocket, exploding

bursts of happiness along the way. It felt empowering to finally be in charge. I knew anger fueled me, but I didn't care. I was going to use whatever I could to my advantage.

I rolled as Anya's ax came down, twisting my body and bringing up my swords. I aimed for the handle of her weapon, keeping my swipes accurate and measured. Without sound, both my blades cut into the wood at the same time, one above where her hands grasped and one below.

There was no resistance.

A moment later, the battle ax broke apart in her hands, the double-edged blade careening into the dirt, slicing through the air with a whizzing sound, the bottom of the wood handle pinging after it a moment later.

Her bellow of rage was nothing short of terrifying as she tossed the middle piece of the handle aside and came at me.

I scuttled back, my weapons still in front of me.

"Fight fair!" she yelled. "With your energy, not with your bastard gifts."

I stood, taking a few steps back, making a decision as I sheathed my swords in one motion. "I'm not going to fight you," I told her. "I already defeated you. You are without your weapon and have no way to defend yourself." I grinned. "I win."

"Any Valkyrie worth the skin covering her knows how to fight with her power," Anya said. She stood not even three feet from me. "If we cannot use our weapons, we use what resides inside us." She raised her hands toward the sky and closed her eyes.

She began to gather energy and was planning to unleash it on me.

I wasn't skilled enough to battle her with lightning of my own, since I hadn't yet learned how to channel it, so I did the only thing I could do. I closed the gap between us in one big step and threw a punch.

My fist landed solidly against her cheek. She went down instantly, crumpling at my feet like she'd been unplugged. The satisfaction I'd felt before doubled. I'd been working out with Ingrid, specifically on hand-to-hand combat, and it had paid off. I was strong and toned, Yggdrasil fortifying me.

Anya hadn't been expecting a physical attack, so the advantage had been mine.

There were noises, and I glanced up.

Valkyries two deep stood watching us, their weapons drawn.

I was so surprised I dropped my fists, which I hadn't even realized I still had clenched in front of me. I turned toward the spectator area. Sam and Junnal both stood poised at the edge of the fence, ready to help. Sam's face was a mask of concern.

I met her gaze, and she mouthed something I couldn't understand, but it looked like, *You're growing*, which was weird. I glanced down at my adversary.

Anya wasn't moving.

Flustered, I crouched down beside her. When I reached out to touch her neck to feel for her pulse, I realized what Sam had been trying to tell me.

I wasn't growing. I was *glowing*.

7

There wasn't just a little bit of light filtering out of me. I was *bright white*. Trying to ignore the vibrant color of my skin, I forced myself to check Anya's pulse. Luckily, her heart was beating and she was breathing. She was fine.

I'd just knocked her out.

On my first try.

An inner whoop of joy was dying to make its way out, but I didn't have time to congratulate myself. Ingrid and Rae walked purposefully toward me.

I rose to meet them, straightening. I'd be damned if I was going to apologize. "I didn't mean to knock her out"—I kind of did—"but she forced me to fight. After I dismantled her weapon, I had no other choice but to..."

"It's okay, Phoebe." Ingrid's voice was cautious, like she was speaking to a horse she didn't want to spook. Living on a farm for most of my childhood, I knew that tone well. Ingrid extended a hand in front of her like she wanted to ward something off, but then thought better of it. "No need to explain. We witnessed the entire thing. That Valkyrie had it coming. But we're just...we just..." She dropped her arm and rubbed the back of her neck. "Well, we don't glow like that. I mean, we do, sometimes, like right after we've eaten, or when we get into an extremely euphoric state, usually after battle. But, honestly, it's just a teensy glow, like a bit of our energy seeps through our skin. I'm not quite sure what's going on with you, but I think it might be a good idea to take a break. Let's head someplace where you can rest and get yourself back to normal." She finally clasped my shoulder, and I relaxed a bit. "That was some fighting, though. I couldn't even track some of your moves. Outstanding!" Her jovial tone returned.

Rae stood next to her. "Take a ten-minute break," she ordered. "I'll deal with Anya." Her voice held respect, and a hint of weariness. "That was a fair fight."

As we walked out, Ingrid tried to assuage my fears. "Don't stress, kid. I think glowing that brightly means you're finally coming fully into your immortality. It takes time for our bodies to adjust after they're struck. Depending on our parents, and what's in your gene pool, each Valkyrie brings something different to the table. With your father being the biggest god around, it shouldn't really be a surprise that you would light up like the Fourth of July. We've just never seen it before."

"That's what Fen says," I mumbled. "He says I burn brighter than any other. I just...I thought all Valkyries glowed at odd times. I had no idea I was the only one."

"Like I said, we do glow. We just manage it on a smaller scale." We stopped in front of Sam and Junnal. "How about we stroll to the next valley over?" Ingrid suggested. "You can hang out there for a bit and get yourself back together. Take all the time you need."

I felt fine.

I didn't need to get myself back together.

This was Anya's fault, and now I felt like a pariah. My unease turned to ire. "You know what?" I told the group. "Getting myself back together sounds like a great idea, but I'm going by myself. I want to be alone."

Judging by her face, Sam was chomping at the bit to tell me something.

"Okay, that's fine," Ingrid agreed. "When you get back, everything will work itself out, you'll see. You did the right thing. In Asgard, we come to blows a lot. It's just a rite of passage."

"I understand," I said. "I'll be back in ten."

Ingrid nodded and headed back into the Park.

Sam grabbed on to my arm, her nails digging in. "Holy crap, Phoebe! That was so intense. Your fist swung so fast I didn't even know you'd clocked her until she was a sack of bones on the ground! She so had it coming. It was beyond satisfying to see her crumple."

"When did I start glowing?" I whispered, leaning in.

"Pretty much when you turned around and decided to go after her. It was a slow build at first, but when you chopped her ax up, you really started to burn. You don't even need a flashlight anymore. You're a human glow stick!"

"It only happened because I was pissed off." I think. "My adrenaline was racing, and my blood was pumping. The weird thing was, once I decided I was going to fight, everything kind of slowed down. It made it easy to see what Anya was going to do."

"It didn't seem like that to us," Sam said. "You were both going at warp speed."

I glanced up at Junnal. "Did it look fast to you?"

The big guy nodded.

"Junnal wanted to step in," Sam said, a hint of pride in

her voice. "But I held him back." I arched my eyebrow at her. "Okay, I didn't actually, like, physically *hold him* back. I sort of grabbed on and pleaded for him to stay out of it. If he'd gone in there, it wouldn't have been a fair fight, and they would've kicked us all out before you could say *trolls kick ass.*"

"That's true." I addressed the giant, my voice grave. "You have to stay back unless I'm in serious trouble. Especially with the Valkyries. They barely tolerate you here as it is. Now I'm going to do what they want and have some alone time. Apparently, I need to get my thoughts back together." I stifled a snort. It made me feel like I was in grade school.

"Your thoughts are fine," Sam scoffed, swishing her hand. "You gave it to Anya fair and square. You should be on top of the world, not skulking off someplace to brood."

"I hear you, Sam. But I'm going to take a few and try to de-glowify." I held my hands up to emphasize my point—not that it needed to be emphasized. They were still star-bright. "I also need to figure out how I'm going to play this entire thing. Anya's going to insist that I bested her because I cheated somehow. I'm going to shut her down somehow. I want her off my back permanently."

"Got it," Sam said. "Okay, if you're doing that, I'm going to get something to eat. Some of us still need to eat an actual sandwich to survive around here."

"I'll see you back here in ten." I turned to leave, and heavy footfalls fell in line behind me. I stopped. "Junnal, you don't have to accompany me. I'm just going down the road a bit."

The giant shook his head. "Come…"

"Suit yourself," I replied. It might actually be nice to have the Jotun around. He was a bodyguard on some serious steroids, but one who was totally sweet.

I wove my way through a pathway that led to a small valley next to the Park, and once we crossed into it, I spotted some thick overgrowth to the right. I'd been in this valley only one other time since I'd been here. There wasn't a lot of downtime to explore, but the stronghold was full of nooks and crannies.

I paced over to the dense brush. It was thick and jumbled, like a wall of tangles, with something behind it. I glanced over my shoulder at the Jotun. "Should we investigate?" Junnal stared back. I wasn't sure if the big guy could shrug his shoulders or not. It didn't seem like he cared what we did, as long as he could see me. I glanced around the small valley. I assumed Fen would come find us soon. He likely saw what went down and would want to check in. "I say we go through. It looks like there's a passageway into another valley behind all this stuff." I grasped on to some brush to move it, but it wouldn't budge.

The branches were so overgrown, they were locked in place.

Junnal came forward, and I stepped out of the way. He lofted his massive club and swiped downward, clearing most of the brambles in one stroke.

"You're pretty handy to have around in a pinch," I joked as I took out my weapons, hacking at a few leftover pieces. "Whoa," I said as I glanced through the obliterated brush. "It's a tiny valley inside. It's so lush." It was teeming with trees and greenery, which was surprising for this area. Most of the stronghold was covered in browns and yellows with a few scattered scrubby trees.

I wondered why the Valkyries didn't use this space.

Without hesitation, I headed inside. The area wasn't more than a square block in size, if that. It was surrounded by high rock walls on all sides. Judging by the overgrowth, nobody had been back here in a long time. "There must be water back here," I commented as we moved through more thick brush. "It's so green. This might be my new favorite spot." A big ponderosa pine forced us to one side, and as we passed, I noticed something high up on one of the sandstone walls. "Does that look like an archway to you?" I moved toward it like it was a beacon.

"Yggdrasil," Junnal intoned, slow and steady.

"It can't be Yggdrasil," I disagreed. "I feed from that tree every day. It's way over by the Valkyrie lodgings, at least a mile or two from here. They basically built their homes around it. It can't be in two places at once."

"Tree," Junnal insisted.

"Listen, I can hear trickling water." A babbling brook was not far away. "I wonder why they don't utilize this. It's a great space to hang out. Likely, the Valkyries aren't required to find a place they have to calm down in very often," I muttered. The archway reminded me of the one in Fen's cave. "Let's go check it out."

The mysterious monument was up a short but steep hill, the bottom obscured in dense brush. I had to hack a bunch of overgrowth out of the way to get through. After it was cleared, we climbed up the short distance.

As we came closer, my hands ached to touch it.

To my shock, I realized Junnal might be right. This strange rock face called to me in the way Yggdrasil did, with a pull I felt all the way from my toes. I sheathed my weapons as I came to a stop in front of it, reaching out to allow my fingertips to graze the gritty surface. It was warm to the touch, and within moments I felt a tug.

I snatched my hand back. "What in the world?" I turned to Junnal, my eyebrows raised. "Is this a portal?" It came out as a question, but I already knew the answer. Fen had described some portals as cillars, or offshoot paths, from Yggdrasil, but they were usually dead.

This one was alive and well.

Before the giant could respond, a humming noise issued from inside the stone. We stepped back as a large raven soared out, cawing as he went.

"Huggie!" The bird surprised me, and I had to steady my footing so I didn't tumble backward off the slope. "What are you doing here?" Odin's agent circled in the air twice before finding a branch near us to settle on.

I felt a puff of air a moment before Huggie's words filtered through my mind.

It is time.

"Time for what?" I glanced around. I was missing something.

For you to leave.

"You're not making any sense, bird," I said. "Where am I supposed to go?"

You are ready. You found the path. But you must hurry, or you will be too late.

"Slow down for a minute," I said, suddenly wary. "I haven't seen you since I arrived in the stronghold, and now you're telling me I have to leave?"

Invaldi will not permit the Valkyries to enter his realm, and there are too many to go undetected. Your mother is in jeopardy. She will be moved soon to a place that is unreachable. This is your only chance to slip in unseen.

My heart leaped into my throat. "Where are they taking her?"

The dark elves know the Valkyries seek to hunt them and that they will break in very soon. They have made deals. You are the only one who can go in unseen, through this cillar. But you must go now, with the troll. Have no fear, you are ready.

I was dumbfounded. "You want…you want me to go to Svartalfheim by myself without the other shieldmaidens?"

It is the only way.

"How do you know?" I asked. "We've been preparing for the mission as a team. Rae is leading the Valkyries. I can't do it alone. I'm not nearly skilled enough."

The bird cocked his head at me. *I have been listening and watching. Your skills are sufficient, and your mother needs you, as you are the only Valkyrie who can traverse this cillar. It is a gift you have been given. You will be able to pass into the realm undetected.*

"What about Junnal?" I asked. "Won't the elves know he's there?"

Yes, the elves will know, but trolls come and go in their world regularly, and the Jotun can ride any portal. He will not raise an alarm. That is why he was sent to you. Together, you can free your mother. But you will not get a second chance. You must hurry. The raven gave an irritated squawk. *He comes.*

"He?" I asked, right as Fen's voice bellowed into the small valley.

"Valkyrie!" Fen called. "Where are you?"

Oh, no.

All the pieces began to fall together in my mind. "Are you telling me I have to choose between my mother and leaving Fen without a word?"

The wolf may not accompany you. You would be captured immediately and face death. Once you retrieve your mother, you will take Yggdrasil back here. You have my word. If things change, the wolf will be granted access to the cillar. But he must wait.

"Phoebe," Fen called, his voice getting closer. "Are you up there?" He couldn't see us, because the brush was too thick and we stood behind a few trees.

My disappearing was going to kill him, and if it didn't, he was going to be supremely pissed off. I wasn't sure he'd ever talk to me again. "Can't I just explain to him what's happening?" I pleaded, my voice barely a whisper. "He'll understand." No, he wouldn't. "I can calm his fears and explain that Junnal will take care of me. It'll just take a moment."

Huggie clacked his beak. *The wolf will follow if he gets a chance. He will not listen to reason. I will close the cillar after you go through, but he will attempt to jump through. If he does, there is no way I can stop him and he will be harmed. You must leave now. Your mother's life depends on it.*

My heart clenched painfully.

Fen was going to feel betrayed, but I didn't want him to be hurt, and had to choose my mother. "Will you explain to him why I left?" Panic filled me.

I will try to reason with the wolf, Huggie reassured me. *He will not take this well, but it can't be helped.*

I exhaled. "Okay." I strengthened my resolve. "How do we do this?" I knew Junnal was up for it without asking.

Get on the giant's back and hold on tight. He will get you there safely. Once you land, you will find a cloak. Put it on. It is magical and will conceal you from the dark elves. The Jotun will scent your mother. Take heed, you will have to fight at the end, as the cloak will not fit over you both. But I have faith in you. You must leave now.

"There you are." Fen's voice filled with relief. He was down the hill twenty yards away, glancing up at us.

"I'm so sorry, Fen," I called to him, then pleaded, "You have to understand. There's no other way. I have to go!" As I spoke, I hopped onto Junnal's back.

"What? What are you doing?" Fen yelled, alarmed. He began to run toward me. "No, Phoebe, you can't leave here alone! This is insanity. Don't do this!"

"I have to," I said, tears forming, threatening to fall.

"Please understand. I have to find my mother. This is the only way!"

Now! Huggie squawked, spreading his wings, leaping from the tree branch, soaring toward us.

Junnal lumbered toward the portal.

"No!" Fen yelled, anguish at the forefront.

As Junnal jumped through the cillar, I called, "I'll be back soon. I promise!"

8

I hung on to the Jotun for dear life. The ride through was longer than any I'd taken before, but that wasn't saying much. I'd been in the tree only three times. I fought to stay conscious, air not being a high commodity in the dark, scary vortex. During my previous trips, I'd blacked out, but I wanted to land awake and alert.

We landed hard.

The force separated us, and I tumbled head over heels, not coming to a full stop until my legs bashed into a huge tree. "Ow." I lay there for a few moments, trying to regain my composure.

Junnal hadn't done more than one roll. He waited patiently for me to get up. As I rose, I was happy to see we weren't in a cave. It appeared we'd landed in a dense forest, but I couldn't be sure. It was fairly dark. The trees around us were slumped over, their branches hanging low like depressed willows, leaves brushing the ground, black vines choking their bark. Nothing was green. Everywhere I looked, things were in various shades of browns and ochers.

Not exactly inviting.

My legs were shaky from the ride. I kicked them out as I checked to make sure I had all my weapons and nothing had fallen out. Gundren was secure on my back, and Gram and the ice pick I'd taken off the dark elf I'd killed were in place. My clothing and shoes were all accounted for. That was something to celebrate. "Do you see the cloak Huggie was talking about anywhere?" I asked the giant, scanning the area for something resembling cloth.

The Jotun shook his big noggin.

Both of us began to search, trying to be quiet, which was easier for me than my two-ton companion. After what felt like too long, I began to lose hope, but then I spotted a small leather pouch sticking out from the roots of the tree nearby.

I snatched it up greedily, relief flooding me. I tried not to think about how unready I was for this mission, steeling myself with the fact the mother I'd never met needed me, and I was going to come through for her or die trying.

My mind locked on Fen and his face as Junnal had jumped through the portal. It had been a mask of sadness, like he'd known I was heading for certain death. My heart gave a squeeze. I hated that I'd left him behind and prayed he would forgive me.

Forcing myself to forget about Fen, I unfastened the ties of the pouch and eased it open. The material was silky and thinner than any material I'd ever seen before and completely sheer. I shook it out in front of me. It was hard to believe this would keep me out of sight, but I didn't have reason to doubt it. I didn't second-guess anything anymore.

I upended the bag, hoping there would be a few more things to aid me inside, but it was empty. I was about to let the Jotun know I was disappointed when voices erupted from nearby.

Junnal motioned me to get on his back as he turned to face our company.

Tossing the cloak around me, I climbed on. It had a hood and I pulled it down around my face. I was worried my legs would show, but there was a lot of material, so I tucked it around them as quickly as I could.

From my vantage point over the giant's shoulder, I spotted two dark elves as they came around the corner. They were short, skinny, had pointy ears, overly large eyes and gray, saggy skin. They looked exactly like the others I'd seen in Midgard.

"There you are," one intoned upon spotting Junnal, its voice high and squeaky. "Why you have come this way is beyond me, but you must come along. You are very late. The others have already arrived."

"They are always late." The second one shook its head. "You can never trust a troll to be on time."

"This one seems to be more than a troll. *Hmm?* Are you?" It glanced up, inspecting Junnal. "Are you more than a troll? Come on, spit it out."

"Jotun," Junnal replied, his voice booming around the quiet forest.

"A giant mixed with a troll! Invaldi will be very pleased," the second one said, vigorously nodding its head. "You were to work in the mines, but now we shall see. I think you will make an excellent guard. You are quite a bit bigger than any we've seen in quite some time."

"Come along, follow us, and hurry up about it," the first one intoned. "As we said, you are late."

They began walking, and Junnal followed.

I hadn't been detected. Score one for the green Valkyrie. I somehow couldn't imagine Rae agreeing to cloak herself and ride on the back of a troll, but whatever, if it worked, I was in.

In order to stay on Junnal's back, I'd tucked my knees into the giant's waist, his burly arms covering them tightly, pinning them there. As we moved, I made sure the cloak stayed secure. "I hope where they take us isn't too populated," I whispered into the Jotun's ear. "If they offer, take the job as a guard. Maybe that will take us to my mother."

I had no idea what to expect of this world.

So far it was dark with lots of brown weeping trees. At least we weren't in a cave. I was extremely tired of caves. As we wound our way through a forest, I peeked over the top of Junnal's shoulder. After only a few turns, we emerged into a small clearing, and looming in front of us, as far as the eye could see, was a wall of black rock. An entrance to a tunnel sat no more than ten yards away.

Come on!

What was it with these worlds and caves? "Just my luck," I muttered as Junnal lumbered after the elves, ducking into the mountain after them. "I'm sure this cave will be much more pleasant than all the rest." Yeah, right.

After my eyes adjusted, I saw that this was no ordinary cave. The inside resembled a palace, with huge columns rising up to an impossibly high ceiling, and a granite floor polished to a high sheen. I glanced over Junnal's shoulder. We'd entered through an actual doorway.

Dark elves were everywhere, scurrying this way and that.

"Hurry up," the first elf huffed at Junnal. "You are entirely too slow."

"Yes, come on." The second one gestured, showing its impatience. "We must get to the inner sanctum, as Invaldi will want to meet you himself before you are assigned a position."

Panic welled in my throat. I'd hoped this mission would be quick and relatively easy—we'd be in and out and wouldn't have to encounter Invaldi, especially not this soon. It was likely a pipe dream, but it was *my* pipe dream. Visions of another Surtr encounter had the hair on my arms standing at attention.

We passed through the large atrium with no one the wiser. Not one elf, out of the hundreds passing this way and that, noticed anything amiss with Junnal or the illegal passenger clinging to his back.

Some of the elves held tools, others carried bundles in their arms. One clutched a breathtakingly beautiful necklace made up of a multitude of gemstones that glittered brilliantly, even in the low light.

I was entranced.

As the elf passed, I couldn't tear my eyes away. How strange. I'd never been much of a jewelry gal, but touching those rubies and emeralds was the only thought running through my mind. I had to physically shake myself, gripping the Jotun's shoulders. It was lucky we turned down a hallway and the sparkly jewels disappeared out of sight.

The ceilings were massive everywhere, and this new space was no exception. They were so high I almost couldn't tell where they stopped. The lighting was dim, coming from some sort of sconce lighting attached to the many pillars.

The elves in front of us chattered in animated conversation, but I couldn't make out what they were saying. At the end of the hallway was a huge archway. It was a good thing everything was extra-large, or Junnal wouldn't have been able to get through.

We passed under it, stepping into a room equally as formidable as the main entrance. But this room was octagonal, and each of the eight sides held a different door. All the doors seemed to be made of stone, but I couldn't know for sure.

"Wait here, troll," the first elf instructed. Both elves wore dark-colored pants and light-colored shirts. If their faces weren't so creepy, and their ears so pointy, they could've passed as tiny businessmen.

"Invaldi is very busy," the second one asserted, its shirt a lighter hue than its companions. "He might see you now, or tomorrow, or next week, or never." It cackled at its own joke.

Without glancing back, both elves entered a door to our right, opening it easily and slipping through, even though it was at least twelve feet tall.

"Are we just supposed to stand here and wait?" I whispered. There were no benches or anything that looked like this space could double as a waiting room.

As we bided our time, other elves came bustling into the area, heading for a specific door and disappearing behind it. None of them even flinched at seeing a giant troll standing there or gave him any other notice.

I tried to remain calm, cool, and collected, but my wildly beating heart and my sweaty palms made it hard to be clearheaded. It was taking too long. "Take a causal walk around so we can scout out the doors. Nonchalantly, like you're supposed to be here," I whispered. "Huggie said you'll smell my mom. Let's see if you can pick up on anything." It was better than just standing.

Very slowly, Junnal began to walk toward the door closest to us. He didn't get far when it sprang open and an elf popped out. This one wore an all-black uniform with silver bars on the lapel.

"Are you here for dungeon work?" the elf chirped in a cringe-worthy singsong voice, settling its hands on its small hips. "Well? Answer me!"

"Tell him yes," I said on the slightest of breaths.

"What was that?" the elf asked.

He'd heard me!

I had to be more careful.

"I said take the troll down already," another voice said from inside the door as a second elf emerged. "We haven't got all day."

Relief flooded through me. My cover hadn't been blown. It'd been talking to its comrade, which also wore a similar black uniform, but its had fewer silver stripes.

"I'm asking him if he's here for the job. Well, are you?" the elf asked again impatiently. "Here for the dungeon work, that is?"

"Yes," Junnal said, his voice low, but still booming. That's what happened when you were huge. Your larynx was massive.

"Fine. Then get a move on." The elf motioned its hand for Junnal to follow as it walked back through the doorway it had come through.

Inside was a massive circular stairwell that looked to have been carved out of the mountain itself. It was illuminated exclusively by torchlight. The rugged stone steps were wide enough for the Jotun to walk down, but that was about it.

As Junnal began to descend after the elves, I glanced over the railing, trying to gauge what might be down there. The staircase seemed endless, and it was pitch black at the bottom.

I didn't dare speak, not even a whisper. I couldn't risk my voice carrying.

After we traversed a few flights, each level containing a long, dark hallway with lots of doors, the elf with more silver on its uniform stuck its nose in the air and commented, "Do you smell that?" It peered over its shoulder at Junnal, its eyes accusing.

"Smell what?" the other elf asked.

"I scent white elf magic." It made an exaggerated show of fanning the air as it continued down the steps.

I wasn't sure what white elf magic smelled like, but it could have been the cloak. Ingrid had told me earlier that cloak stones were made of white elf magic, so that would make sense.

"Something from Alfheim in our realm?" the lower-ranked officer scoffed. "Not a chance."

"My nose is one of the most sensitive in all of Svartalfheim," the elf boasted. "Invaldi has been known to use my services to sniff out magic. I'm telling you, I scent white magic, and it keeps getting stronger." They hit the next landing, and both elves stopped abruptly, turning to confront Junnal. "Do you have white elf magic on you, troll? We do not tolerate it in our realm, and it must be handed over immediately."

The other elf sniffed, "You must relinquish any white magics you may be harboring. It's the law."

Junnal did nothing for a few seconds.

Then, slowly, the giant reached into his waistband and pulled out something I couldn't see, extending his hand.

"Is that...is that a *valknut*?" the higher-ranked elf squealed, its voice impossibly higher than before.

"Why would you bring such a thing into our realm?" the other elf barked. "You must get rid of it immediately!"

Junnal held it out to the elves.

"We can't touch it!" the leader cried, taking a few steps back. It turned to the other elf. "Find something the troll can deposit it in." It glanced back at Junnal. "A valknut will not keep you safe." It scowled. "They ward off death, but not in this realm. We shun white elf magic here."

"Should we punish the offender?" the other one called as it began to search for something to contain the offensive valknut—whatever that was.

I was happy Junnal had found something to occupy them with that wasn't my cloak.

The leader puffed up its chest, trying to look like the important decision-maker. "No, this is to be expected. Trolls who come to work often have trinkets and amulets," it scoffed. "They think it will protect them, but they are mistaken." It narrowed its eyes at the Jotun. "Do not ever bring white elf magic here again. Understood, troll?"

Junnal nodded.

The other elf finally rustled up some sort of black box it'd found tucked into the stone wall. It walked up to Junnal. "Drop it in here. And you better not have anything else on you." It angled its nose in the air and sniffed.

I was curious to see what this strange valknut was, so I peered over the Jotun's shoulder and watched him deposit what looked to be a metal object into the box. It resembled three triangles fused together and appeared to be nothing more than a trinket. Something akin to a good-luck charm.

As soon as the valknut hit the bottom of the box, the elf snapped the lid shut, holding it away from its body like it was diseased. Then it walked back to the wall and tucked it in, clapping its hands. "The cleanup crew will find this sooner than later, and they will be in for a surprise."

The other elf snickered. "I hope Ganwick finds it. He'll have hives for a month!"

They chuckled, bantering about allergies and afflictions, as they headed back down the stairs. Junnal followed, and I glanced behind me into the hallway we'd just been occupying, the landing dark and ominous, as all the others had been, when I heard a noise behind one of the doors closest to the stairwell.

A soft "help me" floated down after us, and shivers raced up my spine.

9

We descended impossibly farther, at least ten more levels as far as I could tell. Each landing we passed was full of closed doors. This was their prison. One level in particular was heavily guarded by a pair of elf sentinels stationed out front. It was well lit, and the doors were color-coded, not just plain gray. The guards ignored us as we passed.

Logically, my mother had to be imprisoned down one of these hallways. The urge to jump off Junnal's back and go investigate needled at me, but doing so wouldn't have gotten me very far, so I struggled to be patient.

As we rounded yet another landing, the elf leader finally announced, "It will be good to have someone as big as you down here to keep the others in line." Both elves strode down a hallway with many doors. "This is where we keep some of our worst offenders, as well as a multifaceted chamber of torture. I'm certain you will enjoy your time here."

The other elf snatched a torch off the wall as light was getting scarce the farther down we went.

Junnal lumbered after them with me on his back.

Moaning issued from behind some of the doors, and my stomach lurched, my hands itching to grab my swords. At the end of a long passageway, and beyond many doors, stood an open archway.

Loud sounds and rumbling came from inside, the voices as deep as Junnal's. The elves scurried through, and there, sitting at an enormous table, were five gigantic trolls. They didn't look like giant hybrids either. Their skin was sickly green and sallow. They each had multiple tusks protruding from their heads—some erupted out of their foreheads, while others from their jaws.

They all looked menacing.

Upon our entry, the one in the middle stood up, toppling its chair, its huge fist pounding down on the wooden table, making it shake to the point of breaking. This troll wasn't as tall as Junnal, so I let myself exhale. "Who are you?" it bellowed.

"This is," the elf leader glanced back as Junnal, "what's your name? And hurry up about it." It snapped its long, skinny fingers. "We don't have all day."

"Junnal," the Jotun intoned.

"Yes, then, this is Junnal," the leader addressed the other trolls, not cowed by their height or ferocity. "We've brought him here to join your ranks, as has been decreed. The Valkyries have been denied access once again, but our sacred leader knows those harlots will find their way in eventually. We must guard Odin's favorite with all we've got and then some, so we have hired more help."

They were talking about my mother.

She was here! We'd arrived at the right place.

My joy was cut short as all the other scary trolls stood up, some of them clutching evil-looking weapons like maces and hatchets. Introducing the Jotun into their ranks wasn't going to be as easy as these elves seemed to think. Junnal tensed beneath me, his muscles tightening, his club rising.

"Well," the elf sniffed, "we will leave you to whatever it is you do here." It waved its hand. "You are all to await orders. I'm certain there will be some movement of some prisoners very soon."

Both elves turned and walked out without a second glance, leaving Junnal to fend for himself with five angry trolls looming over him.

The troll who'd stood first snarled, "We don't need your kind here! Get out!" Its forehead tusk quivered with each word.

Junnal shrugged, unperturbed by their assessment of him.

One of the other trolls came around the table, brandishing a short cudgel. "We don't accept *strangers*. You are not of *our* kind."

Junnal's back muscles twitched.

That was my cue to get off.

How was I going to do this so no one saw or heard? The Jotun sensed my predicament and slowly backed against the wall. The trolls took that as a sign of retreat and began to catcall.

"That's right, mixed race, leave us," one growled.

"Be gone, trash!"

"It's better to leave now, with your head still attached."

Junnal stopped a foot from the wall and lifted his club. As he winged it down, I sprang off. The weapon smashed into a chair that sat next to us, blasting it to smithereens. Yanking the cloak around me, I made my escape, hoping these foul creatures didn't spot me. I edged toward the door as the trolls came forward.

Junnal was quick to react, socking his huge fist into the

side of one troll's head, while smacking another with his club.

I had no other choice but to head back the way we'd come. I rushed blindly into the hallway. The dark elves had taken the torch with them, so it was hard to see. Only a flicker of light at the other end allowed any visibility. I counted twenty doors, ten on each side, between where I stood and the stairway we'd taken.

Could my mother be behind one of these doors? The odds were fairly good.

This was a well-guarded level, according to the elves.

Time to find out.

I crept toward the first door, which was made of thick steel, or whatever metal they used here. It held traces of red rust and looked indestructible. There was a small grate at around bellybutton height that must have allowed the dark elves to communicate or give food to their prisoners.

Behind me, smashing noises echoed down the passageway, followed by snarls and bellows loud enough to rattle the walls. I waited a few moments to see if anything happened, but no elves came running. It must be commonplace for trolls to fight like they were in the WWE.

Trying to ignore the pandemonium, hoping Junnal won, I bent down to the grate. I didn't unlatch it in case whatever was in there could sound an alarm, or worse, poke my eye out.

Instead, I put my lips to it and whispered, "Leela? Are you in there?"

Silence.

I was just about to move to the next door when I heard a sinister cackle, followed by a low hissing, "*Freeeeee* me, young Valkyrie, and I will give you all the riches you desire. Sparkly, shiny things for the taking."

The voice held malice. There was no mistaking it.

Nope. Nope. Nope.

Wasn't going to happen.

To my horror, long, creepy fingernails poked around the grate, the voice louder, demanding, "Do not disappoint me, fair maiden," it seethed, "or I will seek my revenge on you."

I backed away. "Um, I think you have me mistaken for someone else. I'm just looking for my mot—my motor...for my...car." *What?* That was the worst backpedal ever. But I'd almost let the freak know I was searching for my mother! And how did it know I was a Valkyrie?

The thing cackled, sounding like a wailing infant—if said infant was a scary, adult, long-fingernailed supernatural creature. "You are Odin's spawn, are you not? The one they fear? I hear them bemoaning your very existence daily. Help me, and I will spare your life."

How did it know that? It was best not to answer. I backed away.

Its voice followed me, taunting me. "I will be set free, mark my words, and when I am, you will perish!"

Sorry, buddy, I'll take my chances, thank you very much.

I turned and rushed down the hallway, skipping a bunch of doors, but I couldn't exactly stay where this creature could torment me. I stopped at the last cell before the stairway, listening for elves and hearing nothing, tucking my cloak hood down over my face even farther, just to be sure.

Fen would have been an asset right about now, but I couldn't think about that. He was likely frantic with worry. I hated that I'd had to leave without telling him where I was going. But finding my mother had always been the mission. It's what I'd been training for since I'd arrived in the stronghold. Huggie had told me not long ago that it would be my mother who would protect me from the Norns, the three fates who wanted my blood. So saving her would also help me.

A noise sounded behind, making me almost jump out of my skin. I whirled around to face the door. "I can help you, Valkyrie," a voice whispered from behind the closed grate.

He sounded male and human.

I crept over, bending down. "How do you know what I am?"

"I can smell you."

Oh.

"You can trust me," the voice continued. "I'm from Asgard, and I'm fated to die soon anyway, so I have nothing to lose." The man's voice held a stoicism I couldn't deny.

"I'm looking for the shieldmaiden named Leela," I whispered. "Do you know where they keep her?"

"Not exactly. They move her around often," he answered. "But I promise I can help you find her if you set me free. I know she's near."

That gave me hope. "If I free you, how do I know you won't try to hurt me?"

"I have no reason to harm you," he answered matter-of-factly, a slight chuckle followed. He sounded like my brother Tyr. He had the same Asgardian accent.

"Maybe not, but why would you choose to help me?" I asked.

"As a gift for granting me my freedom, of course," he said.

I bit my lip.

One of two things could happen. One, he could do as he said, or two, he could try to kill me or turn me over to the elves.

Was I willing to take the risk or not? That was the question.

There was no doubt we needed help. Getting it from someone on the inside would be invaluable.

Bellows echoed down the hallway. The troll-giant fight was winding down.

Sensing my trepidation, the man said, "I know you don't have reason to trust me, but I know this realm. I've been here for years. I can be an asset. Free me, and I will help you find Leela and escape."

It was too tempting to pass up. "I have a hybrid Jotun as a bodyguard," I warned. "If you try anything, he will protect me."

He chuckled. "If you fail to trust me, you may keep me bound."

"Bound?"

"I am...restrained at the moment." His voice was tight.

My eyebrow quirked as Junnal shouted and a troll cried out in pain. I had to make up my mind. I decided to ask him one more question. "Why are you here? Why do the dark elves hold you captive?"

"My mother felt this was the best way to protect me."

He could not have said anything to me that would've shocked me more. "Are you serious? Your *mother* sentenced you here?"

"She pays the elves handsomely to watch me—it's her way of keeping me alive, but honestly, it's not really a life."

"Why are you bound if you're not a real threat?"

"Because I keep escaping."

"Are you a god?" I asked.

"Yes, my name is Baldur. Open the grate."

I unlatched the small opening and bent down.

He pressed his face near the small bars, grinning. He looked completely human. "Your bodyguard must be mighty. You're lucky he's winning. Those trolls are vicious.

But the continued commotion could lead the elves here at any moment. You must free me now."

Making up my mind, I reached for the handle to yank open the door, but of course it was locked. I inspected the front. No keyhole. Instead, a small combination safe lock sat to the left of the jamb. There were no numbers on the face. The entire thing was covered in weird-looking symbols.

A pair of gleaming blue eyes met mine as a wry smile played on his lips. "I know the combination."

10

"Don't make a mistake," Baldur warned. "If you do, alarm bells will ring throughout the realm. They take breaches in security very seriously here." There was a hint of a chuckle was in his voice.

"I'm glad you can be so lighthearted about this," I said, trying not to elevate my voice. "If I make a mistake, and we get caught, I won't get another chance to free my mot—the Valkyrie Leela." *I did it again! Must stop doing that.* Even though this god seemed trustworthy, I'd just met him. "Freeing her is the only reason I'm here. So tell me the combination again, slower this time."

"Triangle, square, prism, back to triangle, then noose." I squinted at the tiny hieroglyphics. The noose was particularly grisly with a limp body hanging from it.

"Which one is the prism?" I was on my knees, trying to discern which was which so I didn't make a mistake once I started. There were a ton packed on the dial.

"The one that looks like a 3-D triangle." He'd left off the *duh.*

"There's nothing here that fits that description—unless you mean the diamond? Or the inverted heart...with an arrow through it? Or maybe that's a flaming sword?" I inspected it more closely in the low light as a commotion erupted behind me at the end of the hall.

Something was storming out of the guard room.

"Go," Baldur urged. "Get clear of the cell. Wait until they leave, then come back."

"Where do I go?" I glanced around.

"There's a small alcove to the right of the landing. It's just an indent in the stone, but judging by your voice, you'll fit. Since you're cloaked, you should be fine. But even though the elves can't smell you, they can scent white magic, so be careful."

I'd already learned that helpful tidbit.

I didn't have time to ask him how he knew so much about me by my voice and scent as I hustled toward the stairs. I ducked into the alcove, narrowly avoiding the huge troll as it limped by. Junnal bellowed his disapproval of the escapee, pounding after the injured green guy at a brisk pace, shaking the floor as he went.

The troll wore a slightly confused expression as it eyed the stairs, seeming shocked it was getting its ass handed to it. It was the leader—the one who had initiated the fight. That had probably never happened. Coffee-colored liquid leaked from several wounds, and its leg was turned at an odd angle.

The Jotun came up behind it and grabbed it around the neck. With one move, Junnal arched over the stairwell and tossed the troll over the railing. As it fell, it roared, something between rage and fear.

A long moment passed before we heard him land with a thud.

Well, if the elves hadn't known there was unrest on this level, they did now.

Junnal turned and walked back, coming to a stop right in front of me. I pulled my hood back. He appeared no worse for the wear, aside from a few minor abrasions. "Can you see me through this cloak?"

He nodded.

"Are all the trolls down for the count?"

He nodded again.

"Super," I said as I moved out of the alcove. "We have to free a prisoner, and then we can go—"

He shook his head no, sticking his massive tree trunk of an arm out to stop my progress.

I put my hands out. "Listen, I know it sounds crazy to spring a prisoner, but you have to hear me out," I argued. "I found a god who says he can help us." Junnal cocked his enormous head, giving me the *inquiring minds want to know* look. So I expounded on the cooked-up details for the breakout plan. "He says his name is Baldur and his mom locked him up. She *pays* the elves to keep him here against his will. Have you ever heard of such a thing?" I sniffed. "It's awful! So, there's this dial thingy, and he knows the code. If we free him, he says he'll help us locate Leela." Score one for not starting to use the word *mother*. "Then we're out of here before Ingrid and Fen can be too angry I disappeared in the first place." Finding my speech fairly eloquent, I took a step forward, assuming Junnal would see the logic and agree with me, only to be stopped by the Jotun again as he put his massive hand in front of him, shaking his head no.

"Why not? He's being held against his will! That's inhumane on every level," I insisted. My voice rose, and I struggled to keep calm. We needed help. "No adult should be kept anywhere without their consent. Fen was treated the same way. Baldur deserves to be free to live his own life."

"He's worried Frigg will take her wrath out on you for springing me." The voice came from the cell, Baldur having heard me loud and clear. "He's right, of course. But that shouldn't stop you. My mother is overprotective in the extreme, and if I've learned anything in all my years, it's that you can't escape your fate. If I'm destined to die and spend my time in Hel until Ragnarok, so be it. It has to be better than this. The food is horrible, if you can even call it that, and they are very low on sunshine. I haven't attended good sporting event in years, and my vessel needs a captain. I'm mad with boredom, and I will likely die in this cell if I'm not freed soon. You came just at the right time."

"See?" You couldn't argue with that. "You heard him. We can't leave him here," I urged. "It's his life to lead, not his mother's. What if Odin decided to lock you up? Would you want me to free you? Because I would."

The Jotun bowed his head and lowered his arm, appearing resigned.

I took a step, smiling at him. "If it makes you feel any better, you can toss him back in his cell if he double-crosses us." I patted Junnal's tree trunk of an arm as I walked toward the cell.

"That won't be necessary," Baldur cracked. "You are my ticket out of this inferno. We gods honor those who do us service. My debt to you will be to find Leela and help you escape, and in the process, I will get to abandon this dreaded landscape forever."

I knelt in front of the door for the second time. "Okay, let me take a look at this combination again," I said through the grate. "When you give me the code, go slow."

"Try to hurry. They will find the troll in the dungeon soon enough and raise the alarms."

If I made a mistake, we were going to pay dearly. My fingertips brushed the surface, and tingles filtered up into my hand. "This device carries a charge." It was a statement, not a question. I was coming to understand my body, and it was highly sensitive to electricity of all kinds.

"It's made of dark elf magic, which does often carry a charge," Baldur agreed. "That's why they will know if you enter the wrong code."

"Why aren't these locks secured by fingerprints or something more technical?"

"The dark elves don't have fingerprints." Baldur chuckled. He politely refrained from calling me stupid. "How old are you? You must be just struck."

There was no time to fill him in on my story, so I settled on, "Yes, I'm young. I'm going to start now. You said turn it to each symbol without stopping, correct?"

"Yes," he said.

"Give me the code."

"Triangle, square, prism, triangle, noose."

"Triangle," I said as I moved the dial. "Square. Though this almost looks like a box. It has weird lines behind it."

"It's likely not a square," Baldur agreed in his affable way, "but it's the only symbol with four sides."

"I'm going to the diamond that kind of looks like a prism," I told him. "The heart thing just looks wrong."

"I'm certain you will get it right."

There was laughter in his voice. "What's so funny?" I landed on the diamond and took a breath before I deftly turned the knob toward the triangle once again.

"I never thought I'd get out of here, and you being my savior was not in any of my wildest imaginings."

I forgot I'd taken my hood down and he could see me. "I can assure you, I'm much fiercer than I look." I turned the dial to the final symbol, a noose with the awful rendering of a dead creature hanging from it. "I'm on the last symbol. Get ready."

A low snarl came from behind me, and I almost dropped my hand.

Junnal was already in motion. One of the trolls had woken up from his trouncing in the guard room. "Get away from that door!" The green troll limped toward me as it shouted. It was covered in blood, multiple contusions leaking the chocolaty-looking stuff down the side of its face. "Do not interfere with our prisoner. The sentence for that is death——"

The troll was silenced by Junnal with a club to the head.

It collapsed, out cold, with a thundering sound, right as the door unlocked with a pop.

With relief, I sprang up, yanking on the handle to hoist it open. A very handsome face wearing a wide grin met mine. The god was very tall, had tousled blond hair, and was built like a train. His eyes were an impossibly bright shade of blue, more so than I'd noticed through the grate.

He moved back a few paces so I could get by. "You must untie me." He lifted his wrists to show they were tethered by a long cable.

"Are you always in a good mood?" I asked. The cord binding him was glittery, made of some material I'd never seen before, and was attached to the stone wall. Baldur was dressed in something that resembled a prison uniform. It was a one-piece black suit, faded with age. He was grimy dirty and in need of a good scrubbing, but that didn't seem to diminish his joy at all.

He was positively glowing with it.

"Being gracious and cheerful is my bane to bear," he told me as I inspected his bindings. "But on most days I think I wear the mantle well."

"You do," I agreed. His charm was infectious. I dropped my cloak to the ground and unsheathed my swords with their telltale *whoosh*. "I'll look forward to learning more about you later."

Baldur's eyebrows rose. "You carry Gundren?" His gaze locked on mine for a full second. I couldn't read his expression.

"Yes," was all I offered.

He recovered in the next instant. "I wasn't expecting something so...regal. But that will surely do." He smiled.

"Are the elves going to know when I cut this?" I asked, positioning myself next to the wall where the chain was hooked.

"Possibly," he said. "But it can't be avoided. After you free me, we will vacate this area immediately."

"Where exactly are we headed?" I asked, raising my right arm.

"There are several compartments the elves don't check. We can hide there if we must."

I swung my arm down, severing the cable with little effort. It recoiled with a pinging sound as alarm bells began to ring.

11

The red alert sounded like high-pitched foghorns. I sheathed my swords and picked up my cloak as Baldur freed himself from the rest of the cable, the mass falling to the ground around his dirty feet.

I donned the fabric as Baldur poked his head out the door. "Your bodyguard is very efficient."

Junnal's footsteps stopped outside the door.

"Yes, he is," I agreed.

Baldur ducked out into the hallway, and I followed. There was a clamor of footsteps and garbled noises on the stairs.

To my surprise, Baldur turned toward the troll room.

I followed, motioning to Junnal. "Secure the door after us," I told him. "Try to keep the elves out to buy us some time." To Baldur, I said, "I hope you know where you're going."

"There's a tunnel entrance here. It's a way for the trolls to get around without using the main stairwell. They aren't supposed to take prisoners this way, but they're lazy." Baldur made a beeline to the back of the room.

I didn't see any door.

Baldur went to the wall and grabbed a lit torch off its mounting. Then he took the iron bracket in his hand and yanked it down. There was a noise to my right as bricks suddenly began to move, and a secret passage opened up.

I was fairly impressed. "I guess freeing you was the right thing to do, though, if I hadn't, there would be no alarm bells ringing." Behind us, Junnal had slammed the door on the dark elves, pulling a big lever in place to keep them out.

"You will pay for this!" an elf hollered on the other side of the door.

Small fists pounded on the wood. "This will not keep us out for long!"

"Release the god!"

They were beyond angry, security being their main business, and we'd just mucked it up.

I hurried after Baldur, who had taken the torch into the passageway. It was a bigger space than I'd thought. I guess it had to be if trolls used it. Junnal came after, ducking to get through, but once in he could stand upright.

"Secure the door the best you can, troll," Baldur ordered. "They will get through the other once the spells arrive. There are several places we can go from here, but the one I'm thinking of gives us a chance to stay hidden longer."

There was no locking mechanism on the passageway door, so instead, Junnal ripped a torch holder off the wall and jammed it into the handle, going through the wood and into the rock.

He shrugged as I looked on.

Hey, whatever worked, right?

"Good job," I told the big guy. Picking up the pace after Baldur, I said, "I'm up for anything that will keep us free and safe."

"Dark elves are extremely superstitious," Baldur explained as we rushed through the tunnel. "There's a floor they haven't entered in years that they believe is cursed. The white elves spelled it when they freed one of their own. It's said that any dark elf who enters will die a horrible death."

"Is it true? Did they curse it?" I asked.

Baldur chuckled. "I have no idea, but it will keep them out while we hatch a solid plan to free the shieldmaiden you seek." We rounded a corner and ran right into a staircase. This one was smaller than the main stairs and closed off by stone walls on either side. They reminded me of something you'd see in a medieval castle. Baldur went up without hesitation, taking two at a time. I kept up, but just barely. "When they figure out we entered the secret level," Baldur called over his shoulder, "they will enlist help, but that will take time. I just hope we can find it before they find us."

I tried not to be alarmed. "What do you mean *find it?* I thought you knew where we were going."

"Don't worry, young Valkyrie. I will know it the instant I see it, as they have the entrance boarded up. It's been a while since I've been back here."

We raced up two more flights.

Commotion in the form of running feet came from somewhere above us. "They know we're here," I said caustically. "We need to find this mystery level quick."

"The fates have our favor. Look." He gestured in front of him.

Where the other passageways we'd passed looked normal, leading off to who knew where, this one was more than covered—it looked as though someone had nailed everything they could think of, including the kitchen sink, in front of it.

Not only was there wood crisscrossing the entire expanse, but there were several weapons, some metal bars, something that looked like a frying pan, and surprisingly, some clothing.

"What's with the pants and shirt?" I asked as we both moved back so Junnal could come forward.

"Like I said, they're superstitious," Baldur replied. "Who knows? Maybe they thought it would ward off the white magic? It's tough to know with these guys. They're odd creatures, and their behaviors even stranger. Why my mother thought to entrust my care to them is beyond me."

"Your care?" I snorted. "Not sure your well-being was on the list. Did she think she was paying them to keep you in a nice apartment?"

"Well, I did start off in nicer accommodations," Baldur admitted, somewhat sheepishly. "But when I became less than a willing guest, they had no choice but to move me. The end result was where you found me. My mother only visits once every few years. When the time arrives for her to check in, they usually transport me to something nicer."

I was stunned. "Why don't you tell her the truth when she's here?" I sputtered. "If she knew where you were really kept, would she continue to insist you stay here?"

"Unfortunately, yes. Because she chooses to believe it's a better sentence than death."

It was hard to argue with death. It was pretty final.

"Well, quality of life is pretty important, too," I argued. "Or why live at all?"

"My feelings precisely," Baldur agreed as Junnal began to rip apart the barricade.

The patter of feet came from below us. The elves were converging from both sides.

"Hurry, Junnal," I urged. "They're coming!"

"We know where you are!" a dark elf shrieked. "You will not evade us!"

Junnal was making headway, but there were a lot of layers to get through. Baldur and I both turned to face the threat. I began to untie my cloak so I could fight.

"No," Baldur ordered, taking my arm. "Put your hood up and stay cloaked. Right now they think the giant set me free. I have very powerful friends, so they will believe he was sent by one of them. If I'm caught, they will simply take me to another cell and bind me again. I need you on the outside if that happens." He propelled me up a few steps, placing me firmly next to the wall. I pulled my hood down around my face. "Don't make a sound." The man still sounded cheerful. "I should be able to talk to them for a while, to buy us some time until your giant can get us through."

The chorus of voices grew. They were going to descend on us any second now. Junnal grunted as he pulled apart more stuff blocking the passageway. He tossed it down the stairs as he went. Hopefully, that would keep them back long enough for us to get through.

No such luck.

A pack of elves turned the corner, racing upward, narrowly avoiding some flying timber. I glanced at Junnal, anxious to see the progress. Still more to go. They really, really didn't like this floor.

"You will not get to the cursed level, god," one of the elves cackled. "We are here to take you back."

"Hold on there, boys," Baldur replied good-naturedly. "There's no rush. We've all been through this before." More debris was hurtled down the steps. Several of the elves had to duck. Some were hit squarely and tumbled backward. "I'm just having a little fun. Have to stretch my legs here and there. You know how it goes."

All these elves were dressed in outfits with silver bars, and most carried weapons that resembled stun guns. "Tell your henchman to stop his assault on the door this instant!"

"That level cannot be breached!" another shouted.

More flying items, including a pair of pants and what was possibly a nightshirt. Junnal was down to the last bits, his powerful fist ramrodding through them like a sledgehammer.

"You were aided by another," a dark elf accused. "The troll is not your only accomplice."

"That's not so," Baldur replied confidently. "I used my wits and the strength of this giant and nothing more."

"That's not what Tallester told us," another one said.

"That old, wizened man?" Baldur scoffed. "He talks to imaginary beings all the time." They must have been talking about the scary prisoner I encountered briefly. "He can't be trusted."

"He is a dwarf seer," an elf from behind piped in. "And he said you were aided by a *Valkyrie!*" Valkyrie was clearly a dirty word around here.

"And not just any *Valkyrie*, mind you," another one added. "Odin's own spawn! The one who is being sought by the Norns. She is highly dangerous and has committed a great crime by coming into our realm without permission. She will pay dearly!"

I watched Baldur's face through the sheerness of the cloak as he took in the information that I was Odin's daughter. I could see only his profile, but I couldn't detect any surprise. In fact, he showed no emotion at all. Instead, he spread his hands out to the sides. "Well, if I had this expert help you speak of, where is this mysterious Valkyrie?"

They seemed puzzled as they glanced around the small space. I stayed perfectly still, the hood low over my face, my hands folded into the sleeves.

Junnal tore the last of the barricade down, tossing it behind him without a care, a long board hitting an elf smack in the chest, sending him flying back into the crowd of elves behind him.

One of the minions in front shook its Taser at Baldur. "It matters not that we can't see her. We know she's here!"

Another elf stuck its nose in the air and took a long sniff.

Oh, no.

It screeched, "I scent white magic! The Valkyrie is hidden!"

"That's where you're wrong," Baldur said, crossing his arms like he didn't have a care in the world and there wasn't an army of dark elves waiting to take him back to a cell and tie him up. "What you smell is the forbidden level." He cocked his head toward Junnal.

A large man-sized hole gaped in the barrier.

All of the dark elves took in a collective breath. "You cannot go in there!" a dark elf shouted, aghast at the prospect.

"No," Baldur corrected, "*you* can't go in there. Me?" He gestured at his chest with a thumb. "I can go in there all day."

A bunch of garbled voices erupted at once, most of them frantic.

Junnal nodded his head ever so faintly and stepped aside, and I hurried up, slipping through the opening, not making a sound.

Behind me, an elf threatened Baldur. "We will stun you now and be done with this nonsense."

I stopped and turned, thinking I might have to double back and aid Baldur, when Junnal bellowed. The Jotun leaped down the stairs, effectively sending the elves scattering like bowling pins, as Baldur slipped behind the giant before the elves knew what happened.

I moved back to make room for Baldur, when a stun gun

went off with a loud clap, much louder than I'd imagined the small thing could make. I reached for my weapons instinctively, brushing back my cloak. I needed to protect my friend and bodyguard who had just risked his life for ours.

Baldur stilled me, his hand on my shoulder. "They will not harm the giant with those guns," he assured me. "He will be here momentarily. Until then, let's find a safe place away from the stairway."

Reluctantly, I let the god lead me away. Junnal's bellows trailed after us, but they didn't sound pained. He sounded pissed off.

Baldur had brought the torch, which was lucky since this level was pitch black. We entered a hallway, just like the one where I'd freed Baldur, cell doors lining both sides. Some of the doors were wide open, others shut.

A squeaking noise shrilled as we passed a cell, and I jumped, clutching my heart.

Baldur found my actions hilarious and tossed his head back as he laughed heartily, his belly shaking. "Is the valiant Valkyrie afraid of a little Muroidea?" He had actual tears in his eyes. "Only the smallest of children of Asgard fear them."

I blamed my human side for startling at the noise, which had most certainly been of the rodent variety. That part of me would likely be forever ingrained to jump where spiders, snakes, and rats were concerned. "If I knew what a *Muroidea* was, I could tell you definitively if I'm afraid or not. But that sounded like a squeak from a *rodent*. I'm not scared of rats, per se, but I don't hold any love for them either." It was good I hadn't unsheathed Gundren, which had been my first instinct. That would've resulted in over-the-top hilarity that I'd never live down.

"A Muroidea is indeed from the rat family. The ones that live here are just bigger and more ghoulish than the ones on

Midgard. When you evolve in a place like this"—he spread his arms wide—"there's no other choice but to adapt. Count yourself lucky you've never seen one."

"I will." I gave an inward shiver. Gross. Bigger, badder rats. And I thought New York City was bad. "As long as the Muroidea stay away from me, they will have nothing to fear."

Baldur guffawed. "They are harmless. Unless they scent blood."

"Great," I mumbled as we continued down the dark, dusty hallway. "I'll be sure not to bleed."

"They are malnourished on this realm, with little to eat. They will attack en masse if they scent blood."

Behind us, Junnal's heavy footsteps finally echoed into the passageway. I was relieved he was back. Baldur and I made it to the end where a big wooden door stood in front of us.

"This should be the guard's room," Baldur said as he palmed the knob.

It opened with no hesitation, and we stepped in.

12

The room was stagnant and musty. It hadn't been used in a very long time. There was one lone table, battered with age, shoved in a corner, and several overturned chairs scattered about the floor. Cobwebs as big as tractor tires hung from rafters just about everywhere. I tried not to envision spiders as large and grotesque as the Muroidea Baldur had described, but something told me they were.

I grabbed a chair with one hand, while the other untied the cloak at my neck. I shrugged out of my best defense and draped it over the newly set up seat before I perched on the edge, making sure my weapons had enough room, because there was no way I was taking them off. I addressed Baldur, who had righted his own chair. "So now what?" I asked. "Where do you think they're keeping Leela? And how are we going to get there?" I was anxious to find my mother.

Junnal stood by the door, his massive arms crossed, his club holstered in a giant belt he wore around his waist. He looked fine, the scrapes from his encounter with the other trolls already healing.

"My best guess is she's being kept on level five." Baldur fit the torch into a holder on the wall, and a low, flickering light bounced around the room as he sat at the table. "That's where they keep their most-coveted prisoners. It's also the level most heavily guarded and spelled."

"I think I saw that level," I said, remembering the two elf sentinels. "So, how do we get from here to there now that they're looking for you? We're not going to gain access easily."

Baldur ran a hand around the back of his neck. The gesture was so like Tyr's that I sat forward in my chair, but before I could say anything, he answered, "It will take some tricks, but I have a few up my sleeve." I waited for more. "I know of a room where they keep weapons and some spells. If we can make it there, we have a chance to break onto level five."

I blew out a breath as a feeling of hopelessness crept in now that our cover was mostly blown. "I was kind of hoping you'd have more of a slam-dunk plan. Plus, Leela might not actually be on level five, or they might move her before we can get there." There were so many things that had to be taken into account.

"There's no such thing as a sure thing in a place like this." He chuckled. "To most, this castle is impenetrable, as it's built deep inside a mountain. It's actually amazing you were able to get this far. You should congratulate yourself. With your weapons and that cloak"—he gestured to the back of my chair—"you must have some powerful allies."

I wasn't ready to discuss the nitty-gritty of being Odin's daughter just yet. I wanted to feel him out first and make sure I could trust him. He seemed honest, and he most certainly had a cheerful spirit and a good heart, but we'd just met. I redirected the conversation. "Is the weapons room you're talking about close to here?"

"You broke me out of level sixteen," Baldur answered. "We went up three, by my count, so that means this is level thirteen. The weapons room I'm thinking about is on level ten."

"I take it there is more than one weapon cache," I said wryly.

"There is one on every level, but only a few contain spells. The dark elves covet spells. Crafting powerful ones takes a long time and effort, so they don't disperse them throughout all the levels."

"How do you know which floor is which? I haven't seen any markings or numbers."

"The elves don't use our number system. They have their own. If you look closely, there are tiny symbols carved into the stone at the beginning of every hallway, but they are hard to see and only come up about waist-high. Over the years, I've gotten good at interpreting their alphabet."

I glanced around the deserted guard room. "So you're telling me this is level thirteen? What are the odds?" I mused.

He leaned back in his chair, genuine curiosity in his voice. "Why is the number thirteen particular?"

"In Midgard, it's a fairly superstitious number. Meaning it's no coincidence that this level would be the one to be jinxed and not another—"

A loud noise came from the hallway, and we both leaped to our feet, upending our chairs.

I had my swords out in less than two seconds, and Junnal was already out the door.

That had been no Muroidea.

It'd sounded like a door slam.

Baldur went first, and I followed, which was silly, because I was the one with the weapons. Junnal moved to the side, and Baldur slipped in front of him. The god was on high alert. He moved with fluid grace, just like Tyr and Fen. His senses were heightened, like any god, and he seemed at ease with the task of discovering what had just gone bump in the night.

He sidled up to a closed door, his left hand aloft. It was dark out here, the soft light from the torch in the other room barely making it this far.

We had clearly missed something when we'd entered this level. It'd been a stupid oversight, and one that could've cost us. Who knew what was lurking in there?

I held my weapons out in front of me, both swords poised to strike. Baldur burst through the door, and I came next, spinning past him, my swords arcing down, anticipating something awful.

I stopped them midair.

My surprise at discovering what was in front of me could've been a deal breaker in the form of a gruesome death by twin sword blades had I not learned to control my swings on a dime.

There, sitting on the floor, back against the stone wall, was a withered old man with a long, white beard.

My mouth dropped open as I lowered my swords to my sides while Baldur confronted him. "Who are you?"

The man appraised us both, blinking a pair of tired-looking eyes, then he turned to Junnal looming in the doorway. He didn't seem fazed by our presence here at all. It took him some time to answer as he stroked his beard. "I am Callan." His voice was broken and raspy.

"Are you a mage?" Baldur demanded. "You smell like both white elf and magician. I don't believe I've ever scented anything like you before."

"Indeed," Callan answered. "I am both. Some here have given me the moniker *whage*, for lack of a more unique term.

There are only a handful of us in existence. Maybe more or less now." He shrugged his frail shoulders. "It's hard to know. Things in the worlds change very quickly, and I've been gone for a long while."

Baldur dropped to a crouch in front of the elf-mage.

Well, mostly eye level.

He was still taller than the wizened old man, his frame seeming massive compared to the older man on the floor. "How long have you been here?" Baldur glanced around the dingy room, full of dust and bones—likely from the carcasses of what I assumed were remains of Muroidea.

Lots and lots of Muroidea.

I bit back the bile threatening to ascend and harnessed my swords, taking a good look around. The small room resembled a typical cell. No windows. Stone walls. A small cot. It was less than rustic—it was a hovel.

"I've been a resident of this realm for far too long," Callan finally answered. His voice was soft and weak, but gaining strength as he continued. "I came to this place to free my king. After he escaped, I was trapped, so I cursed this place. It has been both my refuge and my prison ever since."

"Well, this is your lucky day, white elf," Baldur replied, standing, extending his hand to Callan. "We're breaking out of here for good, and you are welcome to join us."

The mage took Baldur's hand and stood on wobbly legs.

His snow-white hair tumbled down around his shoulders. The color and length matched his beard, which unfurled down the front of his body as he straightened, hitting his waist.

For the first time I noticed his ears were pointed, sticking through the thin tufts of hair. White elves looked nothing like dark elves. They resembled humans in every way, save for their pointy ears and long, extra-skinny fingers. Fingers were almost as bad as teeth around here.

"That would be agreeable," Callan said, nodding. "But how are you going to master such a feat? I have been here many long years thinking of doing just that, but these walls are impenetrable."

"Can you still kindle magic?" Baldur asked, peering down at the old man, who was at least two feet shorter than the god.

"Why, yes, I believe so," he replied, seeming somewhat surprised by his answer. He glanced down and flexed his metacarpals absentmindedly. "But I am not as potent as I once was. I have not eaten a decent meal or felt sunshine on my withered skin for too many years to count. Sunshine is as important to a white elf as breathing." He took in a labored, shallow breath. "We must have it." Dark elves turned to stone in sunlight. I'd learned that fun tidbit from Sam. "Without the rays of the sun, we weaken and decay, as I have done. My death would have come shortly, had you not found me, of that I am certain."

Stepping forward, I said, "If you help us find the Valkyrie we're seeking, I give you my word we will find a way to get you home."

He appraised me, peering at me with his head angled down, like he had imaginary spectacles perched on the end of his nose. He took a step forward. "You," he started, "are something entirely different as well."

I took an unplanned step backward, surprised.

"A Valkyrie born to a powerful god and an ancient queen."

"A *queen?*" No one had said anything about my mother being a queen. "Um, no. I don't think so. My mother is a Valkyrie, that's true, but she's no queen. In fact, we're a very democratic society." There had been a lot of voting going on while I'd been living in the stronghold, for almost everything. Other than deferring to Rae on battle issues, they were a pretty fair-and-square, majority-wins kind of group.

Callan drew close enough to reach out a frail hand. Birdlike fingers curled around my wrist. He immediately closed his eyes, his head dipping backward, his mouth open.

I felt an unmistakable tug.

This guy was siphoning energy from me!

"Hey...*hey!*" I sputtered, pulling back my arm. "Stop that. You...you can't take that without asking."

Callan did not appear abashed by his blatant grab in the least. Instead, he cracked a grizzled smile. His first. "*Ah*, that was just what I needed. I, too, can get sustenance from energy, and you, shieldmaiden, have much to spare. I would not have taken, otherwise. You are very powerful indeed." He rubbed his belly. "It has done me good."

Okay, now I felt like a guilty hag for denying this man a meal. Jeez.

He reminded me of my grandpa Meadows, if my grandpa grew his hair out and stopped eating for a few years. Honestly, if I'd been in the same spot—in need of food after so long without it—I would've done the same thing.

"Well..." I cleared my throat, trying to sound like I had everything under control. "In the future, just ask before you take. Once we get to Yggdrasil, you can stock up."

"What I took will do for now," he told me. "It is enough to sustain me for a time."

A screech came from outside the cell, a cross between a snake hiss and tiger's yowl. Junnal lifted his club and headed out the door.

"I'm afraid they have called in the skogs," Callan said gravely. "They will do almost anything for magic."

"Skogs?" I asked.

"Lizardmen," Baldur answered. "They live in this realm, but deeper than the elves. They keep a missionary relationship, nothing more."

"Meaning," Callan added, "they come up to get paid in magic. The elves must shell out much more than they are willing to part with, so they seldom summon them. This proves that you are worth the cost." He gazed directly at me.

"They're not after me. They don't even know I'm here. When I freed Baldur, I was cloaked." Oh, no! "I left my lucky charm back in the room. I have to retrieve it." So stupid.

Baldur caught my arm as I tried to get by. "It might be best to leave it behind. The skogs will be swarming this level in no time."

A loud commotion came from the doorway as Junnal began to engage the threat with his club. They were already here.

I drew my swords. "I have to try and recover it," I insisted. "It might be the only way we can make it to the weapons room on level ten without being seen."

Baldur dropped his grip and nodded. "I'll back up the giant while you get it. Hopefully, none have gotten past him."

"Sounds like a plan."

Callan cackled, looking pleased. "This will be an adventure. My first in years!"

13

I slipped behind Junnal and raced toward the guard room. I couldn't believe I'd been so green as to leave the cloak behind! Ingrid would be so disappointed in my battle skills. Rookie mistake wasn't enough to cover it.

Once I reached the door, I skidded inside, sliding to a stop in front of my empty chair.

The cloak was gone!

"Looking for this?" The voice, which sounded vaguely like an elf with a severe lisp, came from a darkened corner.

I spun around, my weapons at the ready.

Then I blinked, not believing my eyes.

A giant lizard, roughly as tall as a dark elf, stood upright on two feet in the corner, holding my precious gift in its podlike hands. I watched in horror as it lifted the see-through fabric to its two inset nostrils and took a long sniff.

What in the *hellll?*

"It smells of delicious magic," it sighed in a voice that held an edge. "The elves cannot touch white elf magic, but we can, and desire it above all else."

I shook one of my swords menacingly. "I don't care if you desire it, you can't have it," I told the creepy sniffer. "It's mine and I want it back."

The thing opened its maw, flashing a row of particularly sharp teeth. It snarled and hissed. "If you want it, you will have to take it from me." It waited a moment, then said, "Or we can make a deal that benefits us both."

My eyebrows shot up as Baldur entered the room at a full gallop, coming to a stop right beside me. He wasn't even panting from the effort.

Calmly, I stated, without meeting the god's gaze, "This lizard wants to make a deal with us."

The white-elf-magic-loving lizard stepped forward.

I had to admit it was an interesting creature. It shared some characteristics of an elf merged clearly with a reptile, specifically the kind of lizard that suns itself on a rock, with a long slender neck. It had ears, which looked insane on its long, pointy, scaly reptilian face. It had shoes on its feet, which I assumed were podlike, just like its fingers. It had only four, all of which were still gripping my cloak.

"State your deal, skog," Baldur demanded. "And we will consider it."

"You will give us white elf magic, and we will help you escape." Its lizardy tongue came out of its mouth and then popped back in. It was forked. Oh, goody. "A very simple bargain."

"Why would you broker this deal with us?" Baldur argued. "You are the agents of the dark elves and owe us no allegiance."

The thing shook its head. "We are not anyone's agents," it spat. "The dark elves have not called us from the depths to do their bidding in years, and when they do, they never pay the price we demand. We owe them nothing, and we are interested in forging another deal—with you—for this." It shook the sheer fabric, its nostril slits flaring.

The sounds of scuffling in the hallway ceased, and Junnal's heavy footfalls came to a stop by the door, the slow patter of older feet shuffling right behind.

"He speaks the truth," Callan commented as he came into the room. "The dark elves congratulate themselves on not paying their full retainer every time."

"How can we trust that the skogs will do as they say?" Baldur asked. "I am not familiar enough with them to know if they will honor their end of the bargain."

"The lizard can start by giving me back my cloak," I said. "Then we can go from there." I gave it a pointed look. "If you don't, we know you will honor nothing."

The thing clutched it tightly for a moment, seeming reluctant to give it up, then thrust it forward, dangling it like a fish on a line. "I will keep my word," it claimed. "But if you do not, we will hunt you down and destroy you." He finished on a snarl-hiss lisp.

Well, then.

I walked over and snatched the cloak back, tucking it under my arm, then went to stand next to Baldur. I leaned in, trying to look smooth, like I knew what I was doing. "How do we get our hands on white elf magic?"

Baldur shrugged. "It's not that hard to procure if you have powerful allies in other realms with means. It would not be so difficult." He arched a knowing eyebrow at me and then Gundren.

Point taken.

My mind rushed to Ingrid, Tyr, Fen, and possibly Huggie. If they were still talking to me when this was all over, they would help. Leela's life was priceless, worth all the white elf magic we could amass. It made me feel emboldened. "If you help us free the Valkyrie we're looking for and see us safely out of this realm, the shieldmaidens will gladly pay any price you ask." I addressed the lizardman. "Do you know where this particular shieldmaiden is?"

The thing nodded. "Yes, she is heavily guarded, and they know you come for her."

Me specifically? Or was it lisping in general terms?

I forged on. "Once we have her, will you be able to get us through their barriers and blockades and back to Yggdrasil?" I asked.

"Yes, there is no question." The lizard was supremely confident. "But doing such a thing will cost you seven caskets."

Before I could answer, Callan sputtered, "Seven! That's highway robbery! This mission is only worth five at the most! You rob us blind."

Caskets? I had no idea what the skog was talking about.

"The price is seven," it insisted. "This mission will be fraught with peril. We risk much by helping you."

Before I could ask for more specifics, like what a casket was, Baldur said, "You don't risk that much. Dark elf magic doesn't harm you, and your reptile numbers exceed theirs. The elves aren't fighters, they are craftsmen. The price should be five, as the mage said, not seven."

They were bickering over the price of rescuing my mother!

I couldn't care less if it was five, seven, or twelve. "I don't know what a casket is," I interjected, "but I agree to pay seven. We're short on time here, and the Valkyries will honor any bargain I strike." I certainly hoped and prayed they would. "Leela's life is worth it."

Baldur leaned in. "He is asking for seven large chests filled with white elf magic. It will be tough to procure, but not impossible."

Our heads met in the middle. "How large are we talking?"

"Big." Baldur chuckled.

"We don't have a lot of choices at the moment."

He addressed the lizardman. "Looks like you have a deal, skog. Free the Valkyrie, lead us all to Yggdrasil, and you will get your chests filled with magic."

The lizard nodded its reptilian head once.

I swallowed, hoping I'd made the right deal.

If the Valkyries refused to pay, I'd have to find a way to honor my end of the bargain. But on the flip side, I'd have my mother there to help me.

"But if any of us perish, the deal is off," Baldur added, his voice strong and final.

"We cannot guarantee *your* life, god," the lizard said in a voice full of lispy condescension. "But will promise the others."

Instead of being angry, Baldur laughed and agreed. "You're right, of course. Mine cannot be guaranteed. Get them out alive, and the deal will be seven caskets."

Before I could protest that Baldur's life must be included, the two shook hands.

It was comical how vastly different sizes they were, one huge god hand encircling one tiny pod hand.

The deal was done.

The lizard whistled, which sounded bizarre coming out of its wide, narrow-lipped mouth, and immediately a trampling of feet issued from the hallway as an army of skogs came to its call.

Junnal bellowed at the intrusion.

"It's okay," I said. "They're going to help us get out of here." I muttered under my breath, "The sooner the better."

Baldur grabbed the table and tugged it out from the wall.

"How do we address you?" he asked the skog. "I assume you are the leader here."

The skog picked up a chair and motioned for a few of his cronies to line up behind him, which they did, with their thin arms crossed. They didn't look threatening in the least, even with their chests puffed up. At the tallest they were four feet, and each had on the same comical outfit—a brown toga-type thing with leg holes.

But I was betting they could turn it on if they had to. They did have sharp teeth, after all.

"I am Zetafoula," it said as we all sat. "I am the leader here."

"Can I call you Zee?" Baldur asked, affection in his tone. He really was a good guy—either that, or he was an extremely talented actor. He was infectious and had a way of making everyone feel at ease. I could see the lizardman leader thought so, too. It nodded, and Baldur continued, "We need a rock-solid plan. Our strategy was to enter the weapons room on level ten where they keep spells, but getting there was going to be a challenge."

The skog shook its head. "No, taking their weapons will not be necessary. We will also have no need of their magic. Our plan is simple. We distract the elves by giving them what they want, and while they are busy gloating about their good fortune, we free the Valkyrie and move you out." I raised an eye as the leader continued. I wasn't sure *giving them what they wanted* was the right choice. "Right now, they are betting we will be victorious, meaning we will bring you out as prisoners. Once we do that," it lisped on, "we will demand that we guard you until we are paid. Since they do not settle their debts quickly, it will be granted, and while they are congratulating themselves on their good fortune, we shuttle you out. The elves will not suspect a thing."

Hm. "What exactly do you mean by giving them what they want?" I asked, trepidation at the forefront. "They don't know I'm here. I can be an asset to the mission and stay hidden."

The lizard examined me, its vertical irises expanding and contracting. "They know that the god had help in his escape."

I jerked my thumb toward the Junnal. "Yeah, from this super-strong Jotun."

"It's too risky," Zee said, shaking its head. "If they discover we've hatched a plan, they will unleash their magic, and we lose."

"So you're asking me to turn myself over to them in hopes you can break me out once you find Leela?" I turned toward Baldur. "Does that sound right to you?"

"The lizard does have a point," the god answered. "If the skogs bring them a far greater prize, that being you, they will be distracted. If your end goal is truly to break out the Valkyrie, this might be the best way to do so." Baldur's voice was sincere, but I had a hard time believing that was the plan we should follow.

"I will accompany you," Callan declared, lofting his finger in the air. He stood behind my chair. "They do not know I have been here all these years, so that will be an even greater surprise. We will tell them I am ailing, and they will not think me capable of anything." He directed his sharp gaze at the lizard. "That's the only way we will agree to this, skog." He was firm, his voice no longer shaky. "She will not go into one of those cells unprotected. I shall go with her. Swear it."

"It will be done," the skog answered, appearing a little smug as it looked around the table.

"Um," I pondered. "I have to say, I'm not entirely

amenable to this plan." I fingered the ice pick I still wore harnessed at my waist. I had used it to slay a dark elf that had been attacking me on a rooftop in New York. I hadn't even thought to leave the weapon behind. "I have no idea what the elves will do with me when they find out who I am, but it could be chaos."

Baldur smiled, his dimples flashing. "Okay, I give. Who are you? I've been wondering that since you freed me. You have Odin's favor, to be sure." He inclined his head at my weapons. "And the elves said you are his decedent. Are you?"

Callan cleared his throat, adding, "You are too young to be on your own, isn't that correct? Just struck? You have a powerful bodyguard, it's true, but to enter this realm alone seems folly. Whoever sent you must ache for your death."

That shocked me. "What? No!" I exclaimed a little too loudly. "I was sent here by Hugin, and he doesn't want me dead." I couldn't believe that—not after everything he'd done to keep me alive thus far.

"Ah, Hugin," Baldur commented. "You are right. He would not want you killed. He favors the Valkyrie who is kept here and would want her freed at all costs."

I turned to Baldur, my eyes wide. "How do you know that?"

Baldur shrugged. "Because my father was very smitten with the Valkyrie they call Leela, as was his agent. She has a beauty and gentleness about her, not typical for a shieldmaiden."

"Your *father*?" I swallowed, trying not to cough or choke or pass out. That's why his movements reminded me so much of Tyr. Baldur was my half brother! "Odin's your father?" I asked, stalling, my voice little more than puffs of air.

"Of course," the god answered jovially. "My mother is Frigg. She was with Odin for a time and is still the chief of the gods, but they parted ways years ago. I am the god of light."

Everyone waited for my response. "I'm...I'm Odin's daughter." Swallow, swallow, deep breath. "Leela is my mother."

"Sister!" Baldur's voice rang with happiness. He stood, making his way around the table, and swept me up in a bear hug, my weapons pressed closely against my sides. "I did not know Leela produced a daughter!" He kissed my cheek and held me out so he could inspect me. "So you are here in search of your mother. I can see the resemblance now. I should've known! It will be the happiest of family reunions once we find her."

He was so energetic and sincere, it was hard not to smile, so I gave in and cracked one.

This was *beyond* strange.

I'd inadvertently freed my own brother.

I tried to hug him back, which was a little awkward, since I was holding my swords. I managed to get my fingers around his back without stabbing anyone. "I hope it's a good reunion," I told him, feeling overwhelmed. "I'm looking forward to meeting her."

Before I could say anything more, Zee interrupted. "The elves are restless. We must go." The lizard leader didn't seem fazed by the news that Baldur and I were brother and sister, other than its yucky forked tongue doing double time.

Baldur slung his arm around my shoulders. "We go together."

14

There wasn't much time to argue with the plan. Much to my chagrin, it began to roll on its own. Callan took my cloak and stuffed it inside his ragged tunic. "I smell like white elf magic, because I *am* a white elf. They will not suspect we have it." His eyes twinkled. "Lead us out!" he commanded the army of skogs.

They shoved Baldur, who was now bound by some kind of cord, in front of us. A skog grabbed on to my arm and roughly forced it behind my back. "Hey!" I protested. "No need to yank that hard!" The thing hissed at me as it tied me up with the same thing binding Baldur's wrists.

Junnal gave a disgruntled sound from behind me. We were both uneasy about this. He had not wanted to surrender either.

He was a smart Jotun.

I tried to abandon thoughts of breaking away. I had to trust my newfound brother. He seemed okay with this turn of events and so did Callan. If I made a break for it, the outcome would be unknown.

119

Either plan could lead to capture, or worse.

At least this capture gave us an advantage. Or at least, that's what I was telling myself as we paced forward.

I was told the elves would confiscate my weapons when I was turned in, but Zee assured me that the skogs would be the ones to hold on to them and suggested I hide Gram and the ice pick somewhere the elves wouldn't check.

Without much time to complete the task, we'd strapped them to Callan's stomach with my belt, which now had my cloak piled on top of it.

Callan's thinness had come in handy.

He didn't look remotely big, even with the weapons and the cloak. The dark elves wouldn't physically touch him, as they reacted to white magic, and they had a healthy fear of being cursed.

If they separated Callan and me, it would be very bad.

I tried not to think about it, but I had a sinking feeling things weren't as they seemed. I wasn't naïve enough to think everything would turn out peachy. Having weapons gave me a sense of security.

As we headed down the passageway, I issued up a silent plea to Ingrid and Fen. *Please, please don't be angry with me, especially if I die!* At least they would get Leela back. I'd made Zee promise. My heart threatened to thump out of my chest when I thought of Fen and how much anguish and betrayal he was likely feeling, and how stupid he'd think this plan was. He'd never surrender.

I had no idea if the Valkyries would be able to come after me, or if Fen or Tyr could get to this realm. Huggie had said the portal would open again.

If you're coming, I hope you get here soon, I pleaded in my mind.

We entered the area that we'd demolished. There was no going back now.

There was cheering as they brought Baldur out. Three more strides and I ducked out of the hole to an army of elves amassed on the steps, their greedy faces shining, filled with triumph and unbridled glee at our capture.

"See?" one screeched. "Tallester spoke the truth! The Valkyrie was here all along!" It was one of the elves who'd questioned us on the stairs. Its face took on a dreamy expression, like I was covered in dollar signs or something equivalent—most likely a casket full of whatever they coveted, like jewels or gold.

I was shoved, none too softly, down the stairs. I stumbled, skog hands encircling me, keeping me rooted, but just barely. Their weird pod fingers pressed into me painfully. They were rough like sandpaper.

"Bring the prisoners down!" a dark elf exclaimed with authority.

When Callan emerged, the crowd went nuts.

"The whage is here!" an elf cried. "Look, look! He did not escape after all! I owe my cousin a ruby necklace."

"Don't touch him!" another called. "He will curse you, and you will die a horrible death!"

"Don't look him in the eye!"

Zee's voice interrupted the elves' glee and triumph. "The white elf is ailing. We will put him with the Valkyrie for safekeeping."

Dissents came from the crowd. The area was packed to the brim with elves. They ebbed back slowly as we descended. "Your job is done here, skog," an elf cried. "You will not dictate." It was the one who wore the outfit with the silver circles who had brought Junnal and me down the stairs. "You may leave us now and go back to the underground. We will take it from here."

"Gladly," Zee answered, stopping one step below me.

"Pay us what is owed, and we will vacate." He thrust his arm out, palm extended, in a universal gesture for pay up.

The dark elf looked uncertain. "You will get your reward in due time."

Zee shook his head. "We have heard that one before, Mungad. We want the payment up front. After it is given, we will leave."

I glanced over my shoulder at Callan, who winked at me. I took that as a good sign. At least someone seemed to know what was going on.

The elf made a move to take Baldur without answering the skog, and Zee sent out a chilling hiss. In unison, the same sounds erupted from all over.

Shockingly, the skogs hit the ground on all fours.

They began to scale the walls and ceilings quicker than a horde of angry geckos, their jaws cracking menacingly. It sounded like they could snap us in half, the combined noise of their efforts increasing to a thunderous level.

The elves all took a collective step backward, and so did I, crashing into a few lizards that had stayed put to guard us. "Sorry!" I squeaked. *Please don't eat me or do any other creepy stuff.*

I itched to take out my swords and be done with this place. It was all I could do to contain myself and stay perfectly still.

The elf leader sputtered, "This is not protocol! Invaldi will be very angry! You will leave now, and your payment will be sent shortly. Call off your men!"

Men? Did it not see that there were hundreds of reptiles scaling the walls?

"Summon Invaldi," Zee challenged. "I wish to speak with him. I am certain he will not be pleased we had to be called up from the depths because you could not contain your prisoners. And let's not forget that you let a powerful

Valkyrie sneak into your lair." He eyed me. "There is also the matter of the white elf mage."

He thought I was powerful? Sweet.

The elf paled. "He…he cannot be interrupted right now. He is in a very important meeting…with a guest who has just arrived."

"Until we are paid, we guard the prisoners," Zee said, his voice lispy and unfaltering, much to my relief. "We have done our job and deserve our reward. The prisoners will remain our collateral."

"You ask too much!" the elf scoffed. "You are not in charge here!"

Zee lifted a single finger, and all the lizardmen changed color, melding into the walls, becoming almost completely invisible.

But that wasn't the scariest part.

Their actual features had shifted as they morphed. Their mouths gaped open and their teeth enlarged, poking out like sabers from their thin lips. Gills I'd had no idea were there puffed wide, and their claws lengthened. All in the span of a few seconds.

Holy lizardmen!

How many tricks did they have up their sleeves?

The changes made them look monstrous before they faded into the background, like evil beings who'd slithered up from the depths of hell. They were dreadful, and it was clear the elves felt the same way.

The elf leader finally put its hands up and backed away. "Fine," it squeaked. "You may guard the prisoners, but not for long."

"We will guard them until we are paid."

The dark elf glanced around itself, before shouting, "Move them out! Take them all to level five."

Relief shot through me. Level five! This plan might not suck after all.

As the lizards changed back to their normal state and crawled back to the floor, Callan got close enough to say, "Things will be okay now. We are in control."

"I hope you're right," I whispered back. Before I could say more, Callan and I were wrenched apart. "Hey!" I cried as the elves gestured to the skogs to lead Callan away. "Your leader just told you to take everyone to level five. The white elf is sick. He stays with me!"

"We must contain the whage," an elf sniffed. "He goes to the special chamber made only for evil white magic users."

"Then I go, too!" I argued.

"No, you come with us—"

Zee's voice boomed from the front, much louder than I'd thought he could project. "I will assign my best guards to the Valkyrie and the mage. They go together. The white elf is feeble and needs a nursemaid."

"We do not care if he dies," the elf scoffed. "We take the Valkyrie to level five as ordered." The elves had already led Baldur away, and I could no longer see him.

Behind us, Junnal's club smashed into the wall, sending rocks raining down around us.

The elf glanced wide-eyed behind me. "Fine, you can go with the whage...for now. When Invaldi arrives, he will do as he pleases! And, I promise you, there will be consequences for your actions." The elf turned to a skog who was holding me. "Make sure you lock up the troll with them. We will not have his ilk running around wreaking havoc."

The skog said nothing. Didn't even acknowledge it was being addressed. The elf gestured at a group of elves in front of us. "Lead them to the white-elf containment cell."

We strode purposely down a long, dimly lit hallway.

When we were almost to the end, the group stopped. One of the elves worked the combination on a cell door. It was similar to the one I had opened for Baldur, and this elf finessed it in two seconds flat.

"Where are they taking the god of light?" I asked.

"To level five. High protection," the elf responded in a clipped tone.

"Why does he need high protection?" I challenged. "He's no threat to you."

Another elf smirked. "If something happens to him, the goddess Frigg will rain her terror down around us. We will not take that chance. We will lock him up nice and tight."

The skogs tossed Callan roughly into the cell ahead of me. None of the elves stood within three feet of the white elf mage, their faces upturned in disgust.

I was next.

Before the skogs could shove me in after Callan, an elf cried, "Take her weapons, skog! A Valkyrie with her weapons is a direct threat to our well-being. What's wrong with you? If you are going to guard her, do it right!"

The lizard reached for Gundren, and I almost backhanded him. Zee had gone ahead with Baldur, and we were on our own. "I'll do it myself," I said between gritted teeth, shaking the skog off. With regret, and no other choice left to me, I slid the leather straps off my arms. My body cried at the parting.

I hope I'm doing the right thing.

Inside the cell, Callan beckoned me with his hand. "It will be all right," he intoned. "Do as they say."

With resignation, I moved forward, trying not to react to the skogs, who looked like they'd just been given the greatest gift of their lives.

"Go on, dirty troll! Get in there," an angry elf voice said. "You will stay put."

Junnal bent his head and lumbered in. They slammed the door after him, cackling like fools.

The first thing I noticed were the bumpy rocks, similar to porous lava, dark and jagged, covering the walls. "What is this place?" I turned in a circle. "Why is it covered in volcanic rock?"

Callan smirked. "The elves believe that using earth stone will dampen our magic. They dig it up from a special place in the realm and bring it here."

"Does it work?"

"For true white elves, possibly," he answered. "It might dampen some of their abilities. White elves gather magic organically, straight from the soil, and this kind of rock inhibits the transfer. But for me? Who is also a mage? It does nothing."

"Please tell me you still have the weapons and the cloak?"

"Indeed, I do." He smiled, his crooked teeth thankfully not sharp. He patted his stomach. "They are right where we left them."

I rubbed my shoulder, yearning for the feeling of my swords strapped to my back again. "Well, at least that's something."

As I began to walk around, my hands fisting in frustration, the ground began to rumble under our feet.

15

I glanced at Callan, a single brow angled up. "Do you know what the shaking means?" More tremors ran beneath our feet, and dust and debris in the form of black pellets fell from the walls and ceiling.

"I've only felt this one other time in my residence," Callan answered. "From what I gathered then, it means a guest is arriving who is not invited. The elves will try to prevent it from happening as best they can."

"That really wouldn't be considered a guest, then," I pointed out. "More like an intruder." My brain instantly thought Fen. If he could find a way in, he would. If not Fen, then the Valkyries may finally have found a way to breach the realm with Huggie's help. My spirits lifted considerably.

Callan opened his tunic, moved his long beard aside, and took out my cloak. With authority, the old man said, "It's time to get you out of here."

Huh?

My brows furrowed. "What are you talking about? You made me go along with this plan, assuring me it was the right choice, and now we're stuck here until Zee frees us. We can't just get out of here."

"On the contrary, that skog can't be trusted!" Callan all but snorted as his eyes narrowed. "I went along with Zee's plan to get us off the cursed level. It was the only way. There were too many of us, not to mention"—he jammed his grizzled thumb at Junnal—"the giant would not have gone unseen. But those lizards are dishonest to the bone. They will rob you blind and sell your soul to the highest bidder." He handed me the cloak, ignoring my bewildered look. "You will don this, retrieve your weapons, and go find your mother. Then you must leave this place as quickly as you arrived. If luck is with us, you will go undetected."

I couldn't believe what I was hearing. "What...what about you and Baldur?" I stammered, feeling a little stunned. Why hadn't he just told me?

Callan swiped a hand while making a *pfft* sound. "We will be just fine. The giant here will spring us once you leave. I will find Baldur, and all will be well. There is no time for arguing." He pushed at my back, his bony fingers like prongs urging me toward the door. "But you must hurry. I bet that lowly skog is double-dealing with the elves right now asking for ten caskets. The highest bidder will get his loyalty, nothing more, nothing less."

Well, okay, then.

I wasn't going to leave Callan or Baldur behind, but I wasn't going to tell him that now. "The skogs aren't just going to let me walk out of here," I said, once he guided me to the door. "How is this going to work?"

"I will open the door with magic, and you will slip out."

"I need Gundren," I pointed out. "I can't fight the elves without it."

"Of course you must have your swords. Weapons like

that are hard to come by." Callan held up his withered hand and placed it on the door. He closed his eyes and leaned down, speaking through the grate. "You will open this door and return the Valkyrie's swords to her right now!"

I arched a look at Junnal.

The giant shrugged.

It seemed Callan might be delusional.

Then, to our utter surprise, the door opened. Gundren was tossed unceremoniously through, clattering to the ground.

I bent down quickly, clutching it to my chest, exclaiming, "How did you do that?"

"I still have it," Callan said, his voice gleeful as he held the door ajar. "I wasn't sure I did, as I have neared the end of my life span in this awful place, but it worked. I haven't had a subject to try it on in years." His voice was wistful. "It wasn't until the second month of my stay on the cursed level that I realized my plan to hide out there until help arrived was severely flawed. I could not escape if I had no one to manipulate, and all stayed away. I thought my king would send others back for me." Callan's expression turned downward. "But it was too late when I realized he thought I perished."

I harnessed Gundren on my back, asking in a soft voice, "A subject to try what on?"

"My specialty is mind control," Callan replied proudly, straightening. "It was how I was able to break out of my cell the first few times, but I could never find my way fully out. Directions are not my strong suit."

This white elf mage was full of surprises.

"Callan, you're an extremely talented guy. I'm lucky to have you on my side," I said with sincerity. "Do you have any tips on how to find my mother once I'm out?"

"You must search for a cell with a milf standing in front of it."

"I'm sorry," I sputtered, "but did you just say *milf?*" I coughed. I knew the word wouldn't mean the same thing in this realm as it did on Midgard, but it was still hilarious to hear it come out of Callan's mouth.

"Yes, exactly, a milf," he answered.

"I don't know what you mean by a milf. Please excuse my ignorance," I told him as I donned my cloak, deciding not to explain what it meant in my world, as that would just be totally confusing all around.

"It describes an elf hybrid. Milf means 'mixed elf,' and they are taller and look more human than their dark elfin counterparts. They are sired by elves and another, most often human. They have held this Valkyrie a long time, and they know she's wily. She will prefer to interact with milfs. To ensure that her needs are met, they will have staffed her with them."

"Are they as strong as dark elves?" I asked, readying to make my break.

"Some are. It depends on their parentage. But most are not. Humans do not kindle magic anymore, so they are no threat. The dark elves keep the milfs around more or less as slaves."

"That's helpful to know." I tightened the leather straps on my scabbard. "I was under the impression the elves were torturing my mother down here. Is that true?"

Baldur had appeared grimy and in need of a shower, but he didn't look like he'd been abused during his time as a prisoner.

"They likely have through the years, trying to extract what information they can about the Valkyries. But they also fear Odin's wrath, so they wouldn't have gone too far. But that's just this old mage's opinion. Who knows what they have done? You must go now, before the skog leader comes back. It will not be so easy to fool him."

I was ready. Callan held the door open a few inches. I leaned over and gripped his arms, gazing down at this stranger who was kindly helping me and expecting nothing in return. "Callan, before I go I want you to siphon some energy from me. I want you to be strong so you can escape."

"Nonsense," he chided. "I need no more. What I took was enough. It will last. Yggdrasil will enrich me when I finally leave this place."

"I insist. I need to make sure you have enough to make it to the tree. You've helped me more than I ever could have imagined, and you don't even know me. It's the least I can do."

"Okay, yes, I will take a small amount." He closed his eyes, and I began to feel a draw.

After too short a time, he let go, shaking himself like a dog coming in from the rain. That was peculiar.

I squinted in the low light. Did his hair look different? I was about to ask, when we heard shouting outside the door.

"You must leave now," he ordered. "I am certain we will see each other again." He withdrew Gram and the ice pick, handing them both to me.

I took Gram, Odin's dagger, which had saved my life on more than one occasion, but I told him, "You keep the elf dirk. You will need it more than I do."

He nodded once, thankfully not arguing, and stuffed it back inside his dirty tunic. I pulled the cloak down over my head and addressed Junnal. "Stay here for now. We will meet up soon. I'm not sure how this is going to go, but we're getting out of here together."

Junnal shook his head no and took a few steps toward me.

I raised a hand to stop him. "Listen, I know splitting up isn't opportune," I argued. "But I've got the means to do this now, thanks to Callan. I need to find my mother. It's the only way. You can back me up if anything goes wrong. For now, I need you to stay here so no one notices I've gone missing."

"Not...safe," the Jotun answered.

"I know," I told him. "But we don't have a better plan."

"Promised...Odin," Junnal responded.

"I realize you took a vow to keep me safe, and letting me go is doing just that," I assured him. "I'm going to be okay. No one can see me. We need to find a way out of here, and I'm not leaving without Leela."

The Jotun dropped his arms to his sides, looking resigned.

I reached out and hugged his massive frame. "Thank you. I didn't trust the skogs, and I'm grateful for another chance. I don't want to screw this mission up any more than I already have. It's time to get this done."

Callan began murmuring something through the crack in the door in a language I didn't understand. After a moment, he stepped back. "You may go now. They will not notice you."

I nodded as I slipped out, making sure not to brush up against the guards as I went.

Callan scolded them, and I smiled. "You shouldn't leave the door open. Your leader will be angry at your negligence."

One of the skogs hissed and slammed the door shut.

I heard Callan softly chuckling as I traversed the long hallway, backtracking the way we'd come. I needed to find the stairs, the ones we'd come down as prisoners. I couldn't risk moving through a main artery.

As I moved silently, I realized there were more doors here

than I'd seen on any previous level. Voices came from around a corner, and I dodged to the side, ducking into a doorway as two elves scurried by.

"It stinks of white elf magic here!" one declared.

"That's because the filthy white elf is back," another snorted.

"I cannot wait until Invaldi kills him once and for all. That whage has put us in a very tough position after all these years. If it gets out that we lost him in our own castle, we will be the laughingstock of all the realms! No one will pay us to keep their criminals."

"Yes. Killing him is the only way."

I managed to hold in my gasp until after they passed. No one would be killing Callan. Once I had my mother, getting the white elf out was my next priority.

Once the coast was clear, I hurried along.

There should be stairs back here somewhere.

Where were they?

I was just about to turn back and head for the main stairway when I heard a different kind of noise, like quiet tapping. I splayed my hands against the wall to my left, then rested my ear against it. It sounded like feet going up stairs, and it was coming from the other side of the wall.

The stairs had to be concealed behind this wall. I just had to figure out how to access them.

I ran my hands along the brick. More noises erupted from inside the stone, this time louder. I leaped out of the way just in time, backing up flush against the opposite side of the hallway, making sure I was completely covered by the cloak.

The wall in front of me slid open seamlessly, and two figures emerged.

Zee and the elf leader!

They had their heads together.

Callan had been right all along! I had to wait for them to pass to slip into the stairwell, hopefully before it closed. I was just about to make a run for it when Zee stopped in his tracks, his ugly lizard face pointed upward, his nostril slits flaring.

"Do you smell something?" he lisped to the elf leader.

"Just the smell of victory," the leader replied. "You were perfect in your role of turncoat. It couldn't have worked any better. You will be lavished with gifts. Invaldi will be beyond pleased."

Zee sniffed. "If you do not pay us within the next hour, we shall see what happens."

"You will have your fifteen caskets delivered within the hour."

Fifteen! That dirty double-crosser.

"And our agreement includes the Valkyrie, do not forget," Zee added.

My interested piqued. Were they talking about me?

"The maiden is awaiting transport on level three as we speak. I am certain the shieldmaidens won't be able to recover her from the depths. We will be glad to be rid of her. She has been nothing but a problem, always trying to escape."

They were talking about my mother!

"They will not get through our defenses," Zee said. "We will bury our trail after we descend. It will be impossible to track us."

"The agreed-upon term is three years, no more," the elf said as they began to walk again. "Odin will check in, and we will delay, but three years is the maximum."

"I would gladly trade her for the younger Valkyrie. Talk to Invaldi," Zee said. "She smelled delicious, and Odin will not be checking in for her. A few caskets less for five years."

I shuddered, my blood running cold. Thinking of either one of us as the skogs' prisoner was horrifying, and it wasn't going to happen. I ducked into the stairwell, right as the wall closed. I hurried up the flights, thankful no one else was around. They'd said she was on level three, not five. It had been a lucky break to overhear the conversation.

Zee was likely heading to check on me, so I had to hurry. Once he found I was gone, he would sound the alarms. I rounded a new level, and right before I cleared the next, a large figure barreled into the stairwell. I caught myself just in time, barely edging out of the way, sputtering as I realized who it was.

"Baldur?" I whispered, as I grabbed on to his arm. "What are you doing here?"

He grasped me around the shoulders. "Sister, is that you?" He couldn't see me. "Ah, I smell you now, little Valkyrie. How fortunate to meet up."

"How did you get here?" I asked, keeping my voice low.

"I'm not totally without skills." He chuckled. "I've broken out of almost every cell at least once, and the skogs only kept me tied with that feeble cord. After I was free of it, I used my outstanding strength to break out—meaning I sweet-talked the guards into opening the door to give me food, and then I hit them over the head." He grinned wide. "Worked like a charm."

I slid my hand into his, keeping my cloak hood over my face. "Come with me. My mom is on level three awaiting transport. Those bastards are sending her down with Zee and his two-timing army of lizards."

Baldur swore under his breath. "I knew they were double-dealing." We started to run.

"If you knew they were going to break their word, why

didn't you tell me?" I asked as we rounded the next level. "Callan didn't trust them either."

"Because the only real choice we had was to play along. They saw you with their own eyes. If we had not agreed, they would've sounded the alarms. I'm not extremely familiar with skogs, but I smelled a rat from the start. I thought if we went willingly we might have a chance to break out, and we did."

I came to a stop on what I thought was level three. "Are we here?"

Baldur inspected the markings. They were so small I hadn't even noticed them. "Yes, level three."

"Where were you heading when you almost collided with me?" I asked.

"To find you." He gave me a lopsided grin. It was impossible not to like this guy. Why did he have to be destined for such a dismal future?

It was so unfair.

"Callan said to look for a milf guarding my mother's cell," I told him as we crept into the hallway. This entrance was wide open and not concealed by a magic wall. I reached up to take my cloak down, making it partway before my brother stopped me.

"Leave yourself concealed. Just in case," he warned. "We have the element of surprise, but only for a short time. They will be on to us soon. If they find us here, I will claim the actions, and you can stay hidden."

"Okay," I agreed.

We weren't in the hallway more than a few seconds when a cackle erupted. It was light and melodic. I grabbed on to Baldur's hand and squeezed.

I knew that voice.

"Here to see your dear mother?" a female voice intoned.

"She hasn't had company in such a long time. You really should try and visit more often."

My heart dropped.

"Oh, don't be so surprised to find me here, girl," the singsong voice I knew too well told me. "I do predict the future, you know."

16

"Skuld?" Baldur said with genuine surprise in his voice. "I didn't expect to see you here. This realm is not visited by many."

"Baldur," she cooed. "You're looking fit and fashionable as ever." She made a show of looking him over, and my jaw clenched. "It's been a long time, has it not? Of course you would not expect me. You've been gone from Asgard far too long and do not know what has transpired." She turned her cool gaze on me. She looked the same as last time, like a bad copy of a Disney princess, complete with long, golden locks cascading around her ridiculously petite shoulders. Her features were calculatedly exact. She had bright blue eyes that held a twinkle, perfectly bowed pink lips, and high, candy apple cheekbones.

But it was all a façade.

What lay beneath her glamour was truly hideous—death and decay, peeling skin, and not much else.

Despite her words, I was genuinely shocked to see her here. I shouldn't have been, but my hope for a quick retrieval of my mother before the Norns knew I'd left the stronghold had occupied my brain, likely so I didn't let my worry take over the mission.

But she was right. She did predict the future. This shouldn't be a surprise.

And once I'd left the Valkyrie stronghold, she would've been monitoring my every move, seeing ahead of time what I would do, waiting to pounce like an evil future-reading cat with her claws out.

"Yes, indeed," she answered, like she'd been reading my mind. "So there is absolutely no need to look so stymied. You should really learn to cloak your features as well as you do your body from the elves. Your face is an open book. It relays everything I need to know." It was clear she could see through the cloaking fabric, so I reached up and pulled the hood down. She paced forward, her sky-blue dress swaying. "You might be relieved to hear that I'm not here to whisk you away to a torture chamber. I know! You can imagine my surprise as well." She laughed. It sounded like bells chiming. Ugly, tinny, awful bells. "Oh, no. I can't possibly take you away from here. What they have in store for you is far more fun! And because of this, my sisters and I have decided to let the elves keep you. Verdi was a hard nut to crack at first, you see, because she wanted you to herself. But eventually she gave in. Of course, I had to explain your fate in *graphic* detail before she approved." Verdandi was Skuld's sister, who saw the present, and was no friend of mine. "Knowing that you will never leave this place gives me such delicious feels." She licked her pink lips. "And to think you were so close to reuniting with your precious mummy." She mocked a sad face, like how a child would look if their ice cream cone landed wet side down on the pavement. "So very close, yet so, so far. But you see, it wasn't meant to be." She spread her hands, palms up. "This was the perfect time for me to arrive. It's just too bad my sisters couldn't accompany me here to witness your undoing." She shook her head. "But Invaldi is unpredictable, so it couldn't be helped." She glanced over her shoulder, then back at me, her expression conniving.

"You're admitting Invaldi is unpredictable?" I said. "But I thought you could see all?" I followed the direction of her gaze and noticed what had to be two milfs standing sentinel beside a cell door.

Immediately, two fists pounded on the inside of a door, and a voice, one I'd never heard before, but was low and melodic, yelled, "You will pay for this, Skuld! We will hunt you down! You are not all-knowing, even though you pretend to be. You will not win this fight!"

It was my mother. She was ten feet away.

She sounded a little like me. My heart sped up, and my hands felt tingly. This wasn't exactly the way I'd imagined I'd meet her, but I wasn't going to complain. She was here!

"Ah, ah, ah!" Skuld lifted her index finger in the air, stopping my forward progression. "Don't move." Her eyes narrowed. When she was sure I'd stay put, she tossed behind her, "Shieldmaiden, you've already done enough damage by siring this...this *bastard*"—she directed her gaze back at me and scowled—"and keeping her from us, hidden like the dirty secret she is. You will not be allowed to do any more harm. Your fate is equally as dismal, as you get to go live with the skogs. They love Valkyrie meat, or so I've heard." She tried to affect casual by twirling a finger through her long hair, but I sensed her unease. She wasn't as in control as she'd like us to believe. I held on to that. "Honestly"—her voice was light and airy—"I never met a skog I didn't like. They will tear your mother's flesh apart, wait for it to grow back, and do it all over again."

I took a bold step forward, tossing my cloak away from my shoulders and unsheathing my weapons. "You don't scare me anymore."

She tossed her head back and laughed. "Hear that?" She cupped a hand over her ear. "That's the sound of your fate marching toward us. I wish I could stay for the party, but I must go. Invaldi is already furious that I came to his dismal realm unannounced. He made me meet with him and everything. I told him I was leaving, but decided to take a tiny detour." She shrugged her shoulders. "It couldn't be helped. But now my work here is done."

I raised my swords and prepared to battle the future-seer no matter what the cost. But before I could make my move, a hand landed on my forearm, Baldur leaning in. "I'm not sure this is wise," he said uneasily. "The Norns are protected by the laws of Asgard. You would pay a large penalty, most likely death, if you struck her down."

Skuld giggled. "Listen to your dear brother. He knows the rules, unlike you." She nodded at the god of light. "There is really no need to worry. She will not strike. I've already seen it clearly."

Baldur squared his shoulders. "I don't know what's going on here, but I do know your intentions are harmful," he said to Skuld, then turned to me. "The elves are converging now. We must vacate this area."

"It's too late," Skuld hissed. "They will be upon you in mere moments."

"I'm not leaving without my mother." I stood stoically, my arms still raised. "You admitted the first time I saw you," I said to the faux princess, "you couldn't see my future when I left your lair. I'm living proof you don't see all. And I will not leave here without the Valkyrie I came for."

Skuld's eyes darkened, but I could tell what I said had

struck a chord. She couldn't foresee everything. "I see the totality of your ruin—"

"She's lying!" a voice called. My mother was frantic. "The Norns don't get everything right. Run, Phoebe! Get out of here! Leave while you are able."

My mother knew my name.

I was almost too overwhelmed to move. "I came here to free you!" I called, my voice thick. "I'm not leaving empty-handed."

"Don't worry about me!" she insisted. "I will escape at some point. I want you to stay safe. Go!"

Spoken like a true mother.

Emotion threatened to disarm me, but I held fast. I took another step toward Leela's cell, swiping my blades in Skuld's direction. The witch just cackled, seeming absolute in the knowledge that I wouldn't have a chance to engage her.

High-pitched voices shot into the hallway from both ends, sounding like a chorus of angry schoolchildren. The elves had arrived.

Baldur was right. There were too many to count.

Adding to the chaos, a loud, hearty bellow shook the area.

It took a moment before it sank in. Junnal was here!

"It matters not that your pet has arrived," Skuld said testily. "He is no match for the army of elves that have surrounded you."

I swung my swords menacingly. "I don't care if they come," I told her. "If you're dead, I have nothing left to fear."

She cackled. "That's not going to happen—"

Baldur shot past me and charged Skuld, knocking her into the wall while yelling, "Free your mother!" It was a split-second decision on his part and obviously one the Norn hadn't seen coming. That was even more proof that Skuld didn't see all.

I took the advantage and ran toward my mother's cell. The elves had amassed twenty feet away, crowding the hallway.

"Get the Valkyrie!" a few elves shouted.

"She must not free our prize!"

"The skogs will have her!"

I reached the door, my swords out. The milfs, who appeared more human than elf, glanced at me uneasily. "Stand down or die." My voice did not waver. "Those are your only two options."

They glanced at each other and smartly scampered away.

"Phoebe, you must leave this place! Don't worry about me," my mother called through the closed grate.

"I came here to free you," I cried. "I'm not going anywhere."

"There are too many of them, and they are more dangerous than you imagine." Her voice was insistent. "Their magic can kill a Valkyrie. I do not have my weapon, so I cannot aid you in battle."

Junnal lumbered down the hallway, helping Baldur with the elves that had filled the hallway behind us. I had no idea if Skuld was down for good, and didn't care. I just needed five more minutes.

"The elves don't have a giant-troll hybrid or a god helping them. I'll take my chances." I placed my back against the cell door and waved my swords at the elves in front of me. They seemed hesitant to strike, like they were waiting for something, even though most of them held guns. I reached behind me and grabbed on to the handle of her cell and yanked on it in vain. "Do you know the lock code?" I asked my mother.

"No, they keep changing it." She spoke through the small grate, which was closed.

A sudden chattering and commotion erupted among the elves. My head swiveled in their direction as a loud voice boomed, "What do you think you're doing?" It sounded like a cross between an elf and a human—if the human was a twelve-year-old girl. "Step away from that cell, or I will strike you where you stand." The elves parted down the middle, and what could only be best described as a large man-elf paced to the front of the ranks.

He was too big to be an elf, but too short to be a human. He wasn't exactly a milf either. He was taller—and much, much uglier. His nose was squashed, his ears were overly pointy, and nothing more than a scant pouf of white hair covered a skull that was blanketed in warts.

He was hideous.

I wasn't surprised.

"I am Invaldi, and you have trespassed into my realm," he yelled in a voice that cracked like a teenage boy in puberty. "Those who do so suffer the consequences."

A vicious snicker sounded behind me. I glanced over my shoulder to see Skuld standing between me and Baldur, Junnal just behind the god. "Ta-ta, Valkyrie!" She waved. "Have fun in your new home. I must leave now, or my sisters will worry, and it wouldn't be wise to rile them up any more than need be, as that would mean even more death and destruction."

"Why are you still here, Norn?" Invaldi accused, sniffing. He stood to my right, Skuld to my left. "This was not our agreement. Not even your kind is immune to punishment when you break our laws." His small fists clenched and unclenched.

It seemed hilarious to me that this little runt of a man,

with the weirdly pointy ears and a warty head, could be so authoritative and have everyone quaking in their boots. It didn't look like it would take much to defeat him. But I obviously had no idea. Everyone seemed to respect his abilities, and the elves had to be somewhat skilled to keep Valkyries and gods and whages contained for this long.

I must be missing something key.

"Oh, I was leaving," Skuld said. "Just took a little detour. My apologies. But I brought you plenty of compensation for your troubles." She paced forward, her dress billowing. "I left it for you in the gallery. You will not be disappointed. The wealth is vast, to make up for my untimely intrusion. Had it not been an emergency, I would have stayed home. But this Valkyrie must be dealt with. As you can see, she's a threat to us all."

Invaldi looked mildly appeased as he directed his gaze to me, his face hardening. "She will be locked away. I will see to it."

"He is more fearsome than he looks," my mother whispered as Invaldi and Skuld exchanged a few more words about locking me up. "Do not underestimate him. He wields powerful magic."

I answered under my breath, "I won't. I've learned in my short time in these worlds that the creatures are vile, and they all have the capacity to hurt."

"Indeed," she answered. "I will help you if I can."

My heart sank.

It was supposed to be the other way around.

Huggie trusted me, and I'd failed! Why in the world had the raven sent me here when I was so clearly unprepared? "I'm sorry I couldn't get you out," I told her, emotion thick in my throat. "I won't stop trying."

"Don't worry," she assured me. "When they take you,

wait until you're well away from Invaldi, then use your energy. It's the only thing that will give you an advantage, especially if you have allies here. Then find your way outside and back to the tree as fast as you can."

It sounded like a good plan, except there was a problem. "Um..." I hated to admit that I was even more incapable. "I don't know how to harness my energy yet."

"What?" she gasped. "Then why did they send you here? Without it, you have no advantage!"

She hadn't seen my weapon yet, the swords I held out in front of me. "That's kind of a funny story—"

"No!" Skuld screeched, suddenly charging forward. "Get away from that door!" Her face was red, her hands fisted at her sides, her very carefully placed glamour blinking away for a split second.

I was confused.

Why such an outburst right now?

"Seize her!" Invaldi commanded at the same time, jumping on the Get Phoebe bandwagon, directing a hand with long, grotesquely curved fingernails my way. The elves were going to close in on me.

The only thing that could help me now was Gundren.

I raised my blades high into the air, daring any elves to come closer.

"Phoebe," my mother urged, "you must find your energy and use it. It lies deep within your body. When you bring it to the forefront, it's a Valkyrie's greatest asset. I know you can do it. I can feel your strength from here."

"Shut up!" Skuld raged. Turning to Invaldi, she yelled, "What are you waiting for? Take her already!"

I was puzzled for one more second until a light went off in my head, almost like the elusive lightning bolt I couldn't conjure up on command.

By giving me information, my mother was changing the outcome of the future.

I made a quick decision. "Junnal," I yelled, "take them out!" I dropped to my knees in front of my mother's door, grabbing on to the grate with both hands and yanking it open as Junnal stormed by to take the front as Baldur took up the rear.

Invaldi raged, "You cannot best us, troll! We are large in numbers. It matters not that you are resistant to our magic."

Junnal bashed his club against the wall, and debris tumbled all over, creating a nice distraction as the elves scrambled.

I gathered enough strength to look at my mother. This was not how I'd imagined meeting her. Beautiful green eyes stared back at me. "Tell me more," I urged. "How do I harness my power?"

"It's not that difficult," she hurried, knowing we didn't have a lot of time. "The energy lies in your very cells, and you are always in command of it. Close your eyes and focus on it, and it will heed your wish. Have you ever unleashed it before?"

I bit my lip. "Yes, but only three times. It emerges at intense moments or when I feel severely threatened. It happened twice when I was kidnapped and tortured by the fire demons on Muspelheim, and"—and once when I was intimate with Fen—"one other time." No need to go into details when I was meeting my mother for the very first time through a cell grate. Nor was I about to share that my boyfriend was a wolf who was slated to kill my father, her lover, in the great war of Ragnarok.

Junnal gave a hollow shout that sounded like rage mixed with pain.

The elves swarmed him, and crimson smoke from their

weapons filtered through the hallway. Baldur rushed up to me, grinning. "They are using their dark magic, but the giant is immune to it. Even though he is managing to divert them, we will not escape. Their numbers are too strong. A capture is inevitable. But that doesn't mean we won't break out again." He winked.

"Baldur!" my mother exclaimed, spotting the god for the first time. "Frigg will be most upset to see you free."

Baldur bent down to the opening. "Leela, it's nice to see you again. Our paths have not crossed enough in this wretched place. You are looking well. My sister here has most graciously set me free." He beamed, his dimples flashing. I smiled back in spite of myself. "I am determined to live out my destiny, and there is nothing anyone can do about it. It only took the common sense of your child to see it was the right course of action to take. I will no longer be kept chained like a dog. It is time for me to live again."

I heard my mother's sharp intake of breath. "Phoebe, Frigg is not to be trifled with. If Baldur is hurt—"

A loud sound, like a mini explosion, whizzed near my ear, and a second later flames erupted on my back.

Holy crap, I was on fire!

"They have set your cloak aflame with magic," Baldur said as he ripped the garment off in one motion, stomping it on the ground.

The flames had been dark violet.

Once the cloak was gone, elves surrounded us. Small hands gripped me all over, surprising me with their strength as they dragged me brutally away from the door. But I wanted to hear what Leela had to say about my brother. Her voice had been insistent. "If Baldur's hurt, what happens?" I called. "Mother!"

Skuld's laughter was the only thing I heard as the elves

rushed me away. "Have fun in your new home. And don't bother to try and escape. Your fate is set."

That's what you think, witch.

"No more white elf magic for you!" an elf shrieked.

"Do not fight us, Valkyrie, or your pet dies!" Hands held me tightly.

"We will kill the troll *and* the whage if you resist!"

Was Callan here?

My head shot up as I searched for the white elf. Our eyes met across the sea of elves, and the mage shrugged. He was being led by two skogs, who looked very unhappy.

The elves had managed to pin my swords to my sides with a powerful charm as they hustled me along. I couldn't move my arms at all. I was surrounded by a mob of little, angry bodies.

I tried to concentrate on my inner energy, like my mother had said, but everything was so chaotic I couldn't focus. They shuffled me up next to Callan and manhandled us both farther down the hallway.

"That was quite an adventure!" Callan's voice was animated. "I had the skogs bring me here to find you."

"Is that how you got out?" I asked, out of breath from the ordeal and not able to move my upper body at all.

"Once Zee came to the cell, the deception was up. But your giant came to the rescue and injured the skog leader, and we escaped. I used my power to make the guards do my bidding."

We were shuffled quickly past Junnal, who was out cold on the floor. "Junnal!" I cried, trying to break free.

"Have no fear," Callan soothed. "The troll will endure. His body was made to resist magic. Invaldi carries root magic, which is extremely powerful."

I craned my neck around, searching for the elf leader, but

he was nowhere to be found. The elves had Baldur, but he was resisting, flinging them off left and right. "No one will bind me again!" he boomed. "You cannot keep me here against my will any longer!" He glanced up, met my gaze, and smiled, even as they hit him with magic. "It will be okay, sister. I will find you, and we will rid ourselves of this wretched place once and for all."

Where had I heard that before?

17

I thought the elves would march me down the main staircase, as that's where we seemed to be heading, but at the last moment they veered toward a wall that looked impenetrable. I spotted the combination lock set into the stone a moment before an elf reached out to turn it.

Within minutes, the stone face slid backward to reveal a hidden room. The elves and skogs pushed Callan and me inside. It seemed this place was filled with hidey-holes—you just had to know where to look.

A shriek sounded as the wall slid closed, which was always unsettling.

The elves' voices were like fingernails raking down a chalkboard at high speed. "Look! The whage has Kennik's weapon!" The elf ordered the skog to hand it over and then waved it in the air. "He must have killed Kennik!"

"No, stupid, that's the Valkyrie's weapon," another argued. "She killed him. My brother's sister's husband was there. He witnessed the Valkyrie slay Kennik. It was she who is guilty."

The room began to rumble and move.

It was an elevator.

More elves than I could count had crammed into the space. There must have been twenty-five or more in a room the size of a bathroom, all of them leaving a wide gap around Callan. I had no choice but to ride this out and see what happened. I'd infiltrated Invaldi's realm, and now I was paying the price. I tugged on my arms, but still no give.

"There will be nothing left of you once we're done," one elf warned.

"You will be crying out for your death," another added.

I could only imagine the delights awaiting me.

After a very short ride, the elevator slowed. It was hard to tell which direction it had gone. We lurched to a stop, and the door slid open. The elves poured out, jostling me, Callan, and the skogs along with them. My hands still grasped my swords, which was a good thing.

We'd emerged into a room I recognized. It was the same large, domed, octagonal atrium we'd come into when we'd first arrived. It was where we'd found the two elves who led us down the stairs and started this entire ordeal.

We were tugged none too carefully across the main floor. All the elves who happened to be walking by stopped to gape, the crowd quickly swelling.

"Nothing to see here, folks! Just a captured Valkyrie," one elf called, puffing its chest out.

"Step aside, prisoner coming through."

"We have Odin's daughter. Praise Invaldi!"

A cheer went up in the crowd, some of the elves dropping the packages they carried. These were clearly the workers, not the fighters. I wondered what they did around here. Did they have clothing stores? Grocery stores? Did people shop for casual items and trinkets? Did they have houses? Caves? They were certainly better off than the fire demons, who lived in temporary stick hovels.

"Ow!" I said between gritted teeth as an elf shoved me. "No need to prod me like an animal. I'm coming with you." Not like I had a choice.

Yet.

Callan cleared his throat behind me. "I believe we're headed into the parliament area, which is peculiar. They only bring prisoners here who have a court date."

"Do they try all their prisoners?" I asked.

"No," Callan replied. "They only try prisoners who have stature and clout. Invaldi can be brought to the High Court of Asgard if he fails to give someone a trial. Most realms operate this way. If you're found guilty in Svartalfheim—and let's just say, most are unless the person on trial can summon a representative from their realm to stand by them—Invaldi can do whatever he pleases. The biggest difference here is that other realms pay the elves to keep their criminals. For those individuals, there is no trial, just prison cells and torture. It's a booming business."

Invaldi would likely give me a sham trial for the death of Kennik. When I was found guilty, he would argue to keep me here forever. Something that Skuld likely had seen, or she wouldn't have left so happy.

I had to find a way to change my fate. "I've only spent time in one other realm," I said, "and the fire demons certainly didn't try any prisoners. I saw nothing that resembled any sort of *parliament*. It was Surtr's rule and nothing else."

"Of course they don't have a parliament," Callan scoffed. "They're considered savages at best. That plane is barely habitable."

153

"I know that now," I muttered. "It's not like I had a choice in the matter."

"How long did you spend with those barbarians?" He raised his white, bushy eyebrows.

"Long enough to hurt," I said, blocking out images that threatened to overcome me.

"Well, you lived to tell the tale, so that says something about your strength. Not all have been so lucky."

One of the elves in front of us hoisted open a huge double door and ushered us through. More hands pushed and prodded. They were definitely enjoying their position of power.

"The only good thing that came out of that realm is finding Fen." My insides clenched, and I wondered what he was doing right this minute. Was he worried about me? Was his level of anger at hot lava? Or had he forgiven me?

"Fen?" Callan appeared confused. "Are you talking about Fenrir the Wolf?" He let out a gasp. "The fabled Mad Wolf of Asgard?"

I smiled. Fen did have that effect on people. "Yes, but he's not made-up. He's as real as you and me. He's my boyfriend. At least I hope he still is. He's probably angry with me, because I came here without telling him. So, honestly, there's a good chance that we're broken up."

"I should like to meet him one day," Callan mused.

"You will be meeting nothing but your death!" an elf cried as they shoved us the rest of the way through the doors.

The room we entered was opulent. All polished stone and granite, buffed to a high sheen. Jewels glittered in some of the columns that encircled the room. It seemed to go on for miles, and the ceilings soared so high I could barely make out where they stopped.

The elves turned right and dragged me down a long

hallway that ran around the outside of the massive columns. The skogs followed with Callan. Twenty feet later, we stopped in front of a large door. This one had a key entry, not a combination lock.

The elf in front pulled out a key ring and inserted a key into the door. There was a loud click as a mechanism was disengaged.

"Get her inside!" the elf shouted.

"Seize her weapons first!"

Greedy hands groped my sides, yanking my swords roughly out of my hands. My arms were still locked to my sides, so there was nothing I could do. I tried kindling my energy once again, and I felt an ember fire up, but my excitement was diminished as I was shoved into the room without Gundren before I could get it to grow.

The door slammed, the lock engaging loudly.

Damn.

I glanced around my new surroundings. It took me a moment to realize Callan wasn't with me. My hands shot to the door, pounding as I yelled, "Leave the whage with me! He is no threat to anyone! He's sick and needs help!"

A cackle answered me. "The whage will not stand trial! He is headed to the highest security!"

"Yes, the highest"—a snicker—"to await his death!"

I pounded on the door with renewed vigor. "He doesn't deserve to die! Just let him go!"

"We will not release him," the voice sounded aghast at the idea. "He has already had his trial and was found guilty! He is a tried-and-true offender of this realm. The white elves sent him long ago to avenge their king, as he is the most powerful of their kind. He killed many of us during that fight, and he will die for his deeds!"

Pounding my fist one last time in frustration, I spun

around. I wasn't going to let Callan die. I had to get out of here.

The room was sparsely furnished with a small cot and a tiny toilet the size of an ice cream bucket. It didn't look like it would tolerate my weight. No windows, and the door didn't even have a grate.

I began to pace, wondering for the thirty-third time why Huggie had sent me when I clearly didn't have the skills. I was forced to turn, running out of room in the small space, and felt something press against my stomach as my body changed motion.

Gram!

The elves hadn't checked me for other weapons. It was beyond foolish, but I wasn't about to complain. I pulled the dagger out of my waistband. It'd been partially hidden by an overlap in my tunic, and that's likely why they hadn't seen it. Or they were too cocky about their skills and didn't care if I had a small weapon.

It would be hard to defeat their magic with a dagger, except this was Odin's blade.

I turned it over in my hands.

Now I just had to figure out what to do with it.

Both Ingrid and Fen had told me a little bit about how special the dagger was, but hadn't elaborated. It was made for Odin as a gift from a goddess. The blade could transport me through Yggdrasil, it could cut the hides of most creatures in the seven realms, and was said to have some intelligence. I could really use its smarts right now.

I'd never taken the time to really study it. I'd been too busy with my training and new life at the stronghold.

The depictions carved into the hilt were similar to Gundren, but not exactly the same. They were definitely made by the same creatures. I tried to decipher some of the scenes. One showed the dagger buried in what had to be the bark of a tree. That showed it worked in Yggdrasil. Another showed the dagger cutting the hide of an animal. In the third, it appeared to be piercing something that looked like flesh.

I squinted.

It almost looked like an arm.

That couldn't be right. Could it?

But there were fingers.

I turned it over and followed the last graphic, the one that looked like the dagger had been inserted into skin. It led to the very end of the hilt. I tipped it up and saw the unmistakable glyphs of lightning.

My breath came faster.

Was this made for a Valkyrie?

Was that why my father had it commissioned? To protect someone he loved?

That was definitely lightning.

I traced over the glyph with my finger. I had already used Gram to cut my palms, and afterward I did glow. Maybe the dagger was a conduit of energy? Maybe that was why it worked in Yggdrasil?

It wouldn't hurt to try.

"Why not?" I said out loud. "I've got nothing to lose, and my mother's and Callan's lives depend on me."

I quickly assessed the room and decided the only thing that I could try energy out on was the toilet, which was empty.

Sitting down on the cot, I positioned the tip of Gram against the soft flesh of my forearm and took a deep breath. "Here goes nothing." The tip slid in with no resistance and very little pain. Dark red blood pooled at the point of entry.

For a moment, nothing happened.

Then, all of a sudden, my body began to quiver like a shockwave was running through me.

I began to vibrate, first in my arm, then my entire body.

Then I began to glow. Just like I did when Gram had pierced Yggdrasil. I made a fist with my newly bright hand. I wasn't sure if I was supposed to withdraw Gram from my arm or not for this to work, so I left it.

The pain was nonexistent.

Instead, the weapon that was now inside my body called to me. Not like Gundren, but something near. It beckoned me to use its power. It wanted to help me.

I closed my eyes and tried to focus on what my mother had told me about gathering my energy. Now that I was glowing, my body felt electric.

"Here goes nothing," I whispered. I opened my eyes and focused all my thoughts on the small toilet.

My greatest desire was to smash it to smithereens.

The thought of it blowing to pieces was so vivid as I imagined it breaking apart in my mind. "Get rid of that mockery of a toilet," I commanded as I stretched my arm toward the offending object.

Lightning shot out of my body with so much force, I was tossed backward. I smashed against the wall, the dagger falling out of my arm, clattering to the ground.

The ice cream bucket exploded on impact, sending debris flying everywhere.

I managed to get my forearms up in front of my face, protecting most of my body from the flying shards. Once it was over, I sat up, out of breath.

I had not expected that to happen.

There was a banging on my cell door. "What are you doing in there?" an elf voice yelled.

"Um," I answered.

FREED

Demolishing your stuff?
Playing with Odin's powerful dagger?
Getting ready to kick your ass?
"Just going to the bathroom."
"Keep it down!"
"Will do."
Not.

18

Now that I'd figured out how to use Gram as a powerful weapon, I had to find a way use it to my advantage. I walked around the room, exploring every nook and cranny, kicking scraps of exploded toilet out of my way as I went.

The cell was sealed up tight, and there wasn't anything else to blow up unless I went after the cot, which seemed counterproductive.

After the dagger had fallen out of my body, my glow began to fade quickly. It was nothing more than a soft illumination now.

If I bulldozed my way out of here by blowing off the door, the elves would be on me quickly, and there were too many of them. It was risky. And just because I blew up a toilet didn't mean I had this power under control. Mastering my energy was going to take time.

I was trying to figure out what to do when I heard a noise coming from the next cell over. I walked over and set my ear against the wall. "Callan?" It was a shot in the dark, but I had to try.

No response.

The walls were thick, so I upped the volume and tried again. "Callan? Is that you?"

"Phoebe?" a tentative female voice answered. One I'd never heard before. It was high and slightly nasally.

"Yes," I replied. "Who is this?"

"You don't know me, but I can help you." Her voice was hard to distinguish, as it was muffled through the rocks, but I could make out the words fairly well.

"You're going to have to tell me who you are first."

"I was sent here long ago by Odin to watch over your mother. I am a mixed elf. They got suspicious of me about a month ago when they caught me relaying messages back to Asgard for your mother. They threw me in here, and now I'm awaiting trial."

There was no way to know if she was telling the truth. "How can you help me?"

"The raven, Hugin, got a message to Leela a few months ago saying to expect you soon. The shieldmaiden has been eagerly awaiting your arrival ever since. She was able to secure a few weapons, sent through smugglers from Asgard, and I have placed them around the castle. It was my intention to meet you at Yggdrasil, but they took me prisoner before I could make it. I'm sorry to have failed you both."

I wasn't sure how much to divulge on my end, so I settled on, "I think I might be able to get myself out of the cell, but it will be noisy. If I can break both of us out, do we have a chance of escaping without capture?"

"I know this realm very well, and there is a good chance. But you must wait until the wee hours before you try," she cautioned. "There will be fewer elves around at that time."

"The wee hours?"

"We bed down in the early morning and sleep most of the day. Elves need their daily sleep to survive, and things shut down to a minimum during the wee hours."

Good to know. "Are they really going to shut down if they're in the middle of a crisis?" I asked. That didn't make sense. "There's a high threat to the realm right now. If it were me, I would make elves stand guard even if they were sleepy."

"It's hard to know. They might be forced to stay awake if Invaldi deems it so. They will have reinforcements in place if there are fewer elves, however, so we must take that into account."

"Are you talking about trolls?" That meant I'd have to defeat one of the big green guys without Gundren. That didn't sound ideal, but I did have Gram.

"Yes, but they are slow and cannot fit into all the areas we can. If you free me, I can show you. We can easily outrun them."

"What kind of weapons do you have stashed?" My body was aching for my swords. I would have to find my weapon once I was out.

"Several broadswords, one spear, and some rope."

That sounded promising. "How long until the wee hours?"

"It will be a while."

I sat down on the cot, my back against the wall. I wasn't sure if waiting was the right thing, but I could use some rest. "Okay, let me know when it gets close."

"Sure thing," she answered. "My name is Willa, and I am happy to serve you. Your mother is a wonderful woman."

My heart constricted. The only thing I knew about my mother for sure was that she had green eyes. My fingers drummed the top of my thigh. I'd been so close to freeing her. It was infuriating that her rescue had come so close, only to be snatched away.

My eyelids felt heavy. Relaxing for five minutes was probably a good idea. I couldn't remember the last time I'd slept. Valkyries didn't need sleep like humans did, but they did require some to recharge. I'd been gone from the Valkyrie stronghold for only half a day at the most, but it felt like years.

As my eyes drooped, my mind wandered to Fen, like it always did when I had a moment to spare. I missed him like crazy. What I wanted most in the world was for him to forgive me. I tried to make myself comfortable on the cot, fidgeting with the hem of my tunic. "Please, please understand," I whispered. "I had no other choice. I had to go. Even though I haven't been successful, I would still choose the same path." I propped my arm under my head, curling my legs under my body. I wondered what Ingrid and Rae were doing right now. Were they trying to get the battle unit here? I wondered what Tyr and Sam were up to. I wondered if Tyr would be happy I sprang our brother Baldur. I bet he would be. Or maybe he would sigh in that particular way of his and calmly explain the reasons why it hadn't been a good idea.

I knew nothing of the gods, what their rules were, or how they lived. I could only go by my own code—a life where everybody gets to choose for themselves. What my mother had said about Frigg being angry had me worried, and I desperately hoped Baldur was going to be okay. I would be gutted if anything happened to him.

"Huggie, why did you send me here?" I lamented. "I'm too young and inexperienced to do this on my own. You should've known that. Anya would be a better choice, and that's saying something."

I could worry about all this forever, but it wasn't going to change my situation. I needed to sleep and recharge.

After a moment, my eyes slid shut.

◢

The ground shook, and I leaped off of the bed.

"Whoa." I grabbed on to the wall to steady myself. My cell was pitch black. When did that happen? I pounded on the wall. "Willa! Are you there? Is it the wee hours?" I hadn't been out for very long.

No response.

I tried again. "Willa! What's going on?" The ground had shaken before, but this was bigger, with much more force.

I couldn't see, so I put my hands out in front of me and ran toward the door. When my palms smacked into the cool wood, I rammed my fists against it. "What's going on? Can anyone hear me? Let me out of here!" The ground shook again, and cracks rent open in the floor beneath me. I heard shouts and feet running by. Most of the footsteps sounded heavy, so they were likely trolls. "Is anyone out there?"

"Quiet, little birdie," a booming voice growled on the other side. "You don't want me to come in there." I recognized the voice. If I was right, it was the leader of the trolls. The one who'd started the fight with Junnal earlier, but I couldn't be sure.

"What's going on? I hear a lot of pandemonium," I said, blatantly ignoring his command for me to be quiet. "It's dark in here. Is the power out?" The ground shook again, and this time rocks poured from the ceiling like hail. I grabbed Gram from my waistband. It was time to take action.

"Nothing out here to concern yourself with."

Bull. Concerning myself was a top priority.

I took a few steps back and brought my arm up, yanking back my tunic. The old wound had already healed. The perks of being a Valkyrie. I inserted the tip of Gram into my forearm without flinching.

My body welcomed it.

I closed my eyes and concentrated on the energy the dagger was amplifying. Blood trembled in my veins, and I began to glow, which was even more apparent in the dark. I looked like a human jack-o'-lantern.

I didn't have a better plan than blowing the door off its hinges. It was the only way out. Obviously, something was up, as the guards were in a frenzy. That could mean one of two things. The Norns had come back. Or help was here. I hoped it was the latter. I had no idea what happened to Willa, but I couldn't worry about that now.

"Prepare for lift-off," I intoned as I angled my open palm toward the door. I had no idea if I had enough juice to accomplish this, but I was about to see.

Power shot out of my body in a thick stream, hitting the door smack in the middle. A loud burst of energy followed. The kickback tossed me off-balance, but I caught myself before I fell on my backside.

I paced forward as the smoke settled, eager to see my handiwork. "What the heck?"

The door was intact.

There was a ring of charred black in a perfect circle, slightly smoking, but other than that, it had held. I'd been so sure my power would free me from this place!

I holstered Gram in my waistband, frustrated.

Laughter filtered through the door. "What? You don't think we make these doors and cells Valkyrie proof? Keep trying, little birdie. We have all day."

Disgruntled, I went to the wall separating me from Willa

and pounded my fists on it. "Are you in there? What's going on?"

I was still glowing, so I could see.

No response.

They must have moved her.

The ground shook again, and pebbles rained down. I had to think of another way to get out of here. It was clear something was out there and the elves were panicking. But whoever they'd placed in front of my door was not worried. Trolls must not care what happened here as long as they got paid.

I paced back to the door, placing my palms inside the black ring I'd just created. It was warm to the touch. It was definitely Valkyrie proof. I had to try a different tactic. "So, it looks like you've recovered from that thrashing my friend gave you. What'd it take you? An hour? Maybe a few? You were out cold when I saw you last. I bet the bump on your head is killing you. The elves must frown on their pet trolls getting their asses handed to them down here. I'm surprised you still have a job."

A growl sounded before the troll said, "Keep your mouth running, and I'll come in there and shut it for you."

That's exactly what I want, buddy.

I smiled. "What happens when a troll gets fired? Do you go home with your tail between your legs? I'm assuming you have a tail, but it's just a guess. Is it even possible to get other work once you get canned from a place like this? I bet you'd be a laughingstock of your kind if anyone found out. Makes it tough to get any future dates. I'm certain your females much prefer a big strong *alpha* male, not a wimpy baby who gets thrashed by a Jotun half-breed."

There was a roar, and the handle on the door rattled.

Well, that didn't take very long.

Satisfied my baiting had done the trick, I backed up, readying myself. I wasn't going to be able to physically best the troll without my weapon, but I could hit him with my power and try to get away.

A set of keys chimed as I pulled Gram out of my waistband, holding the dagger steady above my arm. The key engaged, and then all was quiet. Instead of the door bursting open, outside angry shouts volleyed back and forth, and something large smashed against the wood.

I had no idea what was going on, but whatever it was, it was violent. If there was going to be more than one adversary, I had to make sure I had the advantage. I glanced around the room.

There was only one option.

Rushing over to the cot, I plucked up the only blanket and ripped off a long piece. I slipped Gram inside my sleeve and pricked myself then tied the fabric like a tourniquet around my forearm so it stayed in place, tight against my body.

The dagger amplified me immediately, and I began to glow more brightly.

Finally, the key turned in the lock, and there was a pop.

With a loud creak, the door began to swing open.

I held my breath and hoped my energy would be enough to fell this troll. He was huge, almost the same size as Junnal.

But instead of the troll, something else stood in its place.

It took me a second to realize what I was seeing.

I dropped my hands. "Fen!"

19

I raced headlong into his arms. I'd honestly never been so excited to see anybody in my entire life. To my great relief, he welcomed me, dropping his sword to his side to give me a one-armed embrace as I peppered kisses along his neck. "How did you get here?" I was breathless. "How did you find me?"

He kept me close, not letting me go, his arm firmly around me, his face hard to read. "I arrived by Yggdrasil. I refused to leave the cillar after you left. After a while, the raven finally divulged that the portal would open for me at an undetermined time, so I stayed until it did."

"Was your arrival what shook the mountain?" I asked, glancing around. The place was in shambles. Rocks and debris were scattered all over. Some of the columns had cracked. The troll I'd made angry lay off to the side, unconscious.

"No," he answered. "A short time after I arrived, I felt the same quakes. I believe the Valkyries have stormed another entrance, but I can't be certain. The raven told me to tell no other of my plans, and I kept my promise."

"How did you know I was here?" The mountain network was vast.

"I didn't. I came through the main entrance, and to my surprise there were very few elves around, and the ones who were in attendance were in a fright. As luck would have it, I ran into a group leading a prisoner away. I freed her, and she is the one who helped me."

Movement came from my right as a small, slim figure stepped out from behind a column rife with cracks. She stood no higher than my shoulder. She had long brown hair, softly pointed ears, and large eyes.

Otherwise, she looked mostly human.

She gave me a tentative smile. "You must be Willa," I said as I stepped reluctantly out of Fen's grasp, loosening Gram from my arm. Fen hadn't commented on my glow. I would fill him in later.

"Yes, I am Willa," she replied, her eyes cast downward. "The elves came to move me right before the wee hours began. I'm sorry I was not there for you."

"It's not your fault, and you led Fen here, so I'm grateful." I turned to my gallant boyfriend, who seemed to have forgiven me. "We have to find my mother, Baldur, Junnal, and Callan and get out of here."

Fen quirked his gaze at me. "The god of light resides here?"

"He does, and you probably already know he's my brother." I smiled. "He's been helping me. His mother sent him here against his will to protect him from a fated death, but he made up his own mind to be free, so I broke him out of his cell."

Fen said, "I know his story well. I was not aware he was here."

"I can lead you to where your mother was last jailed,"

Willa said. "I am unsure if she still occupies that cell or not, but if she isn't there, I believe we can find her."

"That sounds good," I said. "She is supposed to be taken by the skogs, and I pray they haven't moved her yet. First things first. I need my weapon. Do you know where the elves would have stashed it?" I sensed Gundren close by, and as I appraised the area for a likely location, the ground shook again. Other than the troll out cold there was no one else around. "Why are there no elves here? They should be swarming."

Willa answered, "In this land, the greatest threat is always addressed first. Those who are storming the realm will take priority. Our resources are limited, as we have gone hundreds of years without an invasion of any kind. Most of the inhabitants here work with gemstones and metal. They are craftsmen, not guards. We make the finest pieces of weaponry and jewels found in all seven realms. Gods and goddesses clamor for our work, which is always infused with magic. Since the attack has come in the wee hours, it has made it even more difficult. The timing happened well for you, and I would guess it was not by chance." We likely had Huggie to thank for that.

"You say 'we,' but you told me Odin sent you to watch over my mother. So is your allegiance here with the elves? Or to Asgard?"

She paused before answering. "It's rather complicated. My mother is of Asgard. She lay with an elf and was shunned for it." Willa's voice was tight. "My mother had special talents, which were passed down to me. Odin collects the unique. It's what makes him so powerful." She beamed. "He realized my talents could be helpful and struck up a friendship. He provided for me when no one else would. I owe much to him, so my allegiance is not to Asgard or to Svartalfheim. It is to Odin alone."

Her steadfast loyalty impressed me. "You sounded fond of my mother when we spoke before. Was she kind to you?" I asked.

I spotted a blush creeping along her cheek. "Yes, very much so. She has been treated unfairly here, and for that I will see her freed. Follow me, we should hurry. There are several secret passageways that will lead us to her."

"First, I need my weapon," I said. "I can't leave here without it."

"Try calling to it," Fen suggested.

"You mean like Tyr does?" My brother could call his weapons, and they flew right to his hand, just like Thor called his hammer. It was incredible to watch. "Do you think that will work for me?" If it did, that would be amazingly cool.

Fen smiled. It was the first emotion he had showed. He was a man of few words, and I wasn't going to push him right now. "It's worth a try."

"Do I have to do anything special?"

"I think wanting them should be sufficient."

I closed my eyes as I tried to envision Gundren in all its glory. It wasn't hard. I had already memorized everything about those swords. I pictured the battered leather scabbard, the onyx grips, each rune carved into the hilts. The weapon all but glittered in my mind. I was still glowing when I intoned, "Come to me." It felt foolish to say it out loud, but I had no idea what else to utter. My eyes flew open. "I felt something!" Excitedly, I focused on my swords and how badly my body ached to feel them in my hands. "Come to *me*!" I shouted.

A door rattled from across the atrium, and seconds later it burst open.

Gundren flew through the air, landing with a solid *thunk*

in my outstretched palm. My gaze was pure amazement as I ogled my weapon.

"That seemed to do the trick," Fen said.

"This might be the coolest thing that's ever happened to me. Sam is going to die when she sees this."

We both followed Willa. "It's likely no other Valkyrie has that ability," Fen said. "You can thank your god genes for bestowing it upon you. Many of Odin's children can do the same." I hurried after them, strapping the scabbard on my back. "There will be much you will discover about your abilities in the future. Each immortal is different, and you are still young."

Willa led us through a door and down a long, high-arched hallway. About halfway down, she set both hands against a solid marble wall. There didn't appear to be anything there, but at her slightest touch, the stone moved inward with a scraping noise. It rumbled open to reveal a small passage.

"How many secret rock walls are there in this place?" I asked, glancing around, expecting elves to start coming around the corner any moment.

"There are quite a few," she answered. "Likely the elves are using many of them right now. We are like the ants of Midgard, in a sense. There is an entire network of passageways and secret doors."

"Do you know where they are keeping other prisoners?" I asked. "I'm looking for the one they call a whage—the white elf mage—the god Baldur, and a large giant-troll mix. We can't leave here without them."

"I do not," she replied as she slipped into the passageway and hurried us down a skinny hallway with L-shaped turns. "We can find them once we have your mother. But we must stay away from the guards as much as possible. They possess

magic and will be using deadly spells. Here, come this way."
She put her shoulder against another rock wall, and it swung
open. Fen and I had to duck into it, as it was elf height. The
ceiling was lower, and we were forced to walk with our
shoulders rounded. After a few twists and turns, she opened
another door that led to a stairway. It was tiny and steep.
"Once we are all the way down," she instructed, "we will
emerge at the back of her cell. This is where I bring her food
and clothing. If she is still there, we will be fortunate. But it is
warded, so only I can enter."

"The wards will not be an issue," Fen stated as we trailed
after her down the steep staircase. "The shieldmaiden's
weapon will break the ward."

"If it's resistant to dark elf magic, it will work," Willa
agreed. The staircase was incredibly long, at least three
stories. We were lucky there were torches every fifty feet.

Once we arrived at the bottom, we emerged into another
narrow hallway, except this one had a little more headroom.
I could stand, but Fen had to bend his neck. Willa rushed in
front of us and stopped halfway down, pressing her palms
against the wall.

Nothing happened.

"Is it supposed to open right away?" I whispered, coming
up behind her.

She glanced at me, worry in her gaze as she nodded.
"Yes, it should respond to my touch. Something is wrong."

"If they arrested you and suspected that you were
working for Asgard, it's no surprise if they changed the
wards," I said, unsheathing my swords. "How long has it
been since you were away? They had my mother on level
three recently. Is this the right level?"

Willa looked stricken. "No, this is level five. I did not
know they changed her location."

"Of course you didn't," I said. "You were locked up, and I should've said something sooner." I hadn't even thought to ask her, figuring she knew where Leela was better than I did. "But we need to get to level three in a hurry. The skogs are supposed to take her soon."

Willa turned and raced back to the steps. I sheathed my swords, and we followed her. But before we arrived at the very top, she pressed her small body into the wall, and once again it opened, revealing yet another hidden passageway right in the middle of the stairway. "Follow me," she urged. "It's tight in this particular space, but this is the fastest way to get to level three."

Tight was an understatement.

My shoulders brushed the sides of the walls. I glanced behind me. Fen was walking sideways with his shoulders bowed. The trolls certainly didn't use these spaces.

"It's just a little farther. Then we will hit the ladder," Willa said. "We are in between two levels at the moment, so we have to climb." We reached what I'd barely call a ladder. It was set into a cylindrical hole. The "rungs" were nothing more than hollowed-out indentations in the stone wall at uneven increments.

Willa began to climb with no hesitation. I started up after her, digging my hands into the broken rocks with everything I had and grabbing on tight. It wasn't meant for someone my size. Below me, Fen grunted. He barely fit and had to carefully maneuver his massive shoulders to avoid getting stuck. It took some finesse, but he was managing it.

Above me, Willa stuck her hand out, forcing the rock ceiling back to reveal yet another tunnel. She climbed into it and waited patiently for me to make my way in.

I boosted myself up onto the short ledge. "I owe you," I told her. "The Valkyries will gladly repay the favor." I scooted back out of the way so Fen had room to come after me. "What will you do once you're finished here?" I asked her. "The elves are bound to find out you aided us."

"They will hold a trial and find me guilty." She said it with no ire, purely a statement of what was to happen. "They were going to do it anyway, so it matters not."

Fen made his way in, squeezing his huge frame up into the tunnel. "Once they decide you're guilty, what happens?"

"Most likely they will kill me. But if your mother escapes, they may give me to the skogs instead. The reptiles will demand payment no matter what transpires up top. They always do."

"Can't Odin intervene and help you somehow?" I couldn't believe my father wasn't powerful enough to help this stranded mixed elf. "He's the one who sent you here. You're breaking the law to serve him, right? He should find a way to get you out."

She shook her head. "There is nothing he can do. He would have to come to this realm physically to intervene, and that would be unprecedented. And it is not his fault. He does not know my life is in jeopardy." The same pride as before came through. She clearly thought my father hung the moon.

"Well, there's something *I* can do. You're leaving with us." I stated it as a fact.

Her eyes widened as she wrung her hands and, head bowed, said nothing. She began to hurry down the tunnel.

As we followed, I arched an eyebrow at Fen, hoping he'd help me explain to Willa what I was talking about. He took the cue. "Midgard is a very special realm. It's a place where the inhabitants have retained their empathy. Asgard might have some things to learn yet." To me, he said, "We typically do not help other creatures. They know the consequences of their actions and can choose for themselves. Willa did not have to agree to come on this mission. Odin would not have forced her. She had her own reasons, and it was her decision to make."

Willa glanced behind her, nodding rapidly. "Yes, exactly that. I do not expect to be repaid. I did this willingly. Odin made my life worth living. It was the least I could do."

"Well, where I come from we help each other," I told her, ducking under a lower section. "You risked your life to serve my mother and help me, and your life is still worth living. I'm going to take you back to the Valkyrie stronghold. I'm certain we can find a place for you there." I had no idea if the other shieldmaidens would agree or not, but I knew my mother would have some say. If this mixed elf had served her well by smuggling weapons, she should want to reward her service. Valkyries had a strong sense of loyalty and paid their debts. I wasn't sure if that extended to other creatures, but if it didn't, there was going to be a problem.

"That is very kind of you," Willa said. "We can discuss it at a later date. We are on level three. If your mother is here, we will find her." Twenty yards down, she took a right. There were no doors, only stone, but she stopped and put her ear up to the wall. "Do you remember how far down your mother's cell was?"

"I think it was right in the middle," I told her.

She nodded as she walked down about ten more paces, then she put her ear to the wall again. "This space is heavily warded. There is a good chance she is in here." She tapped the wall. "The wards are imprinted to other mixed elves I know, and they must be broken."

I unsheathed my swords. Fen was right behind me. "How do I break the wards?" I asked him.

"Insert your weapons into the stone. When you feel

resistance, you must push back. If you can send your energy through your swords, you will break them even faster," he answered. "But even without, your swords should be enough to break any magic."

I nodded. I wasn't going to fail my mother a second time.

I positioned myself beside the wall with my weapons out and closed my eyes, thinking about how much I wanted this. I struck out with both hands at once.

My swords landed true, piercing the stone deeply. A reverberation raced through the blades and up into my arms and shoulders, rocking me to the core. I held on, even though this ward definitely wanted to toss me out.

I began to gather what I thought was my energy and aim it toward the wall. I wasn't sure I was doing it right. I was going on pure instinct. I gritted my teeth as my body fought with the magic. I wanted this bad. "Please, please be enough." As I said the words, power flowed through my arms and into the swords.

It was glorious.

I was doing it!

This was what being a Valkyrie meant.

A large *boom!* erupted, and the wall itself began to tumble away like a mini avalanche. I stumbled back, avoiding the rubble, my back hitting the stone behind me. I was exhausted but invigorated.

I'd created a person-sized hole in the wall like a badass.

As the dust cleared, I made out a single figure on the other side.

My mother.

20

For several seconds, I didn't react. I was too stunned to move. Of course I'd hoped to find her, but I hadn't prepared myself at all for how I would feel or what I would do, so my body just locked up.

She was stunningly beautiful.

Her long, straight hair was the same chestnut color as my own. It hung loosely around her shoulders, falling almost to her waist. Her eyes were a bright emerald green. Both surprisingly and unsurprisingly, she didn't look much older than I did, early thirties at most. Valkyries aged slowly. She was dressed in a simple blue robe and didn't look dirty or unkempt. If they'd treated her ill, it hadn't been recently.

I was relieved.

And at a loss for words.

"Phoebe." She uttered it softly as she moved toward me, her voice melodic and sweet. "You are beautiful. I've waited a long time for this meeting."

I lowered my swords and walked forward, tears pricking the corners of my eyes. "You look a lot younger than I imagined you would." I laughed, because it was the only thing I could think to say. "Oh, hell!" I rushed toward her, leaping over the debris and sheathing my swords so I could give my biological mother a hug for the very first time.

She gripped me back fiercely.

Her hands ran over my hair and back as we embraced, like she was trying to take all of me in at once. Her words were filled with the same emotion I felt. "My precious daughter. I have missed you so. You resemble my mother. That makes me happy. I always wondered who you would take after." She patted my back. "You are more than words. You are everything." She brought me out of the cocoon of her arms, kissing my forehead, scouring me with her gaze again like she'd never get tired of looking at me.

"I...I think you're everything...too..." I stumbled over my words as I wiped an errant tear from my cheek. She was a sight. She radiated a quiet, regal power. Callan was right: She could've been a queen. Now I knew what drew Odin to her. She was irresistible. "I'm happy to know that I look like my grandmother. Is she still alive?" My voice was hopeful.

My mother laughed. It was a wonderful sound. "She is. She will be filled with joy when she meets her only granddaughter."

"I'm very sorry to interrupt," Willa said, her voice barely above a whisper. "But the elves will take note of the broken ward and the explosion. We must leave this area right away."

My mother let go of me, and I stepped aside reluctantly, swiping at more tears that had the audacity to tumble down my face.

"Willa," she said to the mixed elf with authority, "you did exceptionally well. Thank you for delivering my daughter to me. I will be forever in your debt. And, yes, we must move.

The Valkyries are here, and they are engaged in battle in the mines. We must join them, defeat Invaldi, and leave this place for good. I have been waiting for this day to come for too many years to count." She radiated happiness.

"The weapons you will need are hidden," Willa said. "I will lead you to them."

My mother made a move to follow, pulling up short. "Fenrir the Wolf?" Her voice held an edge as she saw Fen for the first time. I sensed her uptick in tension. "What are you doing here? Odin cast you to Muspelheim the last I'd heard."

"I aid your daughter in her quest to find you. She is the one who released me from Muspelheim." Fen's gaze was stoic, but not threatening.

My mother glanced at me and then back at Fen.

Before she could make her mind up on the matter, I interjected, "There's a great deal I need to tell you, but that will have to come later. When I was tossed into Muspelheim, Fen was there. He saved my life three times. I owe him, and he's loyal to our cause. He was banished unjustly, and he is not a threat. He's an ally." I moved to stand next to Fen, reaching out to wrap an arm around his waist.

Leela didn't look terribly thrilled, but after a moment, she nodded. "So be it. If you saved my daughter's life, then I owe you mine."

"Come, follow me," Willa urged. "One of the weapons is not far from here, and I hear others approaching."

As we hustled after her, I asked my mother, "How do you know the Valkyries are fighting?" I was relieved and excited to learn that the shieldmaidens had arrived.

"I have many informants here," Leela answered. "But I also have a physical link to my sister, Ingrid. I felt her presence in this realm immediately. I know they are engaged in battle, because once they arrived, all able bodies were summoned to defend against the threat."

"Where are they?" I asked as we followed Willa around another corner. The tunnels were getting impossibly smaller again. Fen had taken up the rear.

"Within the mountain is a vast cavern," Leela said. "It's where the elves mine their rare gems. It will provide the most space to fight. The Valkyries will face off and fight the battle head on. That is our way."

"The elves don't seem skilled at wielding a weapon as far as I can see," I said. "I've been here for a while now, and none of them have engaged me physically."

They definitely couldn't defeat the Valkyries in hand-to-hand combat.

"You mustn't underestimate them," my mother warned. "They will be using magic, along with their war weapons, which are infused with and powered by the darkest magic they have. I have heard recent rumors that Invaldi has a new toy. He will have it with him, and it will be deadly. The elves know their arsenal is mighty, which is why others don't come into this land without permission. They risk the ire of Invaldi and end up paying the ultimate price."

Willa stopped, crouching low. She moved a large stone away from the wall and reached in to grab something. Out came a long broadsword. She smiled as she used both hands to heft it, giving it to my mother.

"Is that your chosen Valkyrie weapon?" I asked curiously. It was bigger than the one Fen currently held in his hand. It was impressive.

My mother shook her head. "No, my weapon is a bow and arrow and is in safekeeping with Ingrid. But this broadsword will do for now." She practiced some maneuvers, whipping it around like it weighed nothing.

What sounded like a loud explosion hit close-by.

We ducked as stones tumbled from the walls and ceiling. "Are more people entering this realm?" I asked, covering my head to block falling debris.

"No," Leela answered, smiling. "The Valkyries are using their energy to blow the place up. In the end, the elves and their weapons will be no match for us. Let's go join them."

Willa said, "There is an easy way to get to the caverns from here, but it's a steep way down—a crude slide hollowed out from the rock. It's used to shuttle things down to the caverns. But some elves use it as transportation when they are in a hurry. Access to it is down two flights from here."

"If we don't use the slide," Fen asked, "how long would it take us to get down to the caverns?"

"The caverns are located twenty stories below," Willa answered. "Unfortunately, the passageways we are currently in don't reach that far. If we do not use the slide, we will have to use a main artery and would encounter resistance."

"Then there's no other choice. We will take the chute," my mother said definitively. "We must aid them as soon as possible. We risk much if we do not defeat Invaldi. Our lives would be forfeit, for one, and I cannot let that happen."

"Agreed," I said.

As we walked, Fen rested his open palm on my back, rubbing slowly. I leaned into him, loving the feel of his energy and warmth, thankful that he was showing affection. He said low into my ear, "You have learned much during your time here. Your glow is even brighter."

"I have," I said simply, refraining from looping my arms around his neck. "Thank you for not being too angry."

"Of course," he replied, like it was a no-brainer to not be mad that I'd left him.

Willa wound us down two more flights quickly, her

brown hair swaying behind her. We encountered no one, but heard voices. It was a miracle no one found us. "The opening to the slide is right around this corner." She made the turn and stifled a scream. I was right behind her and had to stop myself from crashing into her.

I peered over her shoulder.

"Callan!" I exclaimed. "What in the world are you doing here?" I was very happy to see the whage alive and well, and I moved to embrace him.

He chuckled, hugging me back with his withered arms. "I am likely looking for the same way down you are."

"I should've known you'd have no problem getting out of your cell." I grinned. "How did you know about this place?"

"Years ago, I ended up here," he said. "I was able to find the quick way to the caverns below. But I was captured before I could get any farther. They surrounded me with muting magic. It was awful. But now the Valkyries are engaged down there, and it's time to fight once again!" He peered over my shoulder and straightened, bowing his head slightly.

I cleared my throat and stepped back. "That's my mother, Leela. And this is Fenrir, the fabled wolf. Only, he isn't so fabled, as you can see. He's alive and well."

Callan, head still lowered, reached out his hand. "It is a pleasure to make your acquaintance, Leela. You are a very noble Valkyrie, and I have heard much about you."

"It is wonderful to meet you as well," she said, accepting his hand. "You are a legend around here. A white elf mixed with a mage. You have led the elves on a merry goose chase, and that takes talent."

"Callan helped me a number of times," I told my mother as I squinted at the whage. Was his beard a little shorter and darker? Or was I seeing things? "I am grateful for his help and owe him."

"You have my thanks for helping my daughter," Leela told him. "We will all leave this place together. Have you any weapons?"

Callan grinned. "I have no need of such things when I have these." He wiggled his fingers. "It has been many years since I felt a kindle of magic in these old veins. I have your daughter to thank for my newfound energy. I will happily fight alongside you for freedom. I have been waiting and, not so patiently, for my day of retribution." His gaze went past mine and landed on Fen's. "I've heard your legend spoken since the day of my birth. I did not ever think to encounter you in the flesh. You are a mighty warrior." He inclined his head. "I have always believed you to have been treated unfairly. A man of your strength and power should be revered, not treated like an animal." He reached out his hand.

For a moment, I wasn't sure Fen would take it.

But to my relief, he finally grabbed hold. "You will have to forgive me," Fen replied. "I am not used to kindness. It has been many years since I've interacted in a civilized manner. I thank you for your words."

Willa coughed politely into her palm. "If you are all ready, I will open the chute. It is time for us to depart."

"I will go first," Fen announced.

"And I will go next," Callan said. "I will take the wolf's back and your front." He nodded at me.

Before I could react, my mother said, "Agreed. Then Phoebe, then myself. Willa, I want you to stay here and keep your ear out. When you hear the battle lessening, you may come down. If you go with us now, you will be harmed."

Willa was devastated at the news.

I intervened on her behalf. "If she's found here, they will kill her," I told my mother. "She is safer with us. I vowed to take her back to the Valkyrie stronghold. I hope that plan has your blessing. She has served you well and has aided us with no regard to herself." I didn't mention that my father had left her here to die if things went wrong. "It's the least we can do."

My mother met my gaze. "Years ago, I would not have readily agreed with your logic, daughter. We do things differently in Asgard. But I agree and support your decision to bring her to the stronghold. I'm not of the same mind that she would be safer with us than here, so let it be up to her. What say you, Willa?" She turned to the mixed elf.

"I would very much like to accompany you," she answered softly. "Your daughter speaks the truth. I will not be tried in court now, as I am now tagged a traitor, and I will be killed on sight. I will take my chances by going with you."

My mother nodded once. "So be it. You will go down with Phoebe. I will bring up the rear." Once she said those words, a moment of panic hit me. What if something happened to her and some elves snatched her before she could get down? I'd only just gotten to meet her. Something in my face must have shown. "Have no fear, daughter. I will be right behind you. Once this battle is over, we leave together. Nothing will stop us."

"I apologize," I said. "I don't doubt your abilities. I'm just grateful to have found you and don't want to lose you before we have a chance to begin."

My mother smiled, moving forward to cup my face in her palm, her thumb brushing against my cheek. "I love your innocence, Phoebe. It's something only very young children have in Asgard. I come from a world of harsh realities where sons and daughters lose their wistfulness by the age of two. I was robbed of being a part of your life when you were a child, and I'm happy you still carry that tenderness with you now. In time, you will harden, as is our way. But I will always be grateful to have seen this side of you."

I blushed, feeling human and awkward.

I was ecstatic my mother loved that side of me, but in these realms it would hinder me. I looked forward to shedding my soft shell, even though I would mourn who I'd once been.

Willa turned and opened a small compartment in the wall.

Fen moved, sword in hand. My heart beat faster because we were heading into danger. Right before he entered the chute, he turned to me, placing a light kiss on my lips. "I'll see you down there, shieldmaiden. It would be nice if you didn't disappear on the way down." As he broke the short kiss, I reached up, running my hands through his hair, pulling him closer for an even longer kiss.

Oh, how I'd missed this man!

I grinned, murmuring into his lips, "I won't leave, and you have to promise not to get yourself into trouble until I get down there to back you up. Remember what happened with the fire demons?"

He lifted one of his massive legs into the slide. "You shouldn't remind me of your follies just before battle." His tone was light. "It's distracting. And make sure that when you arrive, you stay out of trouble. Keeping you safe is hard work." The small space was barely enough to hold him. He would have to lie flat.

"I'd like to think the benefits of being with me far outweigh the negatives," I quipped.

"Lucky for you, they do." As he disappeared down the chute, weariness crept over me.

This battle wasn't going to be easily won.

21

"Willa, hang on to me." It was our turn. Callan had just disappeared, giving us a cocky wave and a wink. "I'm not sure what we're going to find down there." I had Gundren out and was ready to go. The chute was tall enough for us to sit upright.

Willa climbed in behind me and did as I asked.

"I will be right behind you," Leela told us. "I'm certain this victory will be ours." Her voice held an excitement that didn't match my own mood. Maybe when I was a seasoned Valkyrie, I'd feel some bloodlust before a battle. Right now, zero lust was happening. Well, there was lust, but it was aimed at a big, strong wolf, not at a bloodied sword. "This war has come at exactly the right time."

"Why do you say that?" I asked.

She smiled at me. "Because you have reached your immortality, and I believe it was meant to happen like this. Go now."

I pushed off, and we began to slide. It was slow at first, but it picked up quickly. "You didn't tell me it was as steep as a cliff!" I didn't hear Willa's response, because the air was whooshing by my ears too quickly. It must have been close to a ninety-degree drop. It went on and on for a long time—too long—and just when I thought it would never end, the chute took a sharp right turn, our bodies slamming into the wall. I never thought to ask how we'd land, and now I prayed it was onto something soft and fluffy.

In the next turn I had my answer as we shot out onto some sort of conveyor belt. Nothing soft about it. We landed hard, bouncing along like a kid's toy flung from a slingshot. It took everything I had not to tumble off.

Thankfully, Willa was still gripping me with all she had. The mixed elf had some moxie.

As we slowed, I had to make a decision. Either continue riding the belt through the hole, or get off and investigate. I chose the latter. It was better to figure out where we were first than dive headfirst into the fray. Plus, I wanted to wait for my mother to arrive. "Hang on!" I called to Willa. "We're getting off here." I stabbed my swords into the belt to halt our forward motion as I pivoted.

The drop was farther than I'd anticipated. Luckily, I landed with Willa still on my back, with my knees bent. Willa sprang off, and I stood, catching my breath. "Holy cow, how did the elves get up there to retrieve their things? It must be twenty feet high."

"They do not use this room much. They wait for the items to land in the cavern through that opening." She gestured toward the wall.

Before I could question my decision to get off when we did, we heard voices.

"No more will reach us through here!" an elf voice declared.

"Shall we blow it up?" another elf asked.

I grabbed Willa's arm and tugged her behind a large boulder before two elves entered through a small hole in the rock on the other side of the room.

"I don't know. Invaldi only said to shut it down," the first elf replied. "Do you suppose that means we should blow it up?"

"I see no other option. We could get a troll in here and stuff it with boulders, but that would take too much time. We are in the middle of a crisis and must act fast!"

"Those Valkyries will not win! No matter who comes to their aid." That meant Fen and Callan had indeed made it into the fray. "Invaldi is just playing with them now. Wait until he unleashes the surprise!" Sounds of battle echoed in from the cavern.

My mother was on her way down. I was going to have to stop them. These elves weren't going to blow up anything. I took a step forward to reveal myself, but a small hand stilled me, tugging fervently on my wrist.

I bent down as Willa leaned in, her voice not above a whisper. "It will take them some time to carry out their agenda. Let's see what they do. If your mother comes down and interrupts them, our time would be better spent fighting them before they can alert others to our presence."

I nodded. "You're right," I whispered. "But if they start something, we have to stop them. I'm not risking an explosion. Leela should be down any second." We both glanced toward the entrance of the chute, waiting expectantly.

No Leela.

Where was she?

My pulse started to beat quicker. She should've been right behind us. The elves were busy gathering stuff and heading toward the bottom of the slide. I took a step. I couldn't just sit here. My swords were up and I was just about to reveal myself when a new noise hit the room. One beat later, something crashed onto the conveyor belt, surprising the two elves.

One of them dropped the load it had in its arms, and one of them tumbled off the rocks, screaming wildly as it fell.

My mother recovered quickly and stood, feet splayed, her borrowed broadsword up and at the ready. She was glorious and clearly feared nothing.

"Come on," I told Willa. "We have to help her." We both scrambled out from behind the rock.

At the same time that I cleared my throat to call to my mother, the elf left standing shrieked, "Our prisoner is free! We must alert the others!" It turned to run.

Leela's position shifted smoothly as she faced the threat. "Stop!" She aimed her broadsword at the elf.

It slowly turned around and shook its head. "No need to get overly excited," it squeaked at her. It was not wearing a guard uniform. It had to be a worker.

"You will not stop us," my mother said as a thin bead of energy raced out of the tip of her blade, tossing the elf back into the wall. It had been an extremely precise strike and not overly strong. Just enough to stun him. I waited a second to see if the elf would rise, but he didn't.

"There's another elf below you!" I called as Willa and I climbed up the rocky wall to the conveyor belt.

Without comment, my mother addressed the threat. The elf had been trying to sneak up on her, something in its hand. My mother dispensed another shot of energy, and the elf dropped to the ground. Once she was done, she leaped onto a large boulder. "I'm glad you waited for me," she said. "This way, we can do a little recon before we show ourselves. It always pays to plan."

"The elves know that Fen and Callan used the chute to get here," I told her. "They were planning on blowing it up."

"It matters not," she replied. "The majority of them will be too distracted to come and do anything about it. They sent in workers, not fighters."

A loud roar came from the cavern.

Fen was in his wolf form.

He had to be monitoring the conveyor belt exit and wondering where I was. If I didn't arrive soon, he would come after me. That would leave the Valkyries without a fighter.

"Willa," my mother asked, "are there other ways to access the cavern other than this main artery?" She pointed to the hole.

"I'm not very familiar with this area, but the elves came in that way." She gestured across the room. The tunnel they'd used wasn't visible. It was likely hidden behind some rocks.

"Then that's the way we go," my mother said, taking off. She tossed over her shoulder, "It's an advantage to come from behind. I am certain the elves have created an enchanted barrier that is protecting them while they throw their magic at the Valkyries. If we can break through that, we can give our sisters an edge."

My mother had effortlessly taken up her mantle as Valkyrie warrior.

It was an amazing thing to witness. It was like she hadn't missed a day in all these years, and there was no doubt she was a decorated member of the battle group. She effused power, and her voice held command. Her sisters would be overjoyed to be reunited with her.

We reached the other side in no time. Behind a boulder was a small passageway. We lowered our heads and raced through, winding around a few curves until another opening came into view. My mother put her arms out to slow us as she knelt at the base. I joined her, motioning Willa to stay back.

The scene before us was chaotic.

We were positioned above and behind the elves. The cavern was massive, much more so than I'd imagined. My mother had been right. The elves fought with magic that sailed right through some kind of barrier. It made it impossible for the Valkyries to engage in any hand-to-hand combat. The shieldmaidens stood on the other side trying to defend themselves, rather than being on the offense.

I counted eight shieldmaidens, along with Fen, Callan, Baldur, and Junnal. I was glad to see the Jotun was alive and well and that Baldur had escaped once again and had joined the battle.

Fen was in his wolf form, standing at the forefront. His fur was dark and sleek, his teeth sharp, his growls ferocious.

"What's creating the invisible wall?" I asked. "If the Valkyries could fight, we'd be done here." Even though there were hundreds of elves, they were small and no match for the team that had assembled, each Valkyrie fighting with a powerful weapon.

My mother gestured down into the melee. "Do you see that shiny gold box?" It was positioned exactly in the middle of the elves, almost like they surrounded a sound system at a concert.

"That thing that looks like a huge overstuffed chair?"

"Yes. It's called an enhancer, and it amplifies all the magic from the elves' weapons, as well as creating a line the Valkyries can't cross. The elves craft very powerful weapons with dark magic, and the enhancer makes them even more deadly. Right now, by the looks of it, I believe they are toying with the shieldmaidens and nothing more. There is no doubt Invaldi has a plan up his sleeve."

This was toying? Several elves shot magic out of guns, and we watched as the Valkyries were forced to take cover.

"Will that magic kill?" I asked.

"It could," my mother replied. "So they can't take the chance. That's why no one storms this realm. There are many things of value, including priceless gemstones by the ton, but no one wants to risk dying by elf magic."

"Why would Invaldi toy with the Valkyries? Why not just blow us all up and be done with it?"

"Invaldi has the right, since he didn't grant permission for them to enter, but he knows all too well that if he kills these Valkyries, he will have to face Odin. The god will be very angry, possibly to the point of ending the elf leader's life. Invaldi waits for them to make their move, because if they act aggressively, and he can prove it, his punishment will be less severe."

I surveyed the scene in front of me. "If we take out the enhancer, what happens?"

My mother met my gaze.

It was strange looking at someone who resembled me. I'd never experienced that before. "I do not know for sure," she answered. "I imagine their weapons will be much diminished. And you're right, the elves don't relish combat. If they are overcome, they will flee." I'd seen that firsthand. They talked a big talk, but hid behind their magic. "Since our goal is only to escape, and not loot, it might be best to take it out and cause enough pandemonium that we can slip out."

"How much energy would it take to blow it up?" I asked. "Can you achieve it from here?"

My mother shook her head. "No. Valkyries don't carry

that much power within. We utilize what we have in short bursts in the best ways possible, perfect for combat. From here, the enhancer looks small, but it's the size of two caskets end to end."

I thought about the toilet I'd destroyed in my cell and wondered if I could generate enough power with Gram alone. I glanced around the cavern. I always felt strongest after I fed from Yggdrasil, and I sensed it near. "Is the tree of life in this cavern?" I asked.

"I'm not sure, but I feel its presence," she said. "It calls to me. It's been a long while since the elves let me feed from it. My body aches for pure sustenance."

I turned to address Willa. "Does Yggdrasil reside here?"

"Not now," she confirmed. "But many, many years ago, an arm of the tree ran through the cavern, or so I've been told. There's nothing left but a dead cillar."

A cillar!

I got excited. I'd traveled through a few thought-to-be-dead cillars. I had no idea why they'd opened up for me before, but they had. One took me to Muspelheim, and the other dumped Fen and me in New York City. "Where is it?" I eagerly searched the room, but saw nothing that looked like the archway in Muspelheim.

My mother gave me an interesting look as she moved to make way for Willa. "It seems they have amassed a large army already," Willa commented as she looked out into the cavern. "But this is their full fighting guard. If you defeat them, there is no more army." Her gaze wandered around the room below us. "I've only been inside this cavern a few times, but I think the cillar is there." She gestured below us and to the right. "Do you see the smooth surface against the wall there?"

"I do." Even though it was hard to see from this angle, it

looked similar to the others I had seen, but with no archway. Fen began to pace below us, his head angling to where the conveyor belt ejected, no doubt wondering where I was. We had to act fast. "Can you cover me?" I asked my mother. "If I can get down there, and the cillar opens for me, I believe I can channel power directly from the tree into my weapon. I don't have much experience, but if it worked with Gram, it should work with Gundren. It might be enough to take out the enhancer."

My mother was quiet before she said, "That's not typical behavior for a Valkyrie, though I have seen those who have successfully tapped into Yggdrasil and used the energy as you describe. It's hard to do, and you would need a lot of it."

"Based on my abilities thus far, I think I can do it. Cillars have opened for me in the past, and I recently used Gram to channel energy, and it gave me enough to blow up a toilet." She gave me a look. "I know, long story. But the important thing is it worked, and I don't think we have any other options. As it stands, the Valkyries can't defeat the elves, and they will eventually be picked off, injured, or worse. I have to try."

My mother appraised me. "I feel your strength. I know you have much in you. I'm not surprised, with Odin being your father. You are both a demigod and a Valkyrie, a very powerful being indeed. I will cover you and match your output with my own. If we discharge at the same time, we might be able to do enough damage to the enhancer."

A demigod!

Nobody had ever suggested that, even though it was right in front of our noses. My brother Tyr was a god, both his parents being gods. Fen was a demigod, his father being the god Loki, his mother a giantess.

If one parent was a god, you were, by birthright, a demigod.

But instead of acting surprised at the news, I kept my cool and replied, "Let's do it."

22

The plan was for Leela to cause a distraction while I headed down to the closed portal, hoping it would open once I got there. Gundren was out and ready. That was my ticket in. If the cillar didn't open, plan B was to make it to the other side and help the shieldmaidens fight.

"Ready?" my mother asked. "We risk a lot, but for great gain. In our world, that's a payoff worth taking. If the elves attack, I will be down to fight with you." She smiled. "We will be victorious. I can feel it."

I tried not to think of what it would be like if we weren't victorious. My brain didn't want to go there. But it made me happy that my mother believed in me and my abilities.

That was enough for now.

"On your mark." I crouched down. I had my eye on the prize. Fen would spot me immediately, as would most of the others. "Willa, stay here. If I get the portal open and the elves stay back, then I want you to run to me. If not, we regroup and I will find you. I promise."

She nodded, wringing her petite hands. "I understand. I

have no weapons and cannot fight. I will wait here and hope for a good outcome."

I grinned. "We will change your lack of a weapon once we get home. I think I know of one that would fit nicely in your hands."

Her face brightened for the first time. "You would teach me to fight?"

"Of course," I said. "That's what shieldmaidens do."

My mother aimed her broadsword out of the cave entrance. "Here we go." A burst of light shot out and carried to the opposite side of the cavern, well away from the cillar, causing a small explosion and commotion.

The moment the light left her sword, I was moving.

I sprang from rock to rock, going as fast as I could. I wasn't even halfway there when shouts of alarm echoed into the air. It seemed the entire place had spotted me at once.

Invaldi's voice boomed loudest. "Capture the Valkyrie! Turn your weapons on her."

Fen's roar followed as several explosions raced past me. I was almost to the cillar. This was going to work, because it had to. I sent out a silent plea as I ran. *Open for me.*

Rae's voice rang out, loud and authoritative. "Cover Phoebe, no exceptions. Go!"

I knew exactly when the Valkyries spotted my mother, because there were shrieks and war whoops.

Ingrid shouted, her voice filled with joy, "Sister! Praise Odin you're okay!"

Leela called, "Get to my daughter. Then we fight!"

More magic bursts flew by me, but the cillar was within reach. A few feet from the wall, I slashed out with my left hand, inserting Gundren deeply into the stone.

A glow kindled immediately, and I almost cried out. This

was going to work! With one hand steady on the hilt, channeling all the energy I could, I twisted around and aimed my right hand into the massive crowd of elves.

"Take cover!" I heard on elf cry.

"She is using her energy! Run!"

"She cannot defeat us! Stand and fight, you ninnies!"

There was a large crack as multiple bolts of lightning shot out of my sword, followed by a gigantic boom. The force was intense, and I had to grit my teeth to hang on. Those blasts had gone wide, but the next would be on the money. I squinted, focusing on the enhancer.

With one nod up to my mother, I let the energy loose, this time concentrating my aim. Thick ribbons of energy rocketed out of Gundren. The blast hit dead center, at the heart of the enhancer, sending elves scattering like dried leaves on a windy day.

Fen was almost to me, still in his wolf form, Junnal right behind him, using his club to whale on any elves that dared get too close. The Valkyries followed, Baldur and Callan bringing up the rear.

Then my mother was next to me, grabbing on to my wrist. "You must let go, Phoebe," she urged. "Too much will harm you." She managed to dislodge my grip, and I fell to my knees, struggling to get air into my windpipe.

The energy had consumed me, my fingertips sparking, my body ablaze.

"It worked," I wheezed. "The enhancer is toast." I gazed down at the damage and was surprised to see the elves gathering again. I was confused. "Why haven't they left?"

We were exposed up on a precipice, and if they picked up their weapons, they would be able to pick us off.

Three feet from me, Fen shifted into his human form fluidly midstep. It was beautiful to watch, even through my haze. He knelt next to me. "That was quite a showing, Valkyrie. Are you all right?"

His hand was warm on my shoulder. I glanced up. "It's better than all right. I figured out how to harness my energy. Did you see that? I had some amp from the cillar, but it totally worked."

He chuckled. "I did notice that. It was very impressive. But now we must leave. The elves have the advantage."

Ingrid came racing toward us, picking up her sister, and swinging her around in a bear hug. "I knew this day would come! It has been too long, sister dear. I didn't expect to find you looking so well." She set my mother down. "The years have been kind to you!"

"Ingrid!" my mother answered, hugging her back. "It's good to be reunited. A little birdie told me that you have been keeping watch over Phoebe all these years. I am forever in your debt." My mother kissed her sister's cheek.

Witnessing their reunion was miraculous.

Rae stopped in front of me, the other Valkyries fanning out below her, their attention focused on the elves. "That was a good tactic, well done. But we're not finished yet. The elves are regrouping, and they will start an assault soon. We must find a new place to finish this battle."

I glanced at my sword, which was still stuck in the cillar. "Can we leave this way?" I nodded at the rock wall. "It's open now."

Rae gazed at the portal. "I don't know. This is unprecedented." She moved by me and reached a hand out, pressing her palm against the stone. She flinched back immediately, curling her fingers into a fist.

"Is it still open?" I asked. Even though I had ridden in them, I didn't know much about cillars.

"It is, but it's not reliable. The energy is static, not fluid. I have no idea where it would drop us. Some places could be much worse than this. We use it as a last resort."

Ingrid came forward to embrace me, patting me on the back. "Nicely done, Phoebe. You gave us a good scare when you left. I'm not sure I'm going to give that raven the time of day next time I see him, but Huggie had your and Leela's best interests at heart in the end. Sneaky bird."

Rae moved past me and gave my mother a quick hug, their arms interlocking and their shoulders touching. "It is good to see you, Leela. You look well."

"Ragnhild, you were just a rising star in the ranks when I last saw you," my mother said, admiration in her voice. "Are those the markings of a battle leader?" She was talking about a decorative medal pinned on Rae's tunic. "Congratulations. Well deserved, I'm certain."

Fen said, "The elves are bringing in fortifications. We must make a decision."

Baldur was the last to reach us. Callan had stopped on a rock below, and Junnal stood in front of him, blocking the elves from seeing his location. The whage had his head bowed, and I couldn't tell what he was doing.

My half brother brushed by everyone, taking me up in his arms. "You appeared on this boulder like a festival light atop a twinkling tree!" he boomed. "I'm happy to see you again, sister." He set me down and turned to my mother, reaching out his hand. "Leela the Lovely, it is wonderful to make your acquaintance again. While I was at court, I watched my father dote on you. He held great love for you."

Leela nodded, taking Baldur's hand while reaching out to kiss both his cheeks. "It is good to see you again, God of Light. You have been down here a long while, but our paths have not crossed until today, which is a pity. I respect my daughter's decision to free you, as it is your prerogative whether you choose to live out your destiny or not. But if anything happens, it will be on her to face Frigg. She has no idea what that means, so you must protect yourself and her at all costs."

"That is my intent," Baldur replied good-naturedly. "Once I reach Asgard, I will draw up the paperwork proclaiming her innocence and plan to take a trip to Vanir to confront my mother myself. We will have it out, and it will be epic. But I'm confident I will be the victor this time. All will be well." The god was all smiles, his countenance as sunny as ever. It was impossible for him not to be positive. I didn't understand what they were saying about Frigg, or why it was necessary to file paperwork, but I was glad for it. I just wanted my brother to stay safe. In the short amount of time we'd been together, we had developed a strong bond.

Billie called up to Rae. "The elves have wheeled out something new. It's much larger than the last one. It's time for us to either fight or disperse. What are our orders?"

The Valkyries had already fanned out, weapons up.

They looked formidable, but we were in danger. Ingrid and my mother joined Rae by my side. "How did you enter this land?" my mother asked Ingrid. "It had to be by force, as the ground shook like a massive earthquake, like none I've witnessed in all my years here."

Ingrid answered, "When your daughter disappeared through the closed cillar at the stronghold, we questioned the raven. After much discussion, he told us there was only one way to enter this realm without permission. But to do so, we had to journey to another portal. We left that same night. We traveled two hundred miles to find an old oak tree near the Rocky Mountains. The elves use oaks for travel, as you well know. We waited patiently for it to quiver, and when it opened, we went through. It let us in near this cavern, but our arrival took time and was noisy, which alerted the elves we were here. But there was no other way."

Rae asked, "Is anyone familiar with the layout of this mountain? Are there any places that would give us a greater advantage than this cavern?"

"I have a mixed elf in my service, sent by Odin himself," my mother answered. "She is up in that tunnel." She gestured to where Willa was waiting. "But there are so many of us, I don't believe we have enough time to reach the main artery, which would lead us outside, without coming under fire from the elves. We are in the very bowels of the mountain, and the passageways are narrow and small. It would be an easy ambush."

"I say we use the cillar that Phoebe just opened," Ingrid said, pointing a thumb to the wall. "I don't care where it drops us. The odds are it will be better than here."

"We can only ride two at a time, if that," Rae said. "There is a very high likelihood we will get separated and sent to different places. A cillar is unpredictable at best. As the battle commander, I cannot allow it. It would lessen our strength and place us all in jeopardy."

I didn't want to be separated from my mother after just finding her, but I knew if we had to go, I would go through with Fen. To accentuate that point, Fen settled his arm around my waist. "If we stay here, we are easy pickings," Fen said. "The elves have taken over the entire cavern below and are busy assembling their next weapon. There is nothing to do but fight. We should engage now or leave."

We all glanced down.

The elves looked positively gleeful. The new thing they'd rolled out was bigger than the enhancer and shiny silver.

"Do you think you can blow this one up, Phoebe?" Ingrid asked. "I've never seen a Valkyrie harness that much power, and you're still glowing." She shook her head, clucking. "And here I thought it would take time for you to learn to master your energy, but you're a pro right out of the gates."

"I don't think *pro* is the right word," I said. "I kind of cheated and used Gundren."

Ingrid shrugged. "Hey, whatever works. If I'd had a weapon like that when I was a young Valkyrie, I would've used it, no problem. I would've been blowing stuff up left and right. We will work on your mad skills of harnessing it without Gundren when we get back."

I was going to answer her about blowing up the elves' new weapon, when I noticed Callan out of the corner of my eye.

He'd moved to the edge of the precipice and stood with his arms raised. I nodded toward the whage. "What is he doing?"

"No idea," Ingrid said. "He just kind of showed up. We figured he was with you. He's a white elf prisoner? Looks like he's been here a long time."

"He is actually a very powerful mage," Leela answered. "He came to avenge his king many years ago, but found himself trapped here."

"We found him on the cursed level," I said. "Or what the elves consider to be uninhabitable. When he freed his king, he spread white magic throughout that level. He's been there a long time. Too long. He needs energy and sunlight to survive. He would've died had we not come upon him."

Rae said, "He appears to be trying to channel something."

"I say we let him do his thing," Ingrid said. "If that doesn't work, we take this here cillar out of this crap hole, or Phoebe blows up the silver box with a huge kaboom."

Before I could comment, Callan's voice boomed out. "Drop your weapons!"

23

To the absolute shock of everyone in the cavern, including Invaldi, the elves complied. Their combined weapons sounded like a hundred trays of silverware clattering to the ground at the same time.

The only one more dismayed than we were was Invaldi himself.

The elf leader must have been the only one immune to Callan's magic, and he was beyond furious. His voice boomed, verging on a terrifying scream, echoing against the cavern walls. "You will pay for that, whage!" He shook his fists as he turned to his elves. "Pick up your weapons and fight! That is a direct order." They appeared confused by his anger, glancing down at their discarded guns with blank stares. "What are you waiting for? Pick them up!"

This could be our way out.

I had an idea.

Still glowing with lots of spare of energy, I made my way down to Callan. As I came up next to him, he startled, surprised to see me, his eyes dazed. He looked beyond tired, on the verge of collapse. Performing a mind-meld on the elves had taken everything he had.

I grasped his hand and asked, "Are you ready to do this?"

He gave me a small smile. "Of course. I told you we would prevail."

"Because of you." As we held hands, energy began to flow from me to him. He nodded once and lifted his other arm into the air, clearing his voice before he commanded, "Leave this place!" Callan's voice, even though he was physically drained, was level and certain. "Go back to your homes!" Energy rushed over me, prodding me, causing the hair on my arms to extend. He was clearly a very powerful mage, and I was relieved his magic was not directed at me.

The elves appeared confused by his directive, knocking into each other as they turned in circles.

Invaldi quaked with anger.

But instead of ordering his elves to fight again, he stormed over to the silver box and picked up a large object. It resembled a machine gun—if machine guns were made of a shiny white material and had a barrel opening the size of a grapefruit. The weapon was attached to the silver contraption by a hose. "I will finish you myself. No one comes into my realm without paying the price!" He cocked the thing and pulled the big hook of a trigger.

A large shock of green light raced out, barreling straight at us.

"Disperse!" Rae shouted from behind me. "The magic is concentrated!"

I let go of Callan's hand, pushing him roughly to the ground. The first blast hit five feet to my left. The explosion was intense, and I was thrown backward, landing hard.

Scrambling up, I ran toward the cillar. I needed both swords.

"Phoebe!" Ingrid shouted. "What are you doing? Take cover. Right now!"

I glanced over my shoulder. My mother waited for me ten steps away, her hand extended. "Come, Phoebe," she urged. "We must take shelter. The magic is too strong."

I reached for the sword hilt I'd left in the cillar, energy racing into my arm at breakneck speed. I yanked it out. It came with no resistance. "Take cover!" I shouted. "Gundren can deflect magic." That's what everyone had told me, and I could feel the power deep inside the weapons. "I have to trust in them."

I caught Rae's eye as I passed her. She nodded once and grabbed on to my mother's arm, dragging her to a safer place. The battle captain had given me the go-ahead to try.

Once I reached a good position to take on the dark elf, leaving him no other option than to shoot straight at me, a growl erupted from behind my left shoulder. Fen had changed into his wolf to back me up. It would be futile to tell him no. I just had to make sure he didn't get hit.

Invaldi was livid that he'd missed his mark and was readying for another blast. Lucky for us, the machine seemed to need to charge up after creating a blast that big. The cavern was almost empty of his elves.

My legs were splayed, my swords up.

I was ready.

This was what I'd been training for.

Each shieldmaiden excelled in one area. Some could shoot an arrow true, some had great strength, and some were incredibly fast.

This was my skill. I could combat magic.

Fear left me, and the world steadied.

Invaldi launched another blast, aiming right at me, his lips curling in glee. I could feel his anger, his malice, his negative energy radiating out into the room. He wanted me gone almost as badly as the Norns did.

As the dark magic came hurling at me, I crossed my swords in front of my body, bowing my head. Gathering my energy, I called it forward, infusing it into Gundren.

The clash was intense.

Dark magic hit my weapons with incredible force, spreading like fire into my arms and throughout my entire body. I knew if I let go of the swords, I wouldn't have a chance.

The power of the dark magic threatened to disarm me, but I held firm.

After what felt like an eternity, but was probably only seconds, my swords began to shake, my fists trembling as I struggled to hold on. I focused on the magic that had just infused me, pulling it from my body and settling it back into the swords.

Gundren began to glow green.

The same color as the dark magic.

My eyes landed squarely on Invaldi, and even from this distance, I could see a mixture of disbelief and hatred on his face.

I leveled my swords and shook my wrists, releasing the magic that had gathered inside. Large green ribbons raced toward the elf leader.

"You will not succeed! Dark magic cannot hurt me—" Invaldi was tossed backward, his body smashing solidly against the cave wall.

Green sparks of light glittered around his body for a few moments, then faded.

He didn't rise.

The magic probably wasn't going to do him any long-term damage, but the force of it hitting him was another matter.

"Phoebe, that was amazing! Excellent swordplay. Now it's time to get out of here," Ingrid said, hurrying up to me. "We skedaddle before the elfman wakes up and his minions come back."

My body felt strangely light, like I could float off this boulder, but energized at the same time. I turned, searching for my mother, surprised to see the Valkyries fanned out above me. Billie nodded, giving me a small smile. The other Valkyries looked fairly impressed, their faces showing appreciation for my newfound skill.

Except for one.

Anya had her hands on her hips, a tight look on her face. Thankfully, she chose to stay quiet.

Fen morphed back to human and planted a kiss on the top of my head. "Your prowess is stellar, Valkyrie. I knew you had it in you to do great things. But your aunt is right, we must use this advantage to get out. I suggest heading up to the main stairwell, through the great hall, and back to Yggdrasil."

I sheathed my still-green-glowing swords. "That sounds good to me, as long as Callan can make it."

"The whage is alive," Baldur commented, lifting an unconscious Callan in his arms.

I rushed over, settling my hands on the whage's chest and arms. "Callan, are you all right?"

Callan didn't reply, but Baldur did. "I think the guy's just worn out. Who knew the old man had it in him? I've never seen such a thing in all my years. Even a god would have a hard time mesmerizing an entire room. It's a wonder he was ever trapped here in the first place! They must've kept him unconscious for a long while, enough so he was lacking substantial energy when he awoke."

My eyebrows quirked. "He doesn't seem so old anymore.

Look." I met my brother's startled gaze. "His hair is shorter and decidedly darker, so is his beard. I've been noticing it for a while, but wasn't believing what I was seeing. I blasted him with a ton of energy, and I think it's made him younger. Are you okay to carry him to Yggdrasil?"

"Of course," Baldur said. "This white elf helped save our lives. I would carry him to eternity and back. Plus, he can't weigh more than a few pounds." Baldur chuckled as he moved his arms, with Callan settled in them, up and down. "Lead the way."

There was a bellow, and I glanced down to see Junnal pacing toward Invaldi, who hadn't moved, with a raised club.

A frantic shout came from Rae. "Do not harm the elf! If you do, we would all stand trial, and that is something we don't need right now. We stormed this realm uninvited. Just guard the elf and make sure he doesn't rise again."

My mother came up beside me. "Wonderful job, Phoebe. I have never seen a Valkyrie harness magic like you just did. I'm in awe. I look forward to seeing more. But we must head out. I believe there's a big tunnel behind where Invaldi lies that we can access."

I climbed down the rocks after Leela. We were almost to the floor when I remembered one thing. I turned around, calling, "Willa! It's safe to come out now. Come down here!"

No response.

Where was she? I tried again. "Willa! You can come out now."

My mother grasped my hand. In a low voice, she murmured, "I believe she was taken."

I arched back. "What do you mean taken? By who?" My stomach dropped. She had told us she would be killed on sight. "She can't be gone."

"Possibly the elves that we disarmed near the chute woke up?" Leela said. "It's hard to know. Others could've found their way to that tunnel as well."

"Well, we're going to have to find her!" I cried. "She risked a lot to help us, and I promised to take her home. I intend to keep my word."

"Phoebe, I know you care about her well-being, and I do, too," my mother said. "She has served me well for many years. But we can't risk the lives of all of those here for one. It's not our way. She is not one of us. She knew the risks."

I shook my head. "I don't accept that. She took risks because she felt she owed my father. And leaving her here is not *my* way. I made a deal to help her, and I'm not going to go back on it. In my world, we value all lives equally. In Wisconsin, my parents taught me to keep your promises and look out for those in need. Willa needs our help, and she's going to get it."

My mother appeared resigned. "We will look for her up top. She is no longer down here."

She was right. The elves who took her wouldn't have stuck around. There was a large tunnel off to the side that led to the main staircase Junnal and I had been on before.

"It doesn't surprise me that you'd be selfish," Anya huffed in an irritated tone as we walked. "I'm not going to let you put the rest of us in jeopardy for an *elf*." She spat the word *elf* like it was diseased.

I stopped, reaching over my shoulder to draw a sword. Anya took two steps back as I brought it in front of her face. I was done. "No one is asking you to stay, Anya, so please feel free to head home. Helping the elf is *optional*. I wouldn't expect you to know what the word honor means anyway. But when I make a pledge, I uphold it." Watching my rival flinch back was rewarding.

I was about to say more when a hand on my arm stopped me.

Ingrid leaned into me, muttering, "Your glow is bordering on sun outputs, kid. No need to get all riled up." She addressed the group. "Whoever wants to stay and help Phoebe is free to do so. All others can go home. We will treat this like any mission—it's your choice to participate. But we make the decision upstairs. Staying down here is pure stupidity. I'm not waiting for Invaldi to wake up."

"Ingrid's right," Rae added. "We discuss up top, where we're that much closer to home."

I sheathed my sword without a second glance at Anya and followed the group.

We passed Invaldi, where Junnal stood sentinel.

The elf leader was still out cold, but I could see his legs and arms beginning to twitch. When he awoke, he would be beyond angry. He would seek retribution at all costs. This wasn't going to be the last we'd see of him.

I gave the Jotun a quick hug.

"Stay...here," Junnal said. "Not...wake up. My watch."

I nodded. "We appreciate that. Give us an hour and we should be good. Will you be able to get home safely?"

He nodded his huge head.

"Are you going to ride the cillar?" He nodded again. What couldn't this giant troll do? "Will you return to the Valkyrie stronghold? Or are you going home?"

"Stronghold."

It was good enough for me. I nodded. "Once we have Willa, we will head back there as well." I prayed there were no other issues. "I'll see you then."

Not one second later, the ground shook beneath us.

Something else was on its way in.

Figured.

24

The ground rattled again as the barometric pressure in the cavern dropped.

"Something's on its way!" Rae shouted. "Everyone move!"

We all took off, heading to the main staircase. It was big enough for two Valkyries at a time. All eight shieldmaidens were in the lead. I ran behind my mother and Ingrid, Fen just behind me. Baldur, carrying Callan easily, barely breaking a sweat, bringing up the rear. The white elf looked to be coming around, but he was still weak.

The Valkyries had their weapons out.

I had no idea what would be waiting for us in the main hall. "Fen," I called over my shoulder. "If an elf gets close enough, let's grab it. It may be able to give us information on where they're keeping Willa." I refused to think that she could already be dead. There was too much chaos happening. They couldn't kill her without Invaldi's consent, right? My hope was they'd taken her back to the same cell area we'd been in when we first met. At least that would be easy enough to find once we got to the main hall.

"If one gets close, consider him caught," Fen answered.

We rounded yet another level. "How many stories are we talking about here?" Ingrid complained. None of us was out of breath, but we all wanted out. "Leave it to Invaldi to dig into this anthill as deeply as he could."

Baldur spoke up. "We just passed level seventeen. There are small markings on the columns on each level. They are written in elfish, if you know how to interpret it."

Ingrid snorted. "I know a little elfish, but not enough to decipher those glyphs at a quick clip. God of Light, how did you end up down here anyway?"

"It's a long, dense story filled with drama," he answered. "The bottom line is my mother loves me and was worried about my untimely death, so she made a deal with the elves to keep me safe." He chuckled. "Meaning she's paying them untold riches to keep me here, alive but devoid of a life. But that's all about to change. I'm looking forward to getting back to my ship, Ringhorn, where I can live out my days on the sea. I figure my death will be a lot less likely at sea."

"And why's that?" Ingrid asked as we rounded yet another level. "There's plenty of stuff that can still get you at sea."

"Yeah," Baldur answered, "but my mother made a deal with all of them not to harm me. In fact, she made deals with most things in the world. There are only a few things that can fell me. I've always told her she shouldn't worry so much."

We passed two more levels before another earthquake shook the mountain.

This one was near cataclysmic.

We had to stop and grab on to the walls of the stairwell for support. Something huge was coming, and it was taking its time getting here.

"The elves may have called in reinforcements," my mother said as we began our climb again. "I've been here a long time, and I've never felt such a force. It feels like the entire mountain is going to split in half."

"Let's hope we're out of here before that happens." We were moving fast. "Baldur, which level is this?" I asked as we passed a column.

Fen answered, "Fourteen."

I peered at Fen as we ran. "I didn't know you could read elfish," I said, impressed.

"Shieldmaiden, what I know could fill volumes."

We rounded four more levels. Once we hit level ten, a few elves lingered in the hallway. Before I could react, Fen passed me, backing them up against the wall. I followed.

I called to the others, "We will be right behind you."

Rae nodded, and they kept going. My mother and Baldur stopped.

Fen looked like a giant compared to the elves. One said, "You don't scare us, beast."

"You think to escape, but we have other plans!" the other squeaked.

Fen grabbed one by the neck, bringing his face close and growling. The elf visibly quaked.

I recognized this one. It was the elf Junnal and I had followed down with the leader. I'd never seen the other elf before. "You fear me enough," Fen rumbled, "and you are without magic. If you do not answer my questions, they will be the last ones you ever hear."

The thing gave a squeaky cackle. "I will not answer—"

Fen held it so tightly its response was cut off. The other elf backed against a wall. Fen leveled his gaze at it. This one wore regular clothing, unlike the other, which wore a guard uniform. "Is this elf your kin? Do you care for him?" Fen asked. The elf looked uncertain. Apparently, that was enough for Fen. "If you do not answer my questions, I will rip his head from his body. And you will have to go home and explain to your family what happened. Are we clear?"

The elf nodded once.

The other began to struggle in Fen's grip, likely trying to tell its pal or family member not to divulge any secrets. But it couldn't speak, because its trachea was a little tied up. Lanky fingers tore into Fen's hand to no avail. The demigod did not loosen his grip.

I stepped up to the worried elf, my mother behind me. "This is an easy question to answer," I said. "There was a mixed elf helping this Valkyrie, Leela, while she was your prisoner." I gestured to my mother. "This mixed elf has been taken prisoner, and we need to know where she is. As I said, this is a very simple question. Cooperate, and nothing happens to either of you." I inclined my head knowingly. "But if you don't, well"—I shot an elbow toward Fen—"the wolf is unpredictable. Your friend will likely lose his head."

The elf shot nervous glances at all of us. "Um...well..." It wrung its hands.

"It's okay, you can tell us," I coaxed. "It's just one small mixed elf. She is sentenced to death. We will harm no others. Just tell us what we want to know, and we will leave."

"They took her to the sacrifice stone!" the elf blurted. "She helped our enemy, and the payment is immediate death!"

My heart sped up. "Where is this sacrifice stone?" We had to get to her in time. I was reaching for my sword when my mother's hand stilled me.

"I have heard of this place before," she commented. "It is outside the fortress, correct?"

The elf nodded vigorously. "Yes, it lies outside. There is a clearing not far from here. The death of a traitor is never carried out inside our walls. We do not want their stain to remain."

Of course not, that would be silly.

I needed more specific directions than just "outside." I leaned in. "Once we leave the mountain, which way do we head? And be quick about it. We have to save a life."

"Down the path and to the right. It is the only clearing in the dense forest," it sputtered. "You can't miss it."

"You better be right," I said in my best threatening tone. "If we have to come back here, I will search you out. Your life will be over."

The elf smiled crudely, flashing broken teeth. "Not before you die. You think you are free, but you are wrong." The mountain rumbled. The elf gloated. "See? We have many allies, and they are on their way."

I shot a glance at Fen, who shrugged, appearing unfazed about any threats. With no preamble, he dropped the elf he was holding, and it tumbled to the ground. "They are not allied with gods or demigods, nor with giants. We can handle all the others."

"Agreed," my mother said, her voice firm. "But whatever's coming will be unpleasant and may take time. If we can find Willa and head to Yggdrasil, we have a chance not to engage."

The sounds of yelling and clashing weapons carried down the stairs.

The Valkyries had encountered a problem.

Engaging was certain. I just hoped the threat was an easy one to defeat. "Let's go," I said. "We have to get through whatever's upstairs and get outside as quickly as we can." As we raced up the stairs, my thoughts were on Willa. I hoped she wasn't in any pain, and I prayed like crazy we could find her and get back to the tree quickly.

As we sped up, the levels blurred together. Once we reached the top, we rushed down the hallway to find the Valkyries engaged in a full-on battle in the huge atrium with what looked to be some sort of cross between dark elves and dwarves.

The newcomers were armed with sickles and axes. They were heavily bearded, and their hands and legs looked human, albeit stubby. But their eyes and ears looked like dark elves', overly large and pointy. They were holding their own with the Valkyries.

"Who are they?" I asked as we slid to a stop. I had Gundren out and ready to go. There were at least a hundred of them. The Valkyries were fighting two or three at once. Without waiting for an answer, I said, "Fen, make sure Baldur gets Callan to the door unharmed. We'll be right behind you after we help the shieldmaidens." He gave me a look. "I'll be fine. If we don't make progress, you can change into your wolf and have at them." I jumped into the melee, my swords clashing with three at once, my mother right behind me.

Leela brought her broadsword up, and with one slice, she cut down four or five dwarves at once. I didn't think they were dead, because they were writhing around on the ground, moaning and cursing shieldmaidens with words too colorful to repeat.

Leela fought close as we pushed our way through the crowd. When Gundren encountered a weapon, it sliced and diced it, much to the dismay of any adversary who stood in my way.

"What in the bloody damn billa-a-hoolie is this?" A stunned dwarf inspected the steel ball of his mace, which had been sheered in half.

"That's my weapon defeating yours," I told him as I passed.

When we got to the other side of the fight, near the doors that led outside, my mother said, "These are the dwarves of Myrkheim, cousins to the dark elves. They also mine gems and are excellent craftsmen, but they lack magic. They share an alliance with each other, of course, to protect both realms, but are not hard to best. In Myrkheim, they have great numbers, but here there are just a few."

"What we don't have in magic, we make up for with stout fighting and courage!" one of them yelled as he charged. He sounded a bit Scottish, but then, everything around me had an Asgardian accent mixed with something else.

I lifted my foot and shoved it into his belly.

My swords would kill him, and I wasn't interested in felling these dwarves. As the dwarf stumbled back, he shook himself and readied to come at me again.

"You might want to think twice about that." I raised Gundren, power and electricity racing along my arms and into the blades, making them jump and spark.

The dwarf stopped in his tracks, his bushy eyebrows heading up his forehead. "Now there's a neat trick, lassie," he said. "But that won't stop me—"

I leveled my sword three feet from his belly, producing just enough spark to hit him squarely in the stomach. He flew away from me, landing flat on his back, gripping his stomach, rolling back and forth on the floor, groaning, "Oh, my aching innards!"

I glanced over my shoulder to see Fen clearing a path for Baldur as he carried Callan. My brother looked like he didn't have a care in the world.

The god of light met my gaze. "This is the most fun I've had in about a hundred years. I love these dwarves! I haven't seen them in a long while. I used to barter my Asgardian weapons for their jewels and household items. They make the best ale cups."

One dwarf said, "Hey, look, it's Baldur the Bright! Haven't seen you in a while. I still have the bejeweled belt you ordered and never came back for!"

Baldur laughed, his tone joyous. "I'll be back for it any day now," he told the bearded man. "My ship will be sailing within a fortnight. I'll contact you then!"

"Sounds good," the dwarf answered as he went after Fen, his ax raised over his head. "I look forward to doing business once again. You pay well. Not like the others."

Fen batted him away without even the slightest effort. "Come, Valkyrie. I see the door. We are almost clear of this place. The other shieldmaidens have it in hand. If you wish to save the mixed elf and get to the tree of life, we must leave now. I sense danger near." He glanced around at the remaining elves, no more than twenty. "And it does not include this lot."

My mother fought a dwarf five paces to my right. "Leela," I called. "Let's head out."

She nodded once. "I'm right behind you, daughter."

Ingrid and Rae were thirty feet away. I yelled, "We'll meet you at the tree!"

"Will do," Ingrid called, using one powerful leg to down a dwarf in front of her. "It shouldn't be long now."

We met up with the guys by the door. Callan looked weak, but was arguing with Baldur to put him down. "You blasted, big ogre! Put me down right this minute. I am not feeble. I can walk by myself."

"Stop struggling, old man." Baldur chuckled. "I promised

my sister I would carry you to the tree, and that I will do. I will not let you risk your life, so stop trying to get free and enjoy the ride."

Callan openly grumbled, but stopped twisting.

We headed outside. We were so close to freedom, I could almost taste it.

25

"We need to head right," I said as we raced out the door. "Anybody see a clearing?"

Fen called, "Over here!"

He was sprinting, and it was all I could do to keep up.

Fen entered the opening one second before I did, followed by my mother and Baldur. I stopped just past the tree line and tried to make sense of the sight in front of me. My mouth fell open as I glanced around the clearing. Willa stood in the middle, unmoving.

"Um?" I cleared my throat when the word came out stilted. "What...happened here? Willa, did you do this?" The mixed elf looked miserable and a little shell-shocked. I paced forward slowly and, in a coaxing tone, asked, "Are they all dead?"

Around us, prone on the stubby brown grass, were elves. They appeared dead, but I couldn't be sure.

Willa nodded slowly. "I...I think they're dead," she said tentatively. "It's been a long time since I last used my abilities." A horrified look crossed her face as she clutched her fists to her chest. "They...they were going to kill me." Her voice sounded shallow and thin. "I had no other choice. I had to do something..."

"Of course you did. It's okay," I soothed as I put away Gundren. I wasn't sure what she did to render the elves motionless on the ground, and I didn't want to spook her. "They were going to kill you, and you are within your rights to defend yourself. I just don't understand what happened. They don't have a mark on them. You said you hadn't used your talents in a long time. What exactly are they?"

A single tear flowed down her cheek. She didn't bother to wipe it off. "I can"—her voice was barely there— "manipulate liquid."

It took me a second to understand what she was telling me. "You mean, as in blood? You can stop it from circulating?" It was the only thing I could think of as I looked around at the bodies strewn on the ground, some of them already turning blue.

She nodded. "Yes. More or less. My mother was an elemental who had properties over water. My powers are not as vast as hers, but simply stopping blood flow is easy."

I settled a hand on her shoulder. This was the exact reason why my father befriended her. He knew she had a special gift and could pass into this realm undetected. He was smart. "It's okay, Willa. We're leaving this realm, never to return. No one will know it was you who did this—"

The earth shook beneath us, the ground splitting open.

I clutched Willa to my side to steady us both.

Baldur called, "Something is arriving in this space! Brace yourselves."

A giant oak tree bordering the clearing sheared in half with a loud crack, its branches dropping like dead weights, thumping loudly into the dirt.

Fen was beside me. "Valkyrie, we must leave now. Yggdrasil is not far. If we run, we might be able to make it to safety. Whatever is coming is dangerous."

I nodded. "Okay, let's go. We only needed to find Willa—" We all turned to make a break for it.

"Not so fast," a familiar voice echoed out of the clearing where the tree had split open. "We haven't given you permission to leave yet."

Damn.

"Verdandi," I turned, saying her name as sweetly as I could. "I'd say it was a pleasure to see you again, but I'd be lying." I unsheathed Gundren very slowly, taking a little solace in the low zinging noise.

"Your weapons don't impress me." She stalked toward us, wearing the same tattered gray dress she'd had on the last time. She must not have a closet. "Nor will they be any use against me. White elf magic does not affect me." Her gaze settled on Callan, who now stood on his own next to Baldur.

Callan bowed his head, not missing a beat, and said, "We shall see, good Norn. We shall see."

As more dust cleared, I noticed Verdandi was not alone. That would be too easy. Behind her, Urd and Skuld emerged.

The gang was all here.

I positioned my swords in front of me, affecting a cool stance, trying to make my heart beat slower. I decided to address Skuld next. "It appears you were wrong again," I told her, smirking. "I didn't turn out to be anyone's prisoner. And that alone proves that your sight isn't reliable. Sucks pretty bad if you're the one people are counting on to predict the future. You *might* want to look for a new job."

Skuld sauntered into the clearing like she couldn't care less, brushing her long golden hair off of her shoulders, chin out. "My sight does seem to flicker when you're involved, I admit it, but that doesn't mean I'm wrong. As soon as I left, several scenarios flashed before me, and in all of them, you lost. It wasn't until you defeated Invaldi that I saw your true path. And it's so delicious!" She clapped. "We just had to rush here to tell you the good news."

"Enough of this." Verdandi stomped her foot, settling a searing gaze on her sister. "We agreed this would be my hunt, not yours. You had your chance." She left off *and you failed*.

There had been some sisterly infighting. Interesting.

Before I could respond, Baldur rose to the occasion. "It's good to see you once again, Verdandi." Verdandi looked unimpressed. "It has been many years since our last interaction. Can I ask, what is it you want with my sister? I don't understand the intrigue. She should be of no interest to you and allowed to go on her way."

Verdandi clasped her hands in front of her as she stepped forward, her voice taking on a condescending tone. "God of Light, you should choose your sides more wisely. This bastard, sired by your father, will bring ruin to us all, and she must be stopped at all costs. That's why we are here."

"I think not," Baldur replied evenly. "She has done nothing but good since I've met her. Something that shines so brightly can only bring happiness into the world. I should know, as I'm the god of light. I think it's best you three go back to the roots of the tree, where you belong." Baldur's voice hardened. "Before any violence gets started. It is a crime to harm you in Asgard, but we are not there now."

I felt nothing but pride as I beamed at my brother.

Baldur didn't know any details of my life, and we'd met only a short time ago, but he knew I was good. That was enough for me.

Skuld cleared her voice, making sure it carried. "Oh, there will be violence. Mark my word. And you will not leave here without being fractured. All of you." Her gaze roamed over the group.

Urd moved closer to her sisters. She was the only sister who resembled a real, live witch. She was dressed in all black, including a flowing skirt and an honest-to-goodness pointy hat. She looked like a walking, talking textbook Midgard witch. Maybe she had a strange fascination with them? She spoke for the first time. "Skuld was not wrong in her predictions before. I see the past clearly. Choices can shift things around occasionally, more so with you than any other we have encountered, but every scenario moving forward will bring you pain and agony."

"How do you know what the future will hold?" I challenged. "You only see the past, once all the decisions are made. Basing anything on Skuld's sight is not advisable," I told her sweetly. "She's been wrong an unsettling amount of times so far."

I crossed my swords in front of me to accentuate my point. I had no idea if Gundren mixed with my energy would have any effect on the Norns, but I was more than willing to check the theory. I hoped it would at least knock them down for a second so we could haul ass to the tree.

Skuld cackled. "Oh, you're not getting to Yggdrasil just yet." She had to stop doing that! "Yep, I see that. It's not happening. And just so you know, your swords will not incapacitate us." She smirked like she knew everything. It was irritating.

Verdandi moved, her gray skirts swishing, her yellowed, chipped fingernails not any better than the last time I'd seen them. They must be short on manicurists at the bottom of the tree. "What will happen here on this day will cause you pain and agony for years to come. We will revel in it. Where you're going, there is only darkness. You will be there for a long time, and the best part? It won't even be our doing." She tilted her head back and laughed, her teeth barely secure in her mouth, many of them missing.

"I have no idea what you're talking about," I told Verdandi, portraying a confidence I wasn't exactly feeling in my voice, hoping I'd succeeded. "But I hold no stake in you being right. I'm not worried. I have managed to overcome everything else, and I will this time, too."

There was a clattering of footsteps as the Valkyries filled the clearing, weapons drawn. Rae took in the scene in about three seconds. She held her hand aloft, and all the shieldmaidens spread out in their fighting stances.

They weren't going anywhere.

Verdandi was nonplussed as she stalked toward my mother. My fists tightened around the hilts of my swords. There was no way I was going to let them hurt her. "Valkyrie slut of Odin's," Verdandi spat. "It's because of you we are here. And because of you, your daughter will experience pain and agony like none before her. You know I speak the truth, and that we are capable of doing this very thing. Can you guess how we will do it?"

My mother paled. "Take me instead," she answered. "I will pay the price that is owed for keeping the secret. I do it willingly. Just leave my daughter alone. She is young and does not know our ways."

"No!" I yelled. "You can't mean that! We're in this together, and we will fight together. So far nothing they've said has come true. You can't believe them now."

My mother didn't meet my gaze. "Take me instead."

Verdandi laughed. It was an ugly sound laced with malice. "Isn't that sweet? A mother sacrificing herself for her child. Isn't that the way it's supposed to go? Then everyone wins." She clasped her hands in mock sweetness. "Unfortunately, that's not how this is going to work." Her face hardened. "Your child must suffer. She will be shut off from the rest of us so she can cause no further harm. But have no fear, you will suffer as well. Your time in Svartalfheim was not nearly enough to repay the debt of your lying secrets. You will be headed far, far away, separated from your dear daughter for an eternity."

"No—" I tried to lunge, but Fen held me back. "Let me go!" I yelled. "No one is taking her away!" Valkyries moved in formation around us. They wouldn't let her be taken. I tried to relax, but my heart was pumping overtime.

Fen said nothing, but held on tight.

Skuld made a noise in the back of her throat, a cross between a laugh and a cough. She daintily slapped her chest as she came forward. "You are so green it's painful. Not knowing our ways is an understatement. You not only think like a human, you are human in every way. In this world, you do not get a happily ever after." She nodded to my mother. "You will be separated, ripped apart before you even get a chance to learn to love one another." *That's where you're wrong, Skuld. We already love each other.* "We found the most delicious, wonderful way to achieve both. All of Asgard will root for your demise. I can think of nothing better!" She was downright giddy, and my stomach filled with foreboding. This wasn't going to be good. The Norns were too calm, too sure of themselves.

My mother's head was still bowed, her cheeks wet.

I refused to believe this could happen. There had to be a way to change the outcome. I'd been given advantage after advantage. I had weapons from Odin. Protection from the Valkyries. It was no mistake that I'd met Fen, I was sure of it.

Junnal was sent to me, and then we'd found Willa.

It all had to mean something!

What would Sam say? She'd be on my side with this. She'd agree with me. It didn't make sense. I couldn't have been given every advantage only to fail.

This bolstered my resolve. "It's not going to happen the way you see it, Skuld." My voice filled with anger. "I chose to believe I will prevail, and I'll continue to do so."

I was defiant. I refused to cry. I was going to win.

"You think yourself brave?" Verdandi snipped. "We shall see once the pieces fall where they may." She reached into a pocket of her dirty skirt and drew out something that resembled a dart. She held it between her thumb and broken fingernail. "Do you know what this is?"

Fen's nostrils scented the air, and he drew in a sharp breath that ended on a snarl.

That couldn't be good.

Even worse, Verdandi's eyes landed on Baldur.

My heart clenched and threatened never to release itself. She would not target my brother. She couldn't!

She was about to speak again when the ground rumbled under our feet, surprising us all.

"What comes?" Verdandi demanded, turning to Skuld. "Friend or foe?"

"Oh, Verdi, I wasn't aware we had any friends, so it is most certainly a foe." Skuld met my gaze. "The god of war seeks his sister. He's been blocked entry by the wards in this realm, but it seems he has found a way to break through after all."

"Does he come alone?" Verdandi asked, still holding the dart in front of her like a prized possession, clearly peeved that she'd been interrupted.

Skuld cocked her head, like she was listening to the future

instead of divining it. "No, strangely he brings a human. A lone girl who is very breakable. Not very smart of him."

Sam!

"A human?" Urd exclaimed. "That sounds like folly."

"The human is no threat to us," Verdandi stated in a certain tone. "Tyr's arrival will change nothing. He cannot harm us."

How could Tyr bring my best friend into a world like this?

Then I remembered who I was talking about.

He'd likely had no choice.

"Our plan stays the same. Nothing has shifted—" Another loud rumbling cut Skuld off.

The ground near us began to rend open, and we all stumbled backward. Out of the gash, my brother and my best friend appeared like they'd been delivered right from the bowels of the earth.

It was an amazing entrance, and the only thing I could manage was, "Sam? What in the world are you wearing?"

26

"Isn't it awesome?" Sam answered excitedly. "It was the only way he'd allow me to come." She gestured at Tyr, who stood next to her, and the action of moving her arm sounded like pots and pans clanking together. "It took some time to get it together, but I got 'er done." She grinned. "I'm pretty sure I'm channeling a medieval vibe, with a side of badass, of course." She lifted her arms, causing more rattling.

She was dressed in some kind of makeshift armor.

It looked as though she had repurposed household items and quite possibly a shed roof. It didn't matter that she was wearing a homemade outfit that wouldn't protect her from literally anything on this plane, including a Muroidea, I was ecstatic to see her.

I said, "I missed you. And even though you shouldn't be here, because it's dangerous, I'm glad you came."

"Honestly, it was a no-brainer," she said as she moved toward me, clanking the entire way. "When you left, there was total panic all around. Then all the shieldmaidens left. I was so worried, and I was done waiting around. Once Tyr figured out how we could get here, I wasn't about to be left behind. Just ask him." She jabbed a hand that was covered in some sort of chain-mail glove at my brother, who looked resigned, if even a little amused.

"It's good to see you, sister," Tyr said as he walked with Sam. "And yes, it's true. I could not dissuade her from me accompanying me. She threatened untold things, including injury to her own body." He appeared scandalized. "I was left with little choice."

Tyr was covered head to toe in weapons. I'd never seen someone carry so many, especially since he had only one hand.

He truly was the god of war.

I nodded and was just about to say something when I was rudely interrupted. "God of War, your life is forfeit if you harm us," Verdandi said, her voice pinging with rage. "You come too late to intervene. What's done is done."

Tyr took a step closer. He was a huge man covered in an arsenal of firepower. I would think even another god would be quaking in their boots right now. "The time draws near. Your reign of terror will soon be over," he stated confidently. "You three will be relegated back to the roots of the tree for all of your days. You have gone unchecked for far too long. The gods are discussing this at a summit right this very moment." He didn't offer up an explanation of how he knew that, but I trusted him.

My father, it seemed, was still trying to rally support for me.

Verdandi pursed her lips, saying nothing, but her eyes slid to Skuld. Verdandi saw the present, so she knew what Tyr said was true, but she wouldn't know the outcome. Skuld was the only one in attendance who could possibly know how this would end.

Skuld swished her hand, as if to say none of it mattered. "Yes, they are discussing matters, but the end result of what happens here will change that. No need to worry. Odin thinks he has gathered enough support, but it won't last long. Once they find out what his bastard allowed to happen, they will turn on her, and him. They will be united in their wrath. In fact, this is even better than the scenario I had envisioned for her earlier." She brushed her Rapunzel hair off her shoulders. "It's far more dastardly."

My mother took a step, her broadsword raised in the air. "I cannot allow you to do this. If you won't take me instead, I will fight for our lives." Behind her, all the Valkyries positioned themselves to back her up.

Tyr moved as well, signaling for Sam to stay back. I was relieved she listened to him. I leaned over and whispered, "Willa, please go stand with my friend. Protect her if you can. She's fragile under all those layers."

A vicious chortle came from Verdandi, who'd overheard me just fine. "There will be no protecting any of you, from anything. What we will achieve here today will leave you stripped and wounded." She brought the dart up once again, settling it in front of her face, twisting it back and forth slowly. "And this is all it will take to do it."

Willa obeyed me and went to stand by Sam as I moved shoulder to shoulder with my mother. We would face this threat together.

I had no idea what Verdandi was planning, as the dart didn't look like anything that could harm any of us, but I knew I wasn't going to be happy about the outcome. My hands gripped the hilts of Gundren more firmly and clenched my jaw.

Skuld interrupted in her singsong voice. "Verdi, we have places to go. Let's finish this. Odin's meeting will be done soon. It's the exact perfect time to send a rocket through Asgard. I cannot wait to see the response."

Urd stood stoically, and for the first time, I noticed that the third sister looked a little uneasy. Her skin was so pasty it was hard to tell if she was ill. "Are we sure this is the right course?" She addressed her sisters. "This new news about Odin is troublesome. The past has shown us that interfering with gods can come at a great price."

"You would question my sight now?" Skuld said, her light tone belying the hardness underneath. "I told you, I see nothing but gain for us. This will solve all of our problems, and the realms will right themselves. In fact, it's our only option. If we do not proceed, chaos will ensue. Asgard will thank us for this. Eventually." She giggled. "But they cannot do anything about it, not even Odin himself. As Verdi said, once it's done, it's done."

"That's what I'm afraid of," Urd responded in a bland tone. "But of course I trust you. If you see that our future is secure, that's good enough for me." The witch straightened, her black skirts barely moving. "Proceed, Verdandi. I have a kettle on at home that needs tending."

I tensed.

Their conversation was cryptic, but I knew whatever they had planned was going to upset the gods and, ultimately, be blamed on me. I leaned into my mother. "Do you know what they're going to do?"

"I have an idea," she said. "We must not let it happen. The dart is the key."

Verdandi smiled cruelly, her attention on us. "Yes, the dart is the key. How impressive of you to notice, Leela." She raked scorn-filled eyes over my mother. "The Valkyrie temptress who lured Odin down a rabbit hole is proving to be intelligent. But not overly so. Shieldmaidens are forbidden from fornicating with their maker, as you well know. You have committed a crime in more ways than one. Asgard will blame you as much as they will blame your daughter, for it was you who had Odin's bastard and kept her from us. If she had never been born, this tragic event would not have occurred."

"I kept her from you because you would've killed her. I would do it again in a heartbeat," my mother said defiantly, passion infusing each word. "I care not what my future holds. The seer who came to Asgard all those years ago was an impostor. You have to know that by now. Harming my daughter for his prophecy is no longer valid. Odin will be proving that soon—if he hasn't already. Then, what Tyr told you will come true. You will be confined to your hovel underground, never to see the light of day again."

Verdandi laughed, and it sounded like she was gargling with nails. "It matters not what the seer predicted. It matters what *we* see. And Skuld has seen the devastation that your daughter will wreak if she is left alive. We must put a stop to it at all costs. In case you've forgotten, that is our job. We keep things running so that destiny stays on track. Without us, the seven realms would fall into chaos."

"That is doubtful," my mother said. "You three have been running the seven realms by your own agenda for far too long, taking lives and liberties for your own gain. Whatever the outcome of going after my daughter, it is for you alone and has nothing to do with her fated path. Your wrongdoings have had a ripple effect on all of us, and you must be stopped. Your time of unlimited freedom is coming to an end."

"You dare speak to us that way, vixen?" Skuld snarled. "We were born to do this job. There are no others to take our place. Without us, the worlds sink into oblivion. We have ruled for a thousand years, and we will do so for a thousand more."

A thousand years? Was she serious? No wonder she looked like a peeling skeleton without her glamour. Honestly, she made Verdandi look like a teenager.

"The Valkyrie is right," Fen piped in. "You have been given too much power, and you've wielded it unwisely. It's catching up to you, and your time is coming to an end. It was Skuld who ruined my life, and for what reason? When we have the ear of Asgard, they will come to understand what's to be done, and it is you who will pay the ultimate price."

"How do you know such things, wolf?" Verdandi sneered. "We were born into our destiny, just like all of you." Her gaze raked the group. "This is our duty, and we will do it to the death. Nothing stands in our way."

Tyr shifted his weight, his weapons clattering, reminding me of Sam and her armor. They were two peas in a pod. "Except all of us," Tyr boomed, his deep voice echoing around the clearing. "You are not infallible, witch. I've been told tales about your kind since I was a babe. The god of war is prepared to fight all beings, including you three. I suggest you leave this place while you are still able." He aimed a large spear gun at Verdandi.

"You would engage us in battle?" Verdandi half laughed, half snickered. "Then you are more foolish than any other. If you harm us, the price is death."

"Not this time." Tyr's voice was firm. "You cross a line when you hunt my sister. As Leela stated, the seer who made the prophecy was a fake. Right now, my sister should be in Asgard with our father, stating her case to the Council. There is no doubt that Odin has already garnered support for her cause. The only law that was broken was that he lay with a shieldmaiden, which has no impact on Phoebe, and that law has since been abolished. It was written in an older, more stoic time. Phoebe and Leela will be cleared of any wrongdoing."

I should hope so.

My gaze shot to Urd as she adjusted her hat, her eyes pinned to the ground. Something was up. If what Tyr had said was true, then the Norns coming after me was unjust, especially if they knew the seer was a fake.

They had to have an ulterior motive.

"None of what you say is true," Skuld said dismissively, swishing her hand. "That particular seer might've been a fake, but her birth was not supposed to be. I can see the future"—she waved her perfectly manicured finger at me— "and she will bring about Ragnarok if she's not stopped."

There was a collective intake of breath.

The Valkyries around me began to murmur.

Fen had told me bits about Ragnarok, the fated battle between the gods. Many of them would die, including my father, by Fen's hand. It was destined to happen, no matter what, but nobody knew when.

No one said anything for a full minute.

The air was cleared by a snort. Ingrid called, "Bullcrap, Skuld. Ragnarok is *fated*. It will come when it comes. My niece is not the catalyst for anything, because there is not one person who can influence something so big. You don't fool us, and I think you'll say just about anything to get what you want. I haven't figured out what your endgame is, but everyone here knows it has less to do with Phoebe and everything to do with whatever it is you gain. If you're smart, you'll take Tyr's advice and leave us before this gets uglier. I am willing to go to jail, or even die, for my niece. Most of us assembled here are. Not giving a shit is as dangerous for a

Valkyrie. It means we have nothing to lose. And, really, the gods can't kill us all. That would be folly."

"Leaving is advisable," Rae added, looking defiant. "If I lose my life defending Odin's child, I consider it an honor. All the shieldmaidens are prepared to fight to the death." To accentuate her point, she raised her katana. If I came across Ragnhild in battle, I would quake in my boots. She was strong and embodied the word *fierce*.

Skuld didn't change her expression, except to close her eyes.

After a second, she tilted her head back.

She appeared to be divining. I hoped it was bad news for her and good news for us. Verdandi took a tiny step back as her sister continued on in her trance.

I felt hopeful for the first time since they'd arrived.

I sneaked a glance at Sam where she stood in her ridiculous armor. I was happy Willa stood close by her side. My best friend was brave in so many ways. She met my gaze and gave me a small smile and a noisy thumbs-up. I knew if she could, she would let the Norns know exactly what she thought. But Sam was too smart for that. If she called attention to herself, she became vulnerable. Tyr knew she was smart, or he wouldn't have brought her. I smiled, thinking of Sam haranguing my big brother until he finally gave in, finally letting her have her way.

Suddenly, Skuld's eyes snapped open, and she raised her head. "All is well. The meeting is over, and the future is the same." She turned to Verdandi. "You will proceed, dear sister. They will not fault us. I see it clearly. It's our job to protect the realms. We must do this."

Verdandi brought the dart up as a slow, creepy smile spread across her dry, cracked lips. She was more than happy to do Skuld's bidding.

In fact, this was the most joyous I'd ever seen her.

She leveled her eyes on me, and I crossed my swords in front of my body, ready to engage. "Once this dart finds its home," she said with a cackle, "your world will rock on its axis until it finally spins completely out of control. You will be tossed into the darkest, vilest of our worlds, never to return." Her muddy teeth flashed as she drew her arm back, and with a speed I hadn't expected, she launched the dart, sending it hurtling through the air.

I sprang in front of my mother to protect her, Gundren burning brightly. I couldn't tell exactly where Verdandi had been aiming, and the projectile was moving too fast to track.

It wasn't until I heard an anguished cry that I knew the dart had found its mark.

27

Please, no! Please, no! The words raced through my brain as I ran. Tyr and Fen beat me to him. I skidded to a stop, dropping to my knees and tossing my swords to the ground.

Tyr held his brother in his arms, his face betraying nothing.

Baldur lay on the ground, the dart sticking out of his chest. It had penetrated deeply, only the very tip showing. The Valkyries amassed around us, forming a protective circle around the god of light.

"We have to get him out of here," Ingrid said. "I'm not sure what that is, but he seems to be reacting strongly to it."

"It's mistletoe," Fen answered, his nostrils flaring, his voice devoid of emotion. "The only thing that can kill him, which the Norns well know."

Baldur gave us a weak smile. "It's not so bad." He coughed, blood pooling on his chest. "This is an easy death. I would choose it over many others." Baldur smiled up at Tyr. "It is good to see you, God of War. It has been too long between meets. I see you are not without your arsenal, and for that I am grateful. Our sister needs to be protected, and I'm glad you have arrived. You must keep her from harm."

"Until I saw you, I did not know you resided on this plane." Tyr's voice rang of sadness. "Your whereabouts have been kept secret. I searched for you over the years after I found you were gone, hoping to locate you, to no avail. Your ship, Ringhorn, is awaiting your return. It is docked in Vanir, right where you left it. I've visited it many times."

"I'm glad of that. I want you to have her. Ringhorn will do well with you at the helm." Baldur chuckled, which turned into a series of shallow coughs. "My other brothers might argue, but they will honor my wishes." He turned to me, giving me a weak grin. "Take care, sister. Our meeting was too brief, but you are in good hands."

"You're not going to die," I insisted, my voice cracking. I met Tyr's gaze. "Can you pull the dart out?"

Tyr shook his head. "Even if I could get the dart out, the damage is already done. The weapon found true aim."

"Then we have to get him to Yggdrasil." My voice was panicked. "Right now. The tree can save him. We have to try!"

Rae gave the command. "Transport the god of light to the tree. Ingrid and Billie, stay behind. The rest, take him in your arms and go." Rae nodded once at me. "I will expect your return within the hour. If you don't show, we will backtrack."

"Thank you," I told Rae. "We will follow as soon as we can." I rested my hand on Baldur's shoulder. "I will see you soon. Yggdrasil has healed me, and it will heal you, too."

Baldur motioned me down, and I leaned over. He pressed his lips to my cheek. "The only thing I regret is not meeting you sooner. You have a good heart, Phoebe. And remember, don't let my mother scare you." He grinned.

"She will be angry, but it's mostly bluster. She has been good to me—her only crime was caring too much. Tell her all will be well and I love her."

"I will." I swiped my cheeks as the Valkyries gently took him away. He had to be okay. When they disappeared out of the clearing, I turned to the Norns, who stood with satisfied looks on their ugly faces. "Why?" I shouted as I stood. "Why would you hurt him? He has done nothing wrong, and this will achieve nothing. Why not just kill me? Isn't that what you wanted? For me to die?"

"Your death will no longer satisfy fate," Verdandi answered, looking pleased, which made me angrier. "Instead, you will get the torture you deserve, tossed into the deepest pit of our worlds. The gods will see to that, especially Frigg. You will pay dearly, as she loved that boy more than anything in the seven realms. You will feel her wrath."

Urd snagged Verdandi's arm, looking pensive. "We must leave now. If we don't, the outcome may change." It seemed Urd was the only one of them with any sense.

My swords clashed in front of me as I walked. Energy raced through my body in a tight swirl, making me feel kinetic. It surged into my palms, flowing seamlessly into the hilts. The blades began to spark. I was beyond rage as I waved Gundren, light bursting from the ends like a pair of deadly sparklers.

"I'm not letting you get away with this," I fumed. "I don't care what happens to me. Like my aunt just told you, I'm not afraid of death." The need to avenge Baldur's death pressed down on me, more than anything else I'd experienced since becoming a Valkyrie. Once the words were out of my mouth, I knew they were true.

I wasn't afraid to die.

Skuld stepped in front of Verdandi, blocking my path. "It

doesn't matter if you've found your true inner strength," she baited. "It's too late for that, which should be your motto. You don't have enough power to fell us, and it certainly won't bring your dear brother back to life." She tossed her head back and laughed. "That ship has sailed."

I leveled my swords at her heart.

Or where it would be if she had one.

Unleashing my energy would take one shake of my sword. "If the gods sentence me to death for this, it will be worth it." I let it go, and lightning rushed forward, slamming like an arrow into Skuld's chest.

She spread her arms wide as her body shook with the force.

Her tinkling laughter contradicted the physical impact, and as I watched, her glamour flickered like lights during a storm, flashing us her putrid visage like an old film reel.

She was a horror.

"You cannot kill me, bastard child," Skuld spat, her body gyrating with the impact. "Your sustenance comes from the tree, and however potent, Yggdrasil would not turn on me."

My stomach roiled as her frail, gray body exposed itself again and again. Maybe the tree wouldn't turn on her, but it was doing a good job of showing us who she really was.

But Skuld had been wrong too many times already, and I wasn't going to take her word for it. I continued to blast her, relishing in her deterioration. When this was over, there would be nothing more than a wretched half-baked skeleton in her place, if I had any say about it.

I gritted my teeth, trying to keep my focus, my stores depleting quickly. "I can do this all day," I lied. "You will succumb sooner rather than later."

"Never!" she declared, her voice hoarse, her skeletal frame crashing to its knees.

"Cease this nonsense!" Verdandi commanded. "As my sister said, you cannot harm us." She held something in her hand and waved it in front of me. "If you do not stop, I will end your life right here."

"So now you're going to kill me?" I said, my voice dripping with sarcasm, coated in anger. "I thought murdering me was a copout. If you kill me now, I won't get the torture I *deserve*." My body felt like it had run several marathons, but it was worth it to see Skuld falter and collapse.

I knew she'd been bluffing.

With sadness, I realized there was no possible way I had enough energy to finish the job. The Norns were definitely stronger than the energy I had stored inside me right now. But I took solace in the fact that that might not always be the case.

There would be another time.

As Verdandi moved closer, I saw she held a short dagger in her hand. She brought it out in front of her and took aim. Right at my chest. But just before she could launch it, her head whipped back, pain washing over her haggard features.

The dagger fell from her grip, landing on the ground with a soft clatter as she clutched her head with both hands.

I was so surprised that I nearly lost my concentration and broke the flow I had on Skuld.

Verdandi staggered like a drunk, shaking her head, trying to clear it. After a moment, she stopped, standing rigidly still. Slowly, her jaundiced eyes raked the group, malice pulsing. Her gaze landed to my left. "It was you," she accused, her voice harsh. "How dare you try to kill me, you little imp? Do you know who I *am*?" She began to move toward Willa. "I will spill your blood and eat your heart!"

The mixed elf had tried to kill a Norn to save my life!

I couldn't let Verdandi harm her, even if it meant giving up on Skuld.

Skuld gave a strangled laugh. "I know which you will choose. I have already seen it. You are weak and useless. You will never be strong enough to be a great Valkyrie! Go on, save the girl. Get it over with."

Verdandi grabbed Willa, and the mixed elf screamed. Sam pounded her chain-mail fists against Verdandi and cried, "Leave her alone, you wicked witch!"

I pivoted, breaking my connection with Skuld smoothly. "Get out of the way, Sam!" I shouted as my vastly depleted energy hit Verdandi.

I only had enough juice for one lash.

It turned out I didn't have to worry about Sam, because Tyr was already there. He scooped my friend up, settling her securely behind him as he drew his weapons on Verdandi. Fen was close behind.

To my utter satisfaction, even though I barely had any energy left, Verdandi dropped, and Willa stumbled backward. Fen, like the valiant protector I knew him to be, stood in front of the mixed elf, guarding her, ready to shift.

A perfunctory laugh interrupted the scene, and I dropped my arms.

Skuld was on all fours. Her dress, if you could call it that, hung in ribbons around her body, smoking. She was trying in vain to recover her glamour, but it wasn't happening. Her head was half bald, the other half containing only a few thin wisps of gray hair. The skin on her face peeled in a gag-worthy way. Her eyes were bloodshot. "As I predicted, you chose wrong." Her same singsong voice sounded so completely wrong coming out of that frightening body. "Not that you would've won this battle, but it shows your true merit is lacking."

"I chose right," I stated with certainty, my body on the verge of collapse. I struggled to hide my need to gasp for air. "I wouldn't expect you to understand. I would bet the farm you've never loved a single thing in your entire, wretched life. I stopped because there will be other chances to engage in battle with you, but not another chance to save a life. I regret nothing."

Skuld staggered to stand. Her shredded dress revealed more than I ever wanted to see. "There will be zero more chances to engage, as we are finished here. We have done our part. Everything will play out as I've seen it, and you will be tossed into a dark realm where you will linger, gasping for life, destined to live the rest of your days in exile. It is the sweetest fate for you." Her glamour began to stitch back together. Her hair filled in first, then bit by bit, her dress repaired itself, until she stood before us the complete Disney princess again. She appeared proud of herself and no worse for the wear.

I swallowed, biting back bile, knowing that I could do no more today, and even if I could, it wouldn't bring Baldur back. Fen came to stand next to me, his presence calming.

"We shall see what happens," I said. "I don't put much stock in anything you say. There has to be a way to help my brother, and after that's done, I will defeat you once and for all. I won't rest until that day comes."

"There is no way to help the god of light. He will perish, and you will pay." Skuld beckoned Verdandi, who struggled to stand after my blow, Tyr's arsenal still aimed at her.

"Don't forget your dagger, Verdi," I mocked. "You might need it someday soon."

"You haven't won, bastard," Verdandi answered, bending to pick up the weapon. "Your pain is just beginning, and we will delight in it from afar."

The sisters joined hands, backing toward the oak tree. Skuld had an evil smile playing on her lips. The Norns were certain of their victory.

But I had other plans.

As they vanished from sight, noises erupted from inside the mountain. The elves had regrouped and were coming.

"It's time for us to skedaddle," Ingrid said. "The natives are getting restless. Invaldi is likely up and around, furious about being bested. It took time to gather more spells, but they're ready now."

My mother wore a serene expression. I walked over and grabbed her hand as we started moving quickly toward Yggdrasil. "It's going to be okay," I told her as she gripped my palm tightly. "I don't know much about these worlds, and nothing about Asgard or the gods who live there, but what I do know is that nothing is set in stone. The Norns have proven that a few times already. We'll figure it out."

She nodded, a thin smile forming. Her chestnut hair swayed as she moved. "I had just hoped for more time together," she said, sadness at the forefront. "They were not lying about Frigg. She is a powerful goddess and will be devastated at the loss of her son. She will blame you. And even if all the Valkyries banded together, it would not be enough to defeat her."

"Maybe Yggdrasil has helped Baldur?" I said, hopeful.

We increased our pace to a run, the elf chatter getting increasingly louder. Tyr was behind us with Sam and Willa. Sam's clanking was enough to alert all the elves in this realm to our location. I slowed so she could catch up. "Sam, start taking that suit off. You're making too much noise." I had to stifle a laugh.

It was dangerous, not funny, but she looked so cute.

"Do you know how much engineering went into this?"

"We'll make you a new one. Just hurry up about it."

She sighed. "I supposed I can't be responsible for an elf attack." She dropped her helmet first, followed by her armbands.

"Were those old gutters?" I glanced behind as we ran.

"I used what I had," she answered. "No critiquing. You get a shiny new breastplate, and I get gutters, that's the way this works. I had to convince the big guy I was protected so he would bring me along."

"There's no way that Tyr thought that getup would save you," I pointed out as she undid what sounded like Velcro, and her leg shields, made from corrugated metal, dropped to the ground.

"That may be true," she admitted. "But I followed his orders. He said I had to have something between my body and a weapon. He didn't specify. This was my answer. But"—she giggled—"you should've seen his face when he saw me. He's all about honoring his word and stuff, so he couldn't say no."

"He said you threatened to harm yourself."

"Oh, yeah, that, too," she said, dropping her chest plate, which was made of what looked like a garbage can lid. "I said I'd jump in the river and sink like an anchor with all this on. Worked like a charm."

"You have no shame," I told her.

"Nope, none. But I'm in Svartalfheim. Not every girl can say that." She glanced at the dingy forest of trees with weeping branches. "But once is enough. No need to make a return visit."

"Agreed." We slowed, Yggdrasil up ahead. We managed to stay in front of the elf pack, which was a relief.

"We go two by two," Ingrid ordered as we stopped in front of the tree. "No time to waste. Let's go. Phoebe and Fen, Tyr and Sam, Leela and Willa. Billie and I go last."

I grabbed on to Fen's hand. "We will be home soon, Valkyrie."

"I can't wait." As we launched ourselves into Yggdrasil, I realized I had no idea how to navigate where we are going, so I simply closed my eyes and trusted I would get where I needed to be.

28

The tree shot us out at the Valkyrie stronghold. I rolled twice and was up, Fen ahead of me. We immediately took off toward the main living area. He grabbed my hand as we raced down the pathway.

"Let's head to the infirmary," I said. Infirmary was a "light" word for what the Valkyries considered a mending room. Shieldmaidens didn't get sick and didn't get hurt very often, and when they did, they healed quickly. In the stronghold, they had what equated to a space that held a few bandages for deep cuts that took more time to heal, and not much else.

We came around the last bend before the main living area, and Fen pulled up short. I stopped myself in time. They hadn't made it to the infirmary.

Baldur was laid out on a blanket in the middle of the Park. I rushed forward, my heart hammering in my chest.

He wasn't moving.

The Valkyries who stood closest to him parted as Fen and I entered the area. Nobody was going to complain that men were in here now, as this was an exception nobody wanted to give. The vibe was somber. Many of the Valkyries had their heads bowed.

I knelt next to my newfound brother, cradling his head in my lap, resting a palm on his chest. Fen stood behind me. Yggdrasil had energized me, refueling me with potent energy.

It had sadly not done the same for Baldur.

Blood from the wound had spread, covering his entire chest, staining it a deep crimson red. The evil dart was still visible. His breathing was shallow, but he was still alive. Still fighting.

Tears pooled at the corners of my eyes, threatening to cloud my vision completely. If I hadn't freed him, he would still be alive.

Baldur coughed as he opened his eyes. Even on the verge of death, he still smiled. "I know what you're thinking, sister. But you are wrong. This was not your fault. Leaving my cell was my choice. I've been fated to die for longer than I can remember being not fated to die." He chuckled, which ended with a racking cough. I steadied my palm over his sternum, hoping to give him some comfort. "I've known this day would come sooner or later. My mother thought to protect me, first by gathering promises from every living thing in all the realms that they would not harm me, then by keeping me prisoner. But that was no life. It wasn't even a half life. Since you freed me, I've had more satisfaction and adventure than I've had in the last hundred or so years. I would not exchange it for anything." He reached for my hand, grasping it. "My death will be hard for you to accept, but you are strong. I've seen it with my own eyes. Who knows? Maybe I will enjoy my time in Hel." He struggled for breath, blood trickling from between his lips. "I've never been to that particular realm, and some say it's not so bad." He tried to laugh, but no sound come out.

I had never watched anyone die before. It was gut-wrenching.

My heart beat erratically, sorrow sweeping through my body like a tide of unbearable loss.

I closed my eyes for a brief moment and tried to gather myself. "If I hadn't arrived in Svartalfheim, you'd still be alive." My voice was thick as I choked back a sob. "I don't regret freeing you, but I hate this outcome. I'm not afraid to face your mother. I will take whatever punishment she metes out. But if I could somehow change this, I would, even if it meant coming back to get you later. Or staying in Svartalfheim longer."

He gripped my hand tightly. "I do not regret this outcome. It's my time to go. I feel no fear." He closed his eyes. "My destiny in Helheim is unknown, but I won't be alone." He smiled, his teeth stained red. "The souls who reside down there will have to endure my jokes for a millennium."

I knew nothing about Helheim. Fen's sister occupied that realm. Hel, the daughter of Loki and the giantess Angrboda, ruled the underworld.

Maybe that meant it wasn't a true death?

Maybe gods didn't really die?

I was being ridiculously hopeful, but I needed to grasp on to something. Tears ran freely down my cheeks. "I'm sure you will find a good audience. You are so magnanimous, everyone will be drawn to you the moment you arrive."

Footsteps headed into the Park. The others were returning. Tyr knelt on the other side of Baldur and grabbed his hand. "Brother, are you in a lot of pain?"

"No," Baldur answered, his eyes fluttering open, his chest

faltering a little more with each breath. "And, trust me, I am one to complain, unlike yourself." He tilted his head. "You had your face rent open by the jaws of Fenrir and lost your hand, yet I never heard you complain once. In fact, I've never seen you in true distress." He was stalled by a fit of coughing. He managed to continue after a moment, his voice thin. "Is it that pain does not affect you? Or are you just that valiant? I'd love to know. It is my eleventh-hour wish to know your secret."

Tyr's voice was gruff, marked by grief. "I feel pain, brother. But I learned at an early age not to show emotion. It is both my greatest asset and my biggest downfall." He shook his head. "But miracles do happen. I didn't think at my age, after all I'd been through, I could change my ways. But, lo and behold, I am evolving after an impossibly long time of stagnation."

"That's wonderful to hear," Baldur said, his voice barely audible. "We should all grow and change, learning from our joy and happiness as well as our pain and fear. It is something my mother has not learned yet. I'm tasking you to help our sister, as she will be burdened with blame. You know what is to come. Protect her from my mother's wrath. I'm hopeful that the combined powers of the god of war and the great wolf will be enough to save her from an unfavorable outcome."

Tyr nodded. "I will do my best. Lest not forget the Valkyries, who will stand united behind her. I've also been given some knowledge from the raven that will be helpful. Once we are summoned to Asgard, I will appeal to the Council and share that information. If they believe me, which will take time, all will be well."

Baldur seemed appeased, a slow grin sliding across his lips. "Take care of Ringhorn. She sails true. It's time for me to leave now. I feel the telltale tug. Be well. I go in love."

He closed his eyes, his features relaxing. He struggled with one last breath, and as he exhaled, his chest stilled.

His grip went slack.

I inhaled, choking back a sob, bending my head to touch his shoulder while I cried.

He was gone, and there was nothing I could do about it.

After a few minutes, gentle hands gripped my shoulders. "Come, Phoebe." My mother's voice was soft and coaxing. "The Valkyries will ready him for transport back to Asgard. He would not want us to mourn for him. He lived a good life."

I stood reluctantly, not wanting to leave him. What was supposed to happen next? Were we just going to go about our daily lives? Start training again?

My mother led me out of the Park. Everything was foggy with loss.

I turned to her, Fen, Tyr, and Sam coming behind us. I didn't want to talk about my feelings. I just needed to absorb what had happened. "Am I allowed to be by myself for a while? Is that okay? I need to...process this. I've never lost anyone before." I glanced back at the Park. Seeing Baldur's lifeless body lying still on the ground was almost too much. "How will he get back to Asgard?"

Tyr answered, "The gods and goddesses will have received word of his death already. Someone from Asgard will come to retrieve him, as is the custom. When gods or goddesses perish, it is felt by others of their same stature."

I nodded numbly, like I understood, even though I didn't. "Once he's back, what happens?"

"It is typical to send a god or goddess off to sea," Tyr replied. "They are laid on a pyre, and arrows are shot during a ceremony. Once the boat is alight, rose petals are thrown into the bay. It is a send-off of the physical body as well as the soul, to ready the god for the afterlife."

Hope sparked. "And what exactly is the afterlife? Does a god truly die? Baldur talked about making jokes and not being alone. What does that mean?"

Tyr shrugged. So not the response I was hoping for. "I know not, sister. Very few have ever traveled to Helheim. And those who have ventured there have never come back to tell the tale. It's not a place one goes willingly nor takes lightly. It is said that if you go there as a living, breathing soul, you have chosen to forfeit your life. No one would readily take that chance."

I turned my gaze on Fen. "You told me that your sister, Hel, rules the underworld. Is that true?"

Fen nodded. "Yes, but I have not seen her since we were small children. It is her destiny to reign over Helheim, just as it was for my brother to occupy the seas and for me to be banished."

I brought my hands up to my head.

Grief pounded so hard I could barely see. I couldn't think. This was all so confusing and foreign. If you died and went to a different realm, were you really dead?

Someone slid a hand around my waist, taking charge. It was Sam. "Come with me," she murmured. To the others, she said, "We Midgardians are going to go back to our bunks and take a small time-out. Not sure if you know what that is, but it's like a mini break, sometimes taken in the corner if you're naughty. How you guys do things around here is a little freaky. So don't mind us, we'll just be out back trying to wrap our heads around the fact you guys have an *actual* afterlife, but it's called Helheim rather than Heavenheim. And if that's not crazy enough, the person who runs things happens to be the sister of my friend's boyfriend." She tugged me away, muttering, "I mean, hasn't the afterlife always been heaven? If there is any justice in the world, the god of light should go to a place with fluffy clouds, golden gates, and angels holding harps wearing halos making beautiful music. Not Helheim, which sounds like it's covered in pitchforks and flames." She patted my back as we walked, like she was soothing a colicky newborn, and I was grateful. This was exactly what I needed right now.

No one else in this entire stronghold understood what I was feeling except for Sam, not even my mother.

Once we rounded the corner and were out of sight, I stopped and embraced my friend. I had missed her. "Thank you so much for getting me out of there. I owe you. My brain is so scattered, it's hard to know which way is up." My heart was also incredibly sore, still trying to process the loss of a brother I would never get to know.

"I'd love to take all the credit, but a little birdie told me I should bring you back here as soon I had the chance. Actually, it was a large, spooky raven who shot words into my brain with his telepathy. But you catch my drift." She hugged me back fiercely, her blonde curls bouncing. She looked no worse for the wear after her adventure in Svartalfheim. "I'm always going to be here for you, Phoebe. Never doubt that for a New York minute. We have to stick together. I mean, we're living our lives out of the pages of a comic book—which is cool, so don't get me wrong—but most days I can't believe this really exists. I wake up every morning pinching myself." She made a show of examining me, brushing some dirt off my breastplate and fixing an errant strand of hair. "Your time in Svartalfheim must have been tough. You have a harder look around your eyes." She motioned around my face. "And your smile doesn't quite go up as far at the ends like it used to." She brushed her thumbs over my cheeks. "I'm sad to see your innocence fading, but what's in its place is good. It will help you survive this new crazy world we've been tossed into." She grabbed my elbow and steered me forward. "I need you to keep getting stronger."

I blew out a breath. "I feel different, like I finally woke up from a long dream. Being a Valkyrie should seem more foreign to me, but it doesn't. Instead, it feels like I'm finally living in the right skin, if that makes any sense. But the problem is, I don't think like a Valkyrie. I think like a human. I'm worried that the way I react to everything is going to be human forever, and I won't be able to adapt. The grief I feel for my half brother is pressing down on me so hard." I rubbed my chest. The pain was manifesting itself as physical, and the muscles in my chest ached. "Everyone else seems to be taking his passing well, and I don't get it. And just like you said, if Baldur is going to the afterlife in Helheim, one of the seven realms, is he really dead?"

Holding on to that was the only thing keeping me upright at the moment.

"I have no idea," Sam mused. "If we had an afterlife on Midgard, nobody would fear death. He made it sound like there was a whole bunch of people down there. What's that supposed to mean?"

We were almost to our living quarters.

I was beyond fatigued, even though Yggdrasil had just given me an infusion of energy. The tree of life couldn't fix what was wrong with my emotional well-being. I could also use a shower.

"You got me," I told my friend. "What I do know is, we will be figuring it out soon, and it won't be pretty. Everything I've heard about Frigg is terrifying. And you heard the

Norns. My punishment will be harsh. Everyone is going to blame me for Baldur's death."

"You shouldn't be punished for anything! It pisses me off," Sam declared. "How much can a mother really love her son if she pays to keep him in jail for years on end? That's not love! That's selling your child into slavery, except instead of working for half a penny a day in some dark, dank factory, he just sits in a cell all day. Back home, if a mother on Midgard did that, she'd get life in prison!"

I loved the way Sam's mind worked. She was one of a kind.

As we walked up the short hill to our rooms, a shadow dotted the sky above us.

A telltale call came floating down.

CAW-CAW. CAW-CAW.

29

I wasn't sure I wanted to talk to the raven. After all, it was the bird who'd sent me through the portal in the first place. But I didn't really have a choice in the matter. I had to admit I was curious about what Huggie had to say. I prayed he was bringing me some hope in this gloomy, depressing situation.

Giving Sam a quick hug, I headed to my room, unstrapping Gundren from my back as I went. Once inside, I hung it on the edge of the headboard, wanting to keep it close. Then I took off my armbands and breastplate, resting them on a few hooks Fen had fashioned on the wall.

The bed was soft and inviting, a respite from all the crazy that had happened. I sat down with my back against the wall, closing my eyes. I didn't have much time to relax as Huggie settled himself on the perch of my one window in the next moment, which was actually just a cutout in the limestone.

I opened one eye.

The bird took up the entire space.

I laced my hands behind my head and waited. When Huggie didn't speak first, I asked, "Did you know Baldur was going to die when you sent me to Svartalfheim? And, if so, it would've been nice if you had warned me."

The bird squawked, readjusting himself before his words filtered softly into my mind. *I did not know, but I would've sent you all the same. The time was ripe and the objective was to free your mother, which was a success. You mustn't discount the mission. Your mother was held captive for over twenty-four years. It is a shame that the god of light lost his life during these events, but his fate had been decided long before this. He would've lost it whether he was with you or not. His time had come.*

Even though grief pounded at the forefront of my mind, I knew the raven was speaking the truth. I went to the land of the dark elves to save my mother. The mission was successful. I was looking forward to getting to know her, but I needed time to grieve the loss of Baldur.

"Are you here to give me a pep talk about my fated destiny? Because I'm not sure I want to know what's in store for me. Verdandi told me I'm going to face harsh punishment, and I believe she's right—or at least partially correct. Honestly, from the things I've learned already, gods and goddesses don't mess around. They punish people severely at the slightest provocation." I scrubbed my hands over my face. "So unless you have good news, maybe now's not the best time to have a chat."

I am not a seer. I'm an observer who gathers and delivers information. I did not take into account that you would run into your brother, although I was aware he was being held there. I do not fault you for setting him free. Many would do the same. I am here to let you know that the Council has convened. The goddess Frigg is inconsolable about the death of her son. They will be calling for you soon. The Norns have already sent word, backed up by Invaldi, that you have committed the crime of entering a realm without permission and were the one to free Baldur from his cell. Odin had been gathering support for your cause, explaining why he needed to keep the secret all these years, and had been successful. With the news of Baldur's death, some are still on his side, but others have turned away. Frigg is much loved, and her grief is vast.

"Tell me something I don't know." My voice was strained. "They will summon me to Asgard, and when I get there, I have no defense. The only thing I can say for a certainty is that I wasn't the one to throw the dart that ended Baldur's life. What are my chances of getting out of this with a light sentence? Are there any?" I pleaded with the huge, silky feathered raven sitting on my ledge. "I need some good news."

The chances are extremely small of a sentence without some form of punishment. It is the way of Asgard to mete out penalties for wrongdoing. But most of these are given to gods and goddesses, and even if the length of time is vast, they are immortal, so it does not matter in the end. It is a rarity for a shieldmaiden to be punished on the same level as a god.

Great. But technically I was a demigod. "Will they take into effect that I was just turned? And don't know their ways? Or doesn't that matter?" Worrying about my sentence was futile, because there was nothing I could do to stop it from happening. Even if all the Valkyries were behind me, we wouldn't win.

They will take everything into account, but Frigg will have the last word. Since you are responsible for freeing her son, she will not be kind.

"Ugh." I wrapped my arms over my eyes, trying to block everything out. Sleep would be welcome right now. "In Svartalfheim, my mother seemed wary of Frigg," I told the bird, my eyes still shut. "I'm not expecting the sentencing to go well. I know she will be harsh. What I don't understand is how Odin and his wives and my mother all fit into the equation. I imagine it's messy and complicated. There have to be hurt feelings all around."

In Asgard, they do things much differently. Our marriage vows are not sacred and unbreakable. Your mother did not intrude on Frigg's relationship with Odin. You need not worry about that. But Frigg herself is another matter. She will seek retribution for her son. But I have other news to share that may help your cause.

Huggie's cadence had changed, his tone urgent. I lifted my arms, tilting my head up, giving the bird a look. "So let's hear it." There was more hope in my voice than I cared to admit.

Each god and goddess has their own prophecies, their own fates, their own destinies set out since birth, all of which lead to Ragnarok, the fated battle. Most of the gods and goddesses are told what their fate will be from an early age, and there is little escaping it. Some learn it later in life. Baldur's destiny was proclaimed as a teenager. His mother knew he was fated to die, but she chose to believe she could overcome it. To evade his destiny, she elicited promises in the name of her son.

"Yeah, I heard about that. But, honestly, I don't get it. Shocking, I know. I can't wrap my brain around how she went about procuring these promises, but she forgot mistletoe? Is that the reason it worked?" Seriously, it was befuddling.

Frigg exacted promises not to harm her son from every living thing she thought capable in each of the realms, but not from things she thought incapable. Gods and goddesses each have special skills. Frigg can commune with nature. The dart Verdandi threw was made of mistletoe wrapped in a witch's spell. It is not without its irony that the Norn chose mistletoe. Not long ago, Loki asked Frigg if she exacted a promise from mistletoe specifically. She admitted she had not. It is a double insult that it was this that killed Baldur.

I pounded my fists on the sheets in frustration.

Of course Verdandi would add insult to injury. She wanted this to hurt as much as possible.

"Sam's right," I said. "It's like we're living in a comic book or some sort of fairy tale. Even though Frigg went to those lengths and still couldn't save her son from his fate." I left out the fact that he would still be alive, at least for a while, if I hadn't intervened. "Huggie, please, please tell me there's a way to bring him back." I leaned up on an elbow, my expression imploring.

There might be. Baldur's fate is complex. Some destinies are simple, and some are woven throughout the fabric of space and time. The god of light is the polar opposite of what resides in Helheim. It is prophesied that once he arrives, Hel will make him her favorite. Honestly, that made sense, because even people in Helheim couldn't help but love Baldur. *It is also said that Hel might agree to set him free if some conditions are met.*

I scrambled up, swinging my legs over the side of the bed. "Now you're talking. What conditions?" My heart raced as hope zipped through me. If there was a possibility I could get my brother back, I would do whatever it took.

It is not clear, as there are different interpretations.

"Yes, yes, but tell me what you know," I urged. The thought of seeing Baldur again gave me great joy.

No matter what the conditions are, you would have to barter directly with Hel for his release.

That took a moment to sink in. "You mean *actually* visit Helheim and strike a deal with her?" Tyr's words ran through my head about living people never coming home. "Or can I do it through some kind of talking device the Valkyries use to call Asgard?"

You would have to journey there, but... Huggie stopped short.

"But what?" I asked, my tone impatient. *Just get on with it, bird.*

Frigg is likely going to exile you there anyway.

I slumped back against the bed. So that's what Verdandi

had been hinting at. "Tit for tat," I said miserably. "I sent her son there, so she sends me."

The difference will be you enter the realm alive, where most enter dead. That is the only facet Odin will be able to influence her on. But there is still a chance for you to gain an advantage. Before the sentence is final, you must convince her that you may be able to free her son.

"How am I going to do that? You said you didn't know the conditions it would take to free Baldur."

In the morning you will meet with the wolf, your brother, your mother, and your aunt. Your mother will know all the tales of Baldur's prophecy. She will be able to guide you through the negotiation, but she must not accompany you to Helheim, as Hel is a bitter rival. Huggie paused for a moment, and I thought he'd stopped again. But then he finished with, *There is only one who can accompany you on your journey.*

Fen.

"You're talking about the wolf, right?" I asked. "That makes sense, because it's his sister who resides there." The thought of having Fen by my side struck fear and relief in me simultaneously.

Precisely. He may be the only one who will be able to give you an advantage. But Frigg won't grant that request. She will both want you to succeed and want you to fail, her pride and grief warring. It is Odin who will send the wolf into exile. This must happen first. Odin will condemn the wolf and declare the banishment a place of his choosing, but he will not announce it before Frigg passes down her own judgment. It is the only way the wolf can accompany you. In order for this to happen, he must accompany you to Asgard.

There was no way Fen would let me go alone, especially not after what just happened in Svartalfheim. I narrowed my eyes at the giant bird perched on my sill. "How in the world did you and my father cook up this plan so quickly? Baldur just died moments ago. This sounds like a fairly complicated plan."

Odin has many skills, some of which I do not understand, even after all these years together. He has known for some time that this might be the end result. He is always well prepared, his mind continuously working. And he knows what lies in Frigg's heart. You must not forget that Baldur was Odin's child, too. The god of light is a favorite of the realm, and he will be mourned by thousands. Odin will do much to get him back, and he feels you can accomplish this.

I was stunned. "Me? Why does he think I can do anything? We've never even met. Without the help of others, I couldn't have freed my mother from Svartalfheim."

Odin sees all. You are a child of his flesh. If you are successful in this mission, you will have succeeded in defeating the Norns, and you will be welcomed back to Asgard as a hero. Your life will begin on its true path, as it is supposed to.

"What about Fen? He will be exiled to Helheim, but if we save Baldur's life, will he be exonerated?" I bit my lip while I waited to hear this important piece of information.

This is unknown.

"What do you mean it's *unknown*? You just told me Odin knows all." Anger roiled in my chest, as it always did when I felt Fen was treated unfairly. I watched my hands as they began to glow. I brought them up in front of my face, fascinated. I was going to have to work on controlling that.

You will have much to bargain for.

I dropped my hands in my lap. "I'm not understanding your angle. You're going to have to spell it out for me. I didn't think I was in a position to bargain. I'm going to Asgard to basically be tried in court, right?"

You will be present when Odin passes his judgment on the wolf, which will come before your hearing. He will ask if any will stand as a character witness to the accused. The last time Fenrir was tried, none stood for him. This time there will be more than one who will.

"Are you talking about Tyr?" My half brother had spent

many years regretting his decision to trick Fen, his ward and student, into being sent away. He had paid dearly, ending up with a facial scar and losing a hand.

Yes, and Leela. Their testimony will have an impact on the end result of getting a shortened sentence.

My mother would stand up for Fen, just like that?

I hadn't thought about it one way or another, but it made me happy that Huggie thought she would. "How long do I have before I go to Asgard?"

In normal circumstances, it would be immediately, but as I said, Odin is prepared. The summons will be for you to arrive a week from now. Once it arrives, you must leave immediately.

I nodded. I was relieved to know I had a week to prepare. Trepidation ran through my barely glowing body, and I blew out a breath. "Okay. I appreciate you coming to let me know. Is there anything else you can share before you leave?"

Only that not many could achieve what you did in Svartalfheim. Not only did you free your brother, but you brought your mother home. The Valkyries have tried in vain for twenty-four years to do the same. Your ingenuity and strength will make you a strong shieldmaiden in no time. You must have faith and keep training.

"I didn't do that alone. I had help, and I was expecting Invaldi and the elves to be much more powerful than they were."

The dark elves are capable of being fierce warriors, but they were expecting a war, not a lone Valkyrie. They let their guard down and paid for it in the end. Invaldi will demand his retribution.

"Figures," I said. "Nothing is simple in these realms."

Huggie flapped his giant wings, half in the room, half outside. The sun had set, darkness beginning to fall. *I will leave you now.*

"Will I see you in Asgard?"

Yes. I will be there.

He jumped off the ledge, soaring into the air. I got up and walked to the opening, watching him disappear, blending seamlessly into the night sky like a dark angel.

I turned.

Fen stood in the doorway, arms crossed, shoulder casually against the jamb. His face was unreadable, but his presence was welcome.

Without a word, I walked into his arms.

30

My head lay against Fen's shoulder. I was content for the first time in a long while. Our lovemaking had been frantic at first, need and grief intermixing, but ended in quiet passion, both of us needing to feel the other. We hadn't spoken about anything of substance yet.

My fingers made lazy circles on his chest. "We can't avoid talking forever," I said. "But just so you know, it was extremely hard to leave without telling you. Huggie said if I waited, it would be bad, and I trusted him. I would've done anything to get my mother back. I hope you can forgive me."

"I will not lie," Fen answered. "It was difficult seeing you go. I felt betrayed for a time, then I understood that you did what you had to do. I would've done the same. Waiting was the hardest part. I did not leave the portal until it opened."

I snuggled even closer. "I knew it would be hard. If you had left me like that, I would've felt betrayed, too. But I'm glad you understand." I settled a kiss on his pec, enjoying his musky scent. "If I hadn't found Baldur early on, I couldn't have done much. Callan, too. Junnal was amazing. Speaking of the giant, have you seen him?" As far as I knew, Junnal hadn't come back to the stronghold. "He told me he would ride the cillar back."

"I have not seen the Jotun, but that does not mean he is in danger. We will search for him in the morning."

"I haven't seen Callan either, but I'm assuming he came back with Baldur and the Valkyries. I should've seen to Willa's needs tonight, since I was the one who insisted she come with us, but I just couldn't think of anything but Baldur." Tears pooled in my eyes. "This entire thing is so messed up. Huggie told me we would meet as a group to discuss plans before I'm summoned to Asgard."

"I overheard your portion of the conversation," Fen said quietly. "We will both be exiled to Helheim."

I glanced at him, trying to get a read on his features. But as ever, Fen kept his emotions close to the vest. "You're not shocked? That's big news."

"It was just a matter of time before the gods caught up with me. I broke out of Muspelheim, with your help, but I'm still a wanted man. They will not let me off so easily. There are worse places for me to be exiled, and I would never let you go without me anyway."

"Huggie says Odin thought this might happen, and there may be a way to save Baldur. From what I understood, your sister will be a tough nut to crack."

"I have not seen my sister since we were children, but we have the same blood running through our veins." He shrugged. "It has to count for something." He tightened his hold on me. "I will not let anything happen to you, shieldmaiden. I swear it. We will fight together and survive."

"I know we will." I believed that. I had to. "But I won't hold you to the keeping-me-safe part. Helheim sounds rough. And as you've just witnessed, I'm not without skills. I hope we can bring our weapons, because if they send us to such a wretched place without them, it will be terrible. Huggie also said we can speak at your hearing as character witnesses, to try to convince them that you are good and don't deserve to be exiled forever. The raven said my mother knows information about Baldur's destiny, and we're going to have to find a way to convince your sister to let him go."

"As I said, I'm not familiar with the underworld or how it works, but if there is a way to do it, we will find it. Have no fear. The god of light is loved by all, and that alone will help our quest."

"Did you know him in Asgard? All those years ago?"

"Our paths crossed a few times. He did not go out of his way to help me, but he was also one who treated me with civility. He is Tyr's half brother, so we were together during celebrations, but mostly he was on his ship. He loved that boat." His voice sounded wistful.

"We have to make sure he gets to captain it again. In the meantime, Tyr will watch over it."

Fen pressed his lips to the top of my head. "We will, Valkyrie."

※

It was after dawn, the sun just slicing over the horizon. We were gathered in a room I'd never seen before. It was carved out of limestone, like everything else in the stronghold, but it was deep within the mesa and had no windows, which afforded more privacy.

We sat at a long conference table surrounded by ten chairs, enough to hold Fen, Tyr, Ingrid, Rae, and my mother.

"So that's all the bird told you?" Ingrid asked. "That

Frigg is going to exile you to Helheim, but there's a chance you can save Baldur while you're there? That's good news mixed with bad." She glanced at Fen. "Then Odin's planning to send Fenrir to Helheim separately, without Frigg's knowledge, but before he does, we have to vouch for his character?"

"That's pretty much it," I answered. "It's imperative that we vouch for him, so if we save Baldur, Fen has a chance to finally be free. I'm not leaving that realm without him." I peered around at the group, meeting each person's gaze. "Fen and I fight together, and we leave together. And since we don't want to spend the rest of our lives on the run, if we can make a good case for Fen in the beginning, I'm hoping Odin will listen to reason." Anticipation fluttered in my chest. It was crazy to think I was going to meet my real father, an actual god, in just a few days. Even though we had gathered to discuss plans, it didn't feel like there would ever be enough preparation to get me ready for that.

Sensing my anxiety, Fen reached under the table and settled his hand on my thigh. I flashed him a smile. We had talked into the night about everything we could think of, but I'd woken up still carrying grief and sadness for Baldur.

"What happens to Fenrir is not Odin's decision alone," Tyr said. "But he will have the last say. I will stand up for you, there is no question. I owe you no less. It has been many years since I've last seen my father, but as the god of war, I should be able to help your cause. After all, I was your mentor and keeper." He winked. "My word should still hold sway."

"I accept your offer to stand and pledge. And though I credit you as a mentor, you were a terrible keeper. I believe that's why we are all sitting here today," Fen said, grinning.

"That may be so," Tyr agreed.

"Huggie also told me that Leela would have knowledge of Baldur's prophecy," I said, glancing at my mother, who sat to my right looking radiant and lovely, even in the early dawn hours. She was freshly showered and adorned in the standard Valkyrie regalia. Her breastplate was polished, and a beautiful bow, with arrows, was attached to her back. I looked forward to seeing her use it later today. She didn't appear older than thirty-five, if that. It was weird to think my mother would seem my contemporary in the eyes of many.

"Hugin is correct," my mother stated. "News of Baldur's uncertain future has been widely circulated for many, many years. It has also been misconstrued by some and interpreted in various ways by others, causing several stories to be popular. But I happen to have been in the right place at the right time, with a true seer, in the company of Odin and Frigg when I heard what I believe is the right prediction. We were told that Baldur would indeed die and that he would descend to Helheim, but he would gain favor with Hel, and she would eventually agree to set him free under certain conditions."

I sat up straighter. This was exactly what Huggie had said. "What are those conditions?" I prayed they weren't going to be too extreme.

"The seer was vague, as they often are, so the interpretation may take a while to decipher," she said. "But one condition stated that Hel would agree to Baldur's release if all the gods and goddesses wept for him."

My mouth fell open. "That's it? Weep for him, and he's free? As in, actual tears?" I asked.

"I think, in this case, 'weep' means they must officially admit that they are sad he is gone and want him back," my mother said. "Or something a little more obtuse. Weep could mean many things. Once we are in Asgard, I will investigate more. I know where this seer resides and will pay him a visit."

Fen made a sound, and I glanced at him. "There will be one holdout. There is always one holdout," Fen concluded. "Which my sister well knows. By agreeing to something like that, she will ensure that she will keep the god of light by her side until Ragnarok."

"Who would be the likely holdout?" I asked. "Baldur is beloved by all."

Fen didn't answer, so Tyr did. "Loki."

"But he's your father." I sat up in my chair. "Wouldn't you be able to sway him?" The thought of Baldur's freedom being blocked by one god made me want to scream.

Fen's face was set in hard lines. "I will try my best, of course," he answered. "But I may have better luck bartering with my sister. Perhaps I can give her something that she desires more than harboring the god of light."

Panic settled into my chest. That sounded like it would be a steep cost. "What could she desire more?" I was almost afraid to ask.

"I know not," Fen replied. "But she has ruled the underworld for many years without journeying to another realm, so there must be something she covets or misses."

What if she asked for a passel of newborn babies to skin alive? Or wanted to rain terror down on Midgard? I cleared my throat. "If she asks for something outrageous, we can't fulfill it."

Fen gave me a long look. Then he nodded once. "Agreed. But then we are destined to reside with Baldur in Helheim forever. Freeing him is our only way out of exile."

I desperately hoped that wasn't true. "We've escaped two other realms. I have to believe we can find our way out of Helheim." We would try, but I wasn't sure we would succeed. With a whole bunch of gods and goddesses against us, the outlook seemed bleak. "We will have to wait and see what Hel has to say. Does anyone know how long it will take after the verdict for us to be sent away?"

"Immediately." Tyr's voice was tight.

My mother stood abruptly, her chair scraping on the stone floor. "You will have to excuse me," she said. "I'm having a difficult time accepting what has happened and need time to think. I waited for years for the day to come when I would be reunited with my daughter, and now she will be ripped away." Her hand rested on my shoulder, her fingers gripping me tightly. "There must be a way we can help Phoebe escape this fate. I'm going to consult with my confidants in Asgard. I will not give up on her. We only have a few short days to figure out how to change the course of these events. Every second is crucial." I held on to her hand where it rested on my shoulder. I understood how she felt. We were all still mourning Baldur, and having to deal with this so soon was excruciating.

The only shining light in all of this was that I might be able to free my good-natured brother from a lengthy stay in Helheim.

"Good idea. Go see what you can find," Ingrid said to Leela as she pushed back from the table. "I'm sure your confidants will be loyal to you, even after all these years. See where the Council is at, if they've reached a verdict, and what the gossip is leaning toward. It's time to wrap up this meeting anyway and go train. Phoebe needs to get as much time in as she can. Plus, I want to see what she can do with her energy now that she can harness it." Ingrid grinned, her hazel eyes sparking with mischief. "That was a hell of a blast you gave Invaldi. I haven't seen energy flow like that in eons—if ever. I have a couple hay bales with your name on them, and I hope when you're done, there's nothing left but smoke and dust."

We all stood.

I was certain we would meet back here again over the next few days. "I'm not sure you'll get smoke and dust, but I'll try my best," I said as I followed my mother out of the room, where we embraced. It felt good to touch her. She radiated positive energy, and my body was hungry for it. "I don't want you to worry," I told her. "I know this all seems dire, but I'll have Fen with me, and we will find a way to get out. I'm confident of that."

"Either that, or we will break you out." She smiled. "The Valkyries will do everything they can to help you, my beautiful daughter." She stroked the side of my face, and I closed my eyes. "You did not kill Baldur, and I will do my best to make sure everyone in Asgard understands that. We will get through this. And once it's behind us, our lives can begin in earnest."

"I look forward to that."

"Now let's get out there," Ingrid said, coming up behind us. "The day's wasting, and we have a hell of a lot of work to do."

"Ingrid, it's barely five o'clock in the morning," I pointed out. "The day hasn't even begun yet."

"You're lucky I let you sleep last night, kid," Ingrid said. "Now let's get cracking. There are a few hay bales out there that need to learn a lesson."

31

I was heading back to the Park, after walking my mother to her quarters, when I spotted someone in the distance I didn't recognize. The figure looked male, but I was too far away to tell for sure. Fen and Tyr had gone to gather more weapons, and their silhouettes were much larger, so it wasn't either of them. The person looked to be practicing with a weapon of some kind, possibly a small sword. His movements were fluid, lithe and agile.

Valkyries did not allow men in the stronghold, so I couldn't imagine they'd let anyone in since last night.

Ingrid was waiting for me, likely impatiently, but I had no choice but to check it out. I approached cautiously, refraining from unsheathing my swords. The person wasn't moving threateningly. He was minding his own business and training, which was commonplace around here. The person was likely a Valkyrie with her hair up, dressed in regular clothes, or some such thing. But I had to be sure.

As I moved closer, my mind shifted to Junnal. The big, lovable troll-giant still wasn't back yet. It made me uneasy.

Fen was going to contact his mother, Angrboda, Queen of Jotunheim, later this morning to see if she had any news. I was cautiously optimistic, since Junnal was so big and strong. But if Invaldi had harmed him in some way, there would be retaliation.

When I was about fifty yards away, I stopped and squinted.

I couldn't believe what I was seeing.

"Callan?"

The man before me was no older than thirty. He was tall, with a full head of dark hair, handsome, and shirtless. He had the sculpted body of an athlete and no beard. All that identified him were his pointed ears.

He spun around, smiling widely. "Phoebe! It's so wonderful to see you." He walked toward me with a bounce in his step, extending his arms in the universal sign for an embrace.

I went in for a hug, still not believing who was in front of me. I pulled back, my hands gripping his noticeable biceps. "Callan, what in the world happened to you? You're going to have to explain this to me. You're supposed to be an old man." My eyes did a once-over again. "I mean, I noticed you looking better with each infusion of energy, but I never expected this. You are utterly transformed!"

He tilted his head back and laughed. It was a soft, masculine sound. "What happened was a hefty dose of Yggdrasil and sunshine." The sun was just rising over the mesa at that moment. "Blessed sunshine is the healer of all." He closed his eyes and opened his arms, drinking in the first rays of the morning. "Oh, how I've missed your subtle kiss on my skin."

He looked free, happy, and rejuvenated.

"Honestly...this is..." I stammered. So strange? "I had

no idea sunlight could make such a difference. It looks like you've shed eighty years. I'm stunned."

"And I owe it all to you, young Valkyrie." Surprising me, he dropped to one knee. I panicked for a brief moment, thinking he might ask me to marry him or something crazy.

"I, um, you don't need to thank me or anything else," I said hastily. "I'm just glad I could help you."

He grabbed my hand, startling me even further. But before I could protest, he stated in a stoic tone, "I hereby pledge my loyalty. It is extremely rare for a white elf of my stature to give it to anyone—especially outside of my species—but nonetheless, I extend it to you. White elves are lone creatures on the whole, but we unite against threats, which makes us strong. You have proven yourself time and time again. I will stand as a character witness for you in Asgard and help you defeat your foes."

"I don't know what to say," I said. My throat felt full. I wasn't expecting this. "Thank you, Callan. I was happy to help you, and your friendship in return is enough."

He stood, and that's when I noticed how bright blue his eyes were. They were as blue as the cerulean sky above us. "Nonsense. My testimony will be unprecedented. It will make the gods think." He tapped a temple. "I have only heard bits about what is to come, but I will do my best to aid your cause. And when this is over, you may call on me at any time. If it hadn't been for you and the god of light, I would be wasting away in my cell, moments from death." He spread his arms wide, a small sword in his left hand. "And now I am back to my true self, full in mind and spirit. I have never felt better."

"I...I accept your help. Thank you." Honestly, I was going to need all I could get. "It fills my heart to see you back to your true self. I had no idea anyone could transform as much as you have. In this time of sadness and loss, you've managed to uplift me."

He slung an arm around my shoulders, and we began to walk. I had to get to the Park, or Ingrid was going to come looking for me. "I am leaving later this afternoon," he told me. "I'm heading back to Alfheim, my homeland, for the first time in many years. The white elves won't know what to make of my sudden appearance. I am certain they marked me dead long ago, or they would have sent a war party to retrieve me. When I was sent to rescue our king, he watched as the elves struck me down while he managed to escape. He likely thought me dead. After I'm done explaining, and relaying all the stories, I will gather prominent white elves, and we will meet you in Asgard. My kind will be talking about my return for the next hundred years."

I was overcome by his generosity. "I appreciate that," I told him, meaning it. "I've never been to Asgard, and I'm a little nervous. It's not opportune that the first time I go, I will be tried for the death of my half brother. Not exactly an ideal time for a girl to meet her birth father."

"You are very strong. Always remember that." He shook my shoulders. "Your bloodline reeks of aristocracy and power. Hold your head high, and you will command respect. Enter the Council like you do not deserve punishment, and they will treat you as such. You have many behind you. Lean on them. Use their help. If white elves lived by this decree, we would've been stronger for it long ago."

I was going to miss my new friend. "Safe travels, Callan. It was a pleasure to make your acquaintance. I'm so glad both Baldur and I could help you. He would be beyond excited to see your transformation."

"He was a good god, light of heart and soul. And you did more than help, Valkyrie. You gave me my life back, and I will never forget it." We came to a stop in front of the Park. The shieldmaidens had already begun to train. Callan leaned over and placed a chaste kiss on my cheek. "I shall see you in a few days."

Rae came up behind us and pulled up short.

Her face registered zero recognition of the man who stood before us. Before she could get a word out, or unsheathe her katana, I hastily explained, "This is Callan, the old man who accompanied us home. I know it looks strange, but it seems Yggdrasil had a hand in transforming him back to his true self. That and, apparently, sunshine. But don't worry, he is on his way back to Alfheim. If I had known he was going to change this much, I would've asked permission for him to enter. I apologize."

Callan extended his hand to Rae. "It's a pleasure to make your acquaintance, battle captain. I watched you train yesterday into the night, and you are an impressive warrior. Your skills are flawless." Rae seemed reluctant to extend her hand. She finally did, much to my relief, and Callan clasped it, bringing it to his mouth in one sly movement. He settled his lips on it in what could only be construed as a casually intimate gesture.

I bit my tongue as Rae whipped her hand back, appearing flustered. "I have heard about you," she managed. "They call you Callan the Capable, one of only a small handful of white elves crossed with mage known to exist. That is why you were sent to rescue your king."

Callan bowed his head at the recognition, smiling. "That is true."

Rae casually drew her long, curved sword from her belt, clearly enjoying the sound it made as she unsheathed it. It was a huge katana, impressive on every level. "Then why is it that the dark elves managed to trap you in their realm for all these years? It seems a better name would be Callan the Captive." Her eyes glinted with something I'd never seen before. Maybe humor? "Now, if you will excuse me, I must attend to my sisters." Rae entered the Park without looking back, her long black hair swaying behind her, the braided plaits glinting in the early morning sunshine.

I expected Callan to look abashed or insulted. Instead, his eyes followed Rae like they were magnetized. He finally pried them away with a wide grin on his lips. "She is truly magnificent."

"That she is." I shook my head, smiling. "I believe she is the fiercest of us all."

"They don't craft warriors like that anymore." He shook himself as he reached out to embrace me again. "I will take my leave, young Valkyrie. But I look forward to our reunion."

"Be well, Callan."

As I entered the Park, where the Valkyries were training, I realized how lucky I was. Even with Baldur's death pressing heavily on my heart, and everything in between, I'd gone from living alone in New York as a lowly shoe clerk to becoming a shieldmaiden with a family to come home to. It didn't get much better than that.

It was full dark before Rae eased up on us. I'd managed to do some major damage to the hay bales, but it hadn't been nearly as impressive as what I'd done to Invaldi when I'd been plugged into Yggdrasil. They'd indeed caught fire. But it was a tiny brushfire, rather than an active bonfire, or a complete incineration. But I was proud of my efforts, because they'd come from my body, not the tree.

Ingrid had been a good sport and had become my sparring partner for the day. I'd rarely had a chance to train with her in the Park, so it had been a good day.

Rae had kept us working so hard, it'd kept my thoughts away from Baldur, and my impending fate, which had been a blessing.

Most of the other Valkyries had left after finally being excused for the day. I was putting my swords away when someone approached from behind. Thinking it was Ingrid, I turned, smiling. My grin quickly turned pinched. "What can I help you with, Anya?" I asked. We had steered clear of each other all day, which had made the day extra special.

"Everyone thinks you've turned into our savior—a powerful Valkyrie who can lead us into war. But I know better. I don't care if you can harness energy, or learn to shear a sheep. You're a fraud. You're not skilled enough to fight even the lowliest dark elf. You got lucky, nothing more." She held her battle ax loosely out in front of her, but the intent was crystal clear. She leaned in aggressively, hoping to intimidate me.

It wasn't going to work.

I straightened and unsheathed Gundren. The blades came out so fast, the whooshing noise was as sharp as a sting. "I might still have a lot to learn, but you're a bully who finally needs to have her ass handed to her."

The Phoebe who worried about consequences was gone. I was done dealing with the Anyas of the world forever. The Valkyrie Phoebe had replaced her. As I brought my swords out in front of me, they kindled with energy, sparks and ribbons of light intertwining the blades, making them look like they'd been plugged in.

I didn't give Anya a warning. I sprang, whipping my blades down in two different directions. She barely had time to get her ax raised as she frantically backed away. I took advantage of the momentum, forcing her to keep moving as I slashed my blades down again, pummeling her weapon with more force than I needed to get the job done.

I didn't have time to register her expression. I was caught up in the fight. It wasn't until her back slammed against the rock wall behind us that I stopped. I hadn't even broken a sweat. Anya was barely clinging to a small portion of her ax handle, her breastplate charred, the steel blade of her ax chipped away.

I glared at her, my weapon still poised, ready to continue this battle to the end. "Do you concede?" I asked, my voice steely.

"Yes." She bowed her head.

"Damn right you do." I lowered my weapons to my sides. "But that's not enough. I want you to admit that I'm a better fighter than you are, or we end this now." When she didn't readily respond, I lifted my right arm, Gundren sparking and dancing with light. "Say it."

Her expression was like ice. "You are more skilled than I."

I stepped back, satisfied.

For now.

I turned on my heel and deliberately walked out of the Park.

Sam was waiting for me, her expression a mix of awe and excitement. She grabbed my arm, hugging me. Once we were out of earshot, she whisper-yelled, "That was awesome! Holy crap! I knew that hag was going to pick a fight with you. She'd been giving you the death stare all day with her beady little eyes. But you handled that like a pro. What'd it take? All of two minutes for you to back her into that wall? I couldn't hear what you guys were talking about, but it didn't matter. She is *so* never coming near you again. It's too bad you can't use your Valkyrie prowess on our crappy manager at Macy's, Nancy. She was the worst."

I chuckled. "She was bad, but using my new Valkyrie prowess on her would be a little unfair."

"Maybe just a smidgen." Sam shook my elbow. "I just thought of something. Imagine what Tom would think of all this! You'd blow that boy's eighteen-year-old head right off his shoulders. Being a stock boy at Macy's is in no way a good preparation for finding out that immortals exist. We *have* to go back to Macy's at some point, with you dressed in full gear. Promise me! To see the look on Tom's and Nancy's face as you walk in—priceless." She clapped. "I cannot wait."

"I never pegged you as a sadist, Sam. And here I thought you were a rule follower with a brain big enough to make all that seem like petty foolishness."

"Yeah, that was before I learned I had Asgardian blood. Now I'm ready to shake this world to its core like you shook up Anya. Seriously, that was bad*ass*." She beamed at me. "Gossip is going to rocket through the stronghold like there's no tomorrow. People will steer clear."

"They better," I said, my tone half serious. "Because there is more from where that came from."

32

I sat shoulder to shoulder with my mother on top of the mesa. We'd spent a lot of time together the last few days, getting to know each other, coming up with plans, then changing them and coming up with even better plans. When she wasn't connecting with people she knew in Asgard, we trained together. My mother was an incredibly skilled archer. Even though she claimed she was rusty after all those years away, she could hit the smallest target at a hundred yards.

"Hawaii is breathtakingly beautiful," I said, the cell phone on speaker so Leela she could hear my parents' voices. "Sam's mom and dad have chartered a boat, and we are going to island-hop."

"It sounds like you're having an adventure of a lifetime, honey," my father Frank said, his tone jovial.

"Yes, it does," my mother Janette agreed, sounding more reserved. "But we miss you so, Phoebe. When are you coming home?"

"We do worry about your safety, even though we know you're in good hands," my father added.

My voice remained as cheery. "I would say in a month or so," I answered, hoping it was true. I had no idea how long I would be in Helheim, but I wasn't going to needlessly worry them. Sam had agreed to call them if I was gone for a longer time and make up some excuses as to why I couldn't come to the phone. I glanced over at my best friend. She sat next to the rickety cell phone tower, waiting for me to give her the signal to shake it. If I'd let them, my parents would stay on the other end of the line forever. "But I'm not sure. Once this beautiful trip ends, real life begins again, so I'm trying to soak in as much as I can."

"Do you have enough money?" my dad asked for the second time. "If not, we can wire you some."

My heart clenched. I hated lying to them. Leela patted my thigh, smiling. I glanced at her, and she mouthed, *They sound like good people.* I nodded. They were good people—the best. I'd already promised to introduce her to them once we got home. She wanted to meet—in her own words—the folks who helped raise a wonderful, caring, smart, brilliant, beautiful daughter.

Her words. Totally.

"I have enough, Dad. I haven't even touched any of my savings, all that money I made working at the hardware store. So I'm fine. And Sam's parents are beyond generous. Speaking of the store, how's business?" Time for a subject change. "With spring right around the corner, sales must be picking up."

My dad laughed. "Business is fine, just fine. I sold Mr. Harper a snowblower the other day. I've been trying to get him to buy one for years, but he's as stubborn as they come. He's got that big double lot, you know, at the end of Fairfield Lane, and he's getting up there in years. Snow is almost gone, but I gave him a deal on last year's model and made him an offer he couldn't refuse."

"That's just like you." I smiled. "Always thinking about everybody else. If Mr. Harper hadn't bought that snowblower, you'd be showing up at his doorstep to shovel his walk for him anyway."

"Well, that's exactly what your father did," my mother said. "Mr. Harper finally gave in, because he didn't want Frank showing up at his doorstep every time it snowed."

I laughed. "Well, that's one way to make a sale. I bet you gave him more than last year's discount. Come on, don't lie."

"Your father practically gave that thing away." My mom's voice was filled with pride. "He made no money. But it was worth it to know that Mr. Harper won't be having a heart attack shoveling snow on our watch."

"Well, truth be told," my dad said, "that old thing had been sitting in the store for two years. It's no loss to me and has a better use for Mr. Harper."

It felt incredibly good to have a normal, everyday conversation. I hadn't realized how much I missed it. Talking to the parents who raised me always eased my stress. "That's great, Dad. I'm proud of you. Mr. Harper has to be close to a hundred years old by now. He was old when I was a kid." As much as I hated to do it, I gave Sam the thumbs-up. I had to get back to training and prepare for another meeting tonight. Tyr had been gone for a day and had come back this morning with new information to share. We were going to try to formulate a solid plan for when my summons came, which would likely be in a day or two. We'd also found out late last night that Junnal had been taken prisoner by Invaldi, and that had to factor into our plans. We couldn't leave the big guy down there.

Sam began to shake the tower, and immediately, crackles

and pops came on the line. My mom was in the middle of saying something about baking pies and the holidays. "Mom, I'm sorry"—*pop, crack, buzz*—"the line is breaking up, and I can't hear you. I'll try to call in a week or two, but likely not before that. We're on a boat in the middle of the ocean, so don't get worried if you don't hear from me!"

"Okay, honey, it was good to hear your voice. We miss and love you," my mom called over the buzzing.

"I love you, too! Can't wait to fill you in on my next adventure." Reluctantly, I disconnected the call.

Leela stood, turning to help me up. "They sound lovely, Phoebe. Odin did well. I can't wait to meet them. They have pure hearts, and that was my only criteria."

We walked toward the edge of the mesa. "They are wonderful parents, and I had an idyllic upbringing. It's incredibly hard to lie to them. It would shatter them if they knew what has happened to me in the past few months, and I want to make sure they stay in the dark."

"Very few in Asgard or any other realm know who they are, and it will stay that way. I give you my word. When we defeat the Norns once and for all, and you are accepted into Asgard, we shall visit them together."

I smiled. That would be wonderful. "It's strange that I'll have to introduce you as my 'good friend Leela,' instead of as my birth mother. Although, that would be incredibly weird as well, since they've never shared with me that I was adopted in the first place."

"Oh, they don't think you were adopted," she said, like it was normal. "When Odin found them, he would have altered reality to make them think you were biologically theirs."

I looked at her, my eyes wide. "I had no idea. My parents did refer to me as their 'little miracle' for years when I was a child. They must've tried, and failed, to get pregnant on their own. They had me in Paris, while my father was doing an internship with a sculptor there. His greatest ambition was to be an artist, but when they had me, they moved back to the States. His father, my grandfather, was a farmer. When they came back, Frank took over the family business. I loved growing up with my grandparents on the farm. When I entered high school, we moved into town, and he bought the hardware store. The rest is history."

"I couldn't have wished for a better life for you. Tranquil and stress free." My mother sounded wistful. "It brings my heart joy to think of you running through the fields, happiness brimming over, even though my mind weeps for missing all those years together. But a cell in Svartalfheim is no place to raise a child, as you saw. Things would've been much, much different if I had kept you, and not at all in a good way."

We joined Sam and began our descent from the mesa. Halfway down, we met up with Fen, who took my hand. "The call went well?"

"Yes," I told him. "I wish I knew when I could speak with them again. They're going to worry about me if I don't check in."

"I'll be sure to call them for you, Phoebe," Sam piped in from behind. "And if you haven't met me yet, I have awesome persuasion skills. I'll tell them you're busy getting a massage, or scuba diving, or on a hot date with a wolf." She winked. "It'll be a piece of cake. They won't doubt me for a second. I don't want to toot my own horn, but I'm *that* good."

I snorted. "You're a master tooter." I laughed. "That'll work once, if we're lucky. The next time I don't call, they will have an APB out on me. But I can't worry about that now." I had enough to think about, like standing in front of the Council in Asgard, trying to convince them there was a chance I could bring Baldur back from Helheim.

Surprisingly, Ingrid and Rae were waiting for us at the bottom of the mesa.

They should've been at the Park training, and judging by Ingrid's face, something was up.

"What is it?" I said. "Please don't tell me Junnal's dead. I'm not sure I can handle another death at the moment." Ingrid shook her head and lifted something. It was a rolled piece of parchment. A large seal of deep-purple wax had been broken. "Is that what I think it is?"

She nodded. "Both of your summonses just arrived." She nodded to Fen. "We must leave immediately."

A low growl issued from Fen's throat. Neither of us had been looking forward to this moment.

"But I thought we had a week?" I balked. "Technically, we should have three more days."

"It doesn't work like that," Rae replied. "Frigg would've wanted you there immediately. Odin has given you a respite for these few days, and now it's time to leave."

A bit of panic welled in my throat, but I tamped it down. I'd made peace with this journey as best I could. There was nothing I could do to circumvent it, so I planned to meet it head on. "Okay, then we go."

"You won't be alone in all this," Ingrid said as we all began to walk. "We're coming with you and will stand as character witnesses. Everything is going to be just fine."

"I know," I told her, even though I had no idea. "We've been over this. The only thing we have to do before we take off is check with Tyr. He said he has some new information that can help with our case. But other than that, I'm as ready as I'll ever be." When we hit the main pathway, Ingrid went right instead of left back to the living area. "Where are you going? The tree is this way."

She grinned. "Tyr brought more home than information. We're going to Asgard in style."

"What are you talking about?" my mother asked.

"Tyr came back in Ringhorn, so we're taking that to Asgard. All of us. We already loaded it with supplies, and Tyr sent word to Asgard that we are on our way." Ingrid settled her arm around my shoulders. "Phoebe, you're going to have to think about this as your next adventure, not a permanent sentence, because that's what it is. A true Valkyrie looks a challenge straight in the eye and gives it the finger." She waggled her middle finger in front of her in true Ingrid style. "You are no exception. Your mother survived all those years in Svartalfheim, and you will get through this one way or another. It might not be pretty, but I have faith in you. You're going to do just fine."

I reached out and grabbed Fen's hand as we made our way to the gates. "We're going to do better than fine. We're going to bring my brother back, whatever it takes."

"That's the spirit!" Ingrid said as we crossed the border of the stronghold and headed toward the San Juan River, where Ringhorn awaited us. "Let the Asgardian games begin!"

Now for a sneak peek of

E ILED

PHOEBE MEADOWS: BOOK THREE

AMANDA CARLSON

– Coming Spring 2017 –

1

"Sweet mother of all that's holy." Sam coughed violently. "Please tell me we're here. My body can't take any more." She lifted her head, dragging her sleeve over her mouth, wheezing, "I'm pretty sure my tank is finally dry, but bile is tricky, as my body is making more of the hot, searing liquid as we speak." Tyr stood next to her holding a clean bucket, his face a mask of concern.

"Aye, we're here," Tyr answered solemnly, bending down to place the new container in front of Sam, who was promptly in need of it.

We stood on the deck of Ringhorn, my half brother Baldur's boat, which had been gifted to Tyr upon his untimely death. I was here to face the Council and Frigg, Baldur's goddess mother, to receive punishment for freeing her beloved son. I'd broken him out of a dark elf prison—the very place she'd put him.

The boat had just taken us through an insane vortex. One that had hauled us straight up in the air at breakneck speeds, only to drop us the next instant. I lost count of how many times my stomach hit my feet.

But I'd fared better than poor Sam.

"Are we really here?" I asked, squinting into the darkness, trying to make out a single shape on the horizon and coming up empty. The boat had lurched to a full stop in what looked to be a void. "I was expecting it to be a little more...vibrant?"

"We are at a holding dock," Fen said, his frame tense behind me. This was his first time back to Asgard in many years and he was ready for any threat, his nostrils flaring, his sword at the ready.

My mother took my hand. "There are various ways in, but if you take magical transportation, like Ringhorn, you must wait to be inspected before accessing the city."

"Yep," Ingrid added, "lots of nooks and crannies on a big boat like this. We might be harboring unknown threats. We'll have to wait for the inspectors to clear us through."

"Why is it so dark?" I asked. The only illumination we had came from the boat itself. We'd left the Valkyrie stronghold so quickly, there'd been no time for questions.

Before anyone could fill me in, a loud grating noise sounded from fifty feet in front of us. It sounded like metal on metal. All at once the scene began to change as bright light shot into the space.

We were in a large cylinder of some kind.

As light penetrated the tunnel, and my eyes adjusted, I began to see my first glimpses of Asgard.

"Brace yourself, kiddo," Ingrid said as she removed her spear from her waistband. "Along with the inspectors, there will be guards. They will be the ones tasked with accompanying us to the Council quarters."

"Why are you drawing your weapon?" I asked. "This is your home."

"Because I'm getting ready to argue, and I do it best with Betsy handy," she shook her trusty spear and it extended instantly, seamlessly morphing into an eight foot killer with a razor sharp blade.

"Betsy?" I chuckled. Ingrid had never shared the pet name before.

"Yep, she was christened my 'Best Bet' when I first got her. Found her in a pile of discarded weapons outside a warehouse in Asgard and never looked back. If these guards try to separate us, Betsy will have her say. And I can guaran-damn-tee there will be no arguing."

Beside me, my mother casually reached for her bow.

Fighting the guards right out of the gates wasn't what I had envisioned for our arrival here, but I was down. I reached around for Gundren, the double swords I wore on my back, only to be stayed mid-grab by Ingrid's hand.

"You can't do that," she told me in a hushed whisper, her fingers wrapped around my arm. "In fact, I hate to say this, but you're going to have to give Tyr your weapon for a teensy bit."

"Say what?" I couldn't believe my ears. Valkyries didn't give up their weapon to anyone.

Before I could protest further, she added, "You carry Odin's personal weapon, and it's one that can harm any god or goddess in Asgard. They won't be amused when they see it in your possession. Give it to Tyr for now, and he'll give you something in return." She grinned. "I'm assuming you can still blow a hole in someone clutching a broadsword. Am I wrong?" She dropped my arm, elbowing me in the side.

She wasn't wrong, I could harness my energy like a champ, better than any Valkyrie, but that didn't mean I wanted to give up my weapon.

It was the principle of the thing.

NOTHING IS CREATED WITHOUT A GREAT TEAM.

My thanks to:

Awesome Cover design: Damon Za

Digital and print formatting: Author E.M.S

Copyedits/proofs: Joyce Lamb

Final proof: Marlene Engel

About the Author

Amanda Carlson is a graduate of the University of Minnesota, with a BA in both Speech and Hearing Science & Child Development. She went on to get an A.A.S in Sign Language Interpreting and worked as an interpreter until her first child was born. She's the author of the high octane Jessica McClain urban fantasy series published by Orbit, and the Sin City Collectors paranormal romance series. Look for these books in stores everywhere. She lives in Minneapolis with her husband and three kids.

FIND HER ALL OVER SOCIAL MEDIA
Website: amandacarlson.com
Facebook: facebook.com/authoramandacarlson
Twitter: @amandaccarlson